THE BLACK PEARLS

Also by Robert Kerr

THE STUART LEGACY

The
Black Pearls

ROBERT KERR

STEIN AND DAY/*Publishers*/New York

First published in the United States of America, 1975
Copyright © 1975 by Robert Kerr
All rights reserved
Printed in the United States of America
Stein and Day/*Publishers*/Scarborough House,
Briarcliff Manor, N.Y. 10510

Library of Congress Cataloging in Publication Data

Kerr, Robert, 1899–
The black pearls.

Sequel to The Stuart legacy.
I.   Title.
PZ4.K417Bl [PS3561.E646]   813'.5'4   74-23423
ISBN 0-8128-1762-1

'Not all Stuarts are sib to the King.'
                    (Old Scottish saying)

Jamie was.

Contents

THE BLACK PEARLS

No Roses Grow on These Rocks

The *Jesus,* a Hanseatic merchantman of 600 tons, was stealing eastwards at the flagging pace set by a sleepy wind which every now and again died away altogether in a shivering of canvas, and a cracking of sheets against timber, and then in a little while took heart and blew once more. But weakly, half-heartedly.

For'ard, a man who could not be seen was calling out every few minutes in a kind of chant some words in a language which was neither English nor French and was therefore incomprehensible to the blond young man with the long hair, whose name was James Stuart.

He was sitting on the poop deck with his back against the post that carried the ship's lantern. But although he did not understand the words he could guess what was signified. The leadsman was calling out the depth of water beneath the keel. And someone else who was likewise invisible was repeating what he called.

They were probably using some German dialect, for the flag that flapped or, more often, hung limp from the staff on the stern was the mercantile ensign of the free imperial city of Lubeck.

The young man with the gleaming yellow curls falling to his shoulders paid no heed to the words that were chanted by the sailors. Now there was a sound of men quarrelling on the deck below them. He paid no heed to that either.

He was writing a letter.

'Ensign Stuart!'

The letter-writer looked up. Before him, looking sternly down, was a man as big as a house. No, as big as a church. A ruined church. He was a professional soldier by the look of him—one of those Scot mercenary officers who sought service —and, with luck, fortune—in the armies of European monarchs whose subjects were too peaceful for the soldier's life. Stuart, the young man with the curls, had joined Sinclair's force when, in an emergency. the war compelled him to leave Scotland quickly.

'Captain Sinclair,' said the young man.

'They tell me there's a girl aboard the ship.'

At that moment, the quarrel below flared suddenly into violence.

'Just a minute. Captain.'

Stuart scrambled to his feet and ran down the companion way. Two men were squirming and writhing on the deck. The one on top was a Highlander to judge by his costume, what there was of it. His fist rose and fell.

Stuart caught him by the shoulders with both hands and violently pulled him to his feet. He was a man with a dead eye. Stuart knew his name. Dugald. A kinsman of his friend Alistair.

Pure rage flamed out of the good eye. Dugald's hand flashed to his belt, to the knife that was there.

At that moment a man barked, 'Dugald!' A stream of Gaelic followed. Sulky and still venomous, Dugald put the knife away.

The man who had been underneath him in the fight scuttled away like a crab disturbed in a rock pool. He had a grey-blue face and a grey-yellow beard. His eyes were damp round the rims. Stuart knew him as Jock Stevenson.

'Keep out of sight, man.' Stuart threw the words after him; then he turned to the man who had shouted the command at Dugald.

'Thanks, Alistair,' he said.

Alistair MacIan had a face badly marked by an old scar under the cheekbone.

'James,' he said softly, 'don't you know it's dangerous to come between the wild cat and the weasel?'

He and Dugald exchanged words in a flow of passionate Gaelic, one expostulating, the other placating.

Stuart went back to the place in the poop where he had been writing. Captain Sinclair was looking over the rail. Now he turned.

'What was all that?'

'One of Alistair MacIan's children having a disagreement with a man named Stevenson. But you were saying something, Captain?'

He had sat down again in his old place and picked up his pen.

'I was telling you about a rumour that's going around. About there being a girl hiding aboard—somewhere.'

'If she has paid the passage money, I don't see the harm.'

'No. But who would have done a thing so foolish? Not one of the officers, I hope.'

'I hope not, Captain. I really hope not.'

Captain Sinclair gave the young man a long, hard look. Then he moved with ponderous majesty to the companion way.

James Stuart bent once more over his writing.

He had been composing the letter ever since the sea had begun to quieten down and the ship had entered calm water as it came into the embrace of the land. That was two days ago.

First, there had been the sea-washed skerries, pink and almost naked. Then a wilderness of grey rock, notched and lined. After that, the land proper, with some green showing here and there—very green—amidst the waste of stone. And at last a dark narrow channel twisting between mountains of incredible height and steepness.

For the greater part of two days, the ship had made its way deeper and deeper into this strange, silent, secret world. A world in which there seemed to be no sound apart from the rhythmic calls of the seamen and the rustle and gurgle of the water through which they were moving. And no sign of life, he would have said, because it was hard to link with any organised rhythm of human existence the lonely little houses, each like a stroke of red chalk above a stroke of white chalk. He could see them far above him, clinging like crimson burrs

11

to the precipitous mountainside. Why were they there? And for that matter, how? Just little boxes with no visible means of support . . .

He took a deep breath. For a moment, he caught an odour fainter and more delicate than the resinous smell of the ship's woodwork. It was the scent of the solemn land that was taking them into its arms. It was the odour blown from a great mass of pines. He bent again to the letter which he had begun so confidently a few days before. A thought that pleased him had come into his head: 'No roses grow on these rocks or I should pluck one and send it to you by the first passing seagull.'

He was writing to a girl in Edinburgh of whom he was fond —as fond, at least, as he could be of any woman. And that, as he would have been the first to admit, was probably not very much. He wrote on cautiously, telling as little as he could about the enterprise on which he was engaged. For he and his companions—above all, Captain Sinclair—had been gathering soldiers in Scotland to fight for the King of Sweden, deadly enemy of the King of Denmark. And the King of Denmark, as well as being a drunkard on a truly heroic scale, was the beloved brother-in-law of the King of Scots. So—it was an enterprise best spoken about in whispers.

James went on with his letter.

As we sail farther along this channel, trees are already showing in places. God only knows how, but they find soil in the crannies of these rocks. Ahead lie higher mountains and darker waters—and more trees. I can smell them from here. I believe people call this the Home of the Gods. If there are gods and not a God, they could well live in some such place as this.

He frowned and lifted his pen from the paper. What he had written was not at all worthy of the theme—the majestic, forbidding landscape with its rich, dark colours, where even the sky was of a blue so deep that it seemed to be a near neighbour of black. The glittering rocks, waterfalls hanging like brides' veils, precipices impossibly steep.

Higher up and farther inland, he caught glimpses of snow-fields and the surly wink of a glacier.

He resumed:

*We are going to land and march. Drums beating and colours flying:
also the pipes playing—the pipes of our country. in which I am
beginning to find a soul-stirring music. Nobody is more surprised at
this than I am.*
*I am told that the people who dwell in the country ahead of us are
friendly—*

That was what Captain George Sinclair had said, veteran
soldier of fortune, presently in the service of the King of
Sweden.

One day on the way over the North Sea, Sinclair had
explained the geography and politics of the march to Stuart,
with a map spread on the table in the skipper's cabin.

'Here is Norway, this long stretch of coastland on the west.
As you can see, it is damnably eaten into by the sea. We land
here'—pointing to a place in one of the deeper inlets. 'The
whole coastline is a dominion of the Danish king. He rules
from the North Cape to Hamburg, fifteen hundred miles as
the crow flies. As far as from Paris to Constantinople.

'Our business is with this part in the middle.' He pointed
with a fat finger at a place about halfway down the map. 'It is
not far from here to the Swedish border. But don't be
deceived, boy. To cross it will be like climbing a wall—and
then walking over the roof of the earth. A roof strewn with
broken glass. After that, we come to this valley running away
to the south. From that point onwards it will be easier.
Provided'—and at this point the captain's lips parted in a grin
which, however benevolent his feelings might be, always had
a hint of the tiger in it—'provided that the peasants are as
friendly as I expect them to be.'

'And how friendly is that?' Jamie had asked.

'They are peaceful people,' said Sinclair, with a trace of
contempt. 'What do simple farmers care about the quarrels
of princes?'

Stuart thought that it might be unwise to take too much for
granted from people who were, after all, descended from
marauding ruffians called the Vikings. Admittedly, that was
a long time ago.

Now the ship had slowed down almost to a standstill. The
water made hardly a murmur as it lapped round the stern.

Seamen climbed on to the poop and began to loosen the rope that towed the longboat.

Stuart made haste to finish his letter.

One day in Scotland you promised you would write to me when you felt you were beginning to be wicked. Do not wait so long.

J.S.

James Stuart folded the paper and rose to his feet. When he looked over the side, he saw that the longboat had been pulled alongside the ship's waist. Two of the hands had dropped into her and were unshipping her sweeps.

A vast figure stood again beside him. Captain Sinclair.

'Another hour and we are there,' he said. 'We shall have to finish the voyage in tow. The wind has fallen to nothing.'

Stuart looked about. The ship was moving imperceptibly if at all on the surface of what seemed to be a lake. On either hand, the rocky walls plunged down from hundreds of feet into an inky mirror. Ahead, the vista was closed by a confined mass of purple mountains.

In a moment, he heard the slow beat of the sweeps, and felt a tug underfoot as the ship slowly gathered way. A seaman ran up on to the poop and lowered the Lubeck ensign at the staff. The skipper had probably decided that he should not be at pains to identify his ship.

Stuart became aware that Sinclair was speaking.

'About this march,' he was saying. 'We shall move off at first dawn tomorrow. Now for the order of battle. Captain Ramsay'—speaking of an officer who had joined the ship at Dundee with a party of followers—'will take command of the main battle, which, as you know, is the central body of the army. I myself will, of course, lead the vanguard. The post of danger. Except that there will not be any danger.'

At this moment he aimed at Stuart a glance of exceptional severity.

Stuart, with a slight bow, which shook golden lights out of his curls, suggested that this aspect of the subject was of the smallest possible significance.

'As for you, Baldur the Beautiful,' Sinclair went on, 'I will entrust the rearguard to your care.'

'To me?'

'An order is an order,' said Sinclair, pulling at his moustache. 'If you think that the post is not honourable enough for you, let me tell you that some of the greatest captains have been proud to—'

'Yes, of course,' said Jamie, impatiently.

'Are you one of those people,' Sinclair demanded, 'who want to be either a field-marshal or nothing? No? Very well. As a concession, you may choose your second-in-command yourself. Whom do you want?'

Stuart answered without hesitation.

'I'll take Alistair MacIan, if he'll come.'

'Of course he'll come. But do you really want that Highland robber?'

'I really do, Captain.'

'He was sick all the way over the North Sea.'

'He wasn't the only one.'

'True enough. Below, the ship stinks like a lazaretto.'

'If it had not been for the sea-sickness we should have had a civil war on board.'

Sinclair inclined his head in his stately way.

'Yes. There was some bad feeling in the ranks, so I hear. Highlanders not liking Lowlanders . . . All that sort of thing will disappear like snow off a dyke when the trumpet blows for battle. Now, as for your request—you can have MacIan. And remember, you will be responsible if any peasant wife misses a cow on the line of march.'

Stuart nodded.

Sinclair went to the poop rail and called down, 'MacIan! A word with you, handsome.'

A lopsided smile, a scarred cheek, and brown hair burnt red by the weather, Alistair MacIan showed above the level of the poop and looked at the two men suspiciously.

Sinclair addressed him.

'This madman, Stuart, wants you to go with him at the tail-end of our march.'

'So that we can keep an eye on those thieving rogues in front of us,' Stuart explained.

'My children will of course be near me.' Alistair was speaking of the clansmen he had brought with him.

15

'That goes without saying,' said Stuart. 'And now, if you'll excuse me, Captain, I'll go to have a word with Alan Beaton.'

'He'll be leaving us today,' said Sinclair. 'A great pity—I see a good soldier going to waste in that young man.'

'He has business that takes him to Copenhagen and on to Hamburg.'

'So he says,' grumbled Sinclair. 'Greed tempts the boy. Sordid love of gold. Sad, sad—at a time of life when the call to glory should be sounding loudly in his ears!

'Buying and selling arms! Blunt swords, damp powder and guns that burst at the first shot! I have seen the scoundrels at their dirty trade. No better than pimps!'

'Shall I tell Beaton what you say?'

'Certainly. Tell him with my compliments.'

Stuart grinned and made his way for'ard. He was looking for the reddest hair, the maddest blue eyes in the ship, for a young man who had the same surname as the girl to whom, a few minutes earlier, he had been writing a letter.

The deck was a mass of excited men, the men whom Sinclair had coaxed off Highland crofts or prised—with the gaoler's connivance—out of Lowland prisons. Dour young men at odds with society and with the hunger of their kind for foreign places and unprofitable adventures; furtive creatures pursued by the memory of a misdeed; mere scarecrows who had not been strong enough for civilian life and now hoped, perhaps, God help them, that a camp would be kinder to them than their native town had been.

Stuart fancied that he detected in the eyes of these waifs some motive at work that was not mere weakness of mind or body—something that was at work in himself, a spark of— what? Wickedness? Self-reliance?˙ Restlessness? Curiosity? He had no time to analyse it more deeply or give it a more dignified name.

When he had discussed with his father, once an officer in the French army, the matter of a career suitable for a gentleman—'and there are damned few, boy, especially as I see no natural love of learning in you. Well, one must take the rough with the smooth—soldiering'—it had been agreed that the best days for Scotsmen in the French service were over. Carried away by a reckless and selfish nationalist sentiment, the French would be likely in future to keep more of their fighting for themselves. His father had thought of Denmark as a possible field for endeavour—a people with well-filled pockets and a peaceable nature.

But when, later on, Stuart had put the proposition to Sinclair, he had brushed it aside with a disdain that Stuart found unmannerly. No! The future of the profession lay in Sweden, rich in potential and with no unreasoning prejudice against the bearers of names like Sinclair and Stuart.

So now he was on the way to Sweden in this ship with the most unlikely troop of comrades that could be imagined.

But where was Alan Beaton with the hair which was unique even in that ship crowded with red-haired young men from the Highlands? Ah, there!

'Alan! I have a note here for your sister. Can I leave it with you to send it to her when you reach Copenhagen?'

'Give it to me, Jamie. It will find her. But you're sure that you won't come with me to Denmark? There is always room for another in the business.'

'The business?'

'Selling guns and powder to Queen Elizabeth's rebels in Ireland. And not in Ireland only. I have a customer in London. The old queen has trouble on her hands nearer home.'

Stuart shook his curls. Alan went on reluctantly.

'Listen. I hinted at this before. Now I'll speak more plainly. In Edinburgh, an Englishman came to me. Rich. A nobleman. He wanted a shipload of arms to arrive on such a date.'

'To arrive where?'

'London.'

'London!' Jamie's eyes had opened wider.

'London. To get it there secretly would be a problem—a hell of a problem. Something for you, Jamie! A ploy to your taste! Up the river! Past the guardship! Dodging the coast-watchers! Putting the arms ashore one night in the dark! Are you no' tempted, man?'

'Who is to get the arms, Alan?'

'That is a secret my Englishman would not tell me. Some man big enough, daring enough to launch a rising in London against the Queen of England. That is all he would tell me.'

Jamie frowned for a second. Then he shook his head and spoke almost angrily.

'I'm bound to go with Sinclair. Honour!'

'Mad!'

'Maybe, but so it is,' said Jamie. 'Now, let me tell you something. Captain Sinclair has the idea there is a woman aboard.'

'Now why in the world should he think a thing like that, James?'

'Someone has been talking.'

'You can trust nobody in this world.' Alan shook his head sadly.

At the memory of some recent events which they had shared, the two young men exchanged a broad, slow smile . . .

On the way over, the *Jesus* had put into Kirkwall harbour for victuals, and Jamie Stuart and Alan Beaton had gone ashore.

'This is the capital of a friend of mine, Lord Orkney,' said James.

'I've heard of him,' said Alan. 'You set a wild cat on him one night.'

'Did I now!'

'That's what they say.'

'If you see anything in the town you fancy, Alan, just take it. His lordship would like you to do that.'

After a bit they found their way to a dram shop. Beaton went ahead to reconnoitre.

'All clear,' he reported with a grin, 'if you are ready to risk meeting a couple of girls.'

'No battle is won without taking risks,' said Stuart.

The two women had gazed at the new arrivals with a cool appraisal.

Each was sturdily built, with high colour and gleaming black hair. One was maybe a dozen years older than the other, a handsome creature with bright black eyes. The younger one was an inch or two slighter in the body and lacked the older woman's hard assurance. But in that lissom waist, Stuart detected a budding talent for dalliance. The evening proved him right.

'Wine,' said Stuart. 'Red wine.'

The wine, when it came, was good quality Bordeaux of a ripe age, no doubt part of the plunder of some piracy.

He beckoned to the younger woman to sit down at the table. 'Jamie Stuart,' he said, tapping his chest. 'And you?'

'Margaret,' she told him. 'Stewart too.'

'Same clan. I hope not within the forbidden degrees.'

She shrugged her shoulders.

'You must ask my mother.'

The older woman had seemed to be deep in conversation with Beaton. Now she spoke sharply.

'I was fourteen at the time. Patrick Stewart was Earl of Orkney then.'

Stuart nodded gravely.

'Blood runs true,' he said. 'And good blood runs truest.'

Across the table, he took the girl's hand. He found it warm and responsive.

Much later, she stretched herself in lazy strength on the bed. Her smooth muscles moulded the light into changing, liquid patterns. She said, 'I hate you . . . I should hate you . . . I shall hate you tomorrow.'

She bit his shoulder.

'Devil!' She had drawn blood.

'Now you're going to remember me. For a little.'

'Remember you! I'm going to take you with me. Across the sea. For a little. Alan will see that you come back safely.'

'So you'll keep the girl below deck,' James said to Alan Beaton, as the *Jesus* crept along the rocky coast of Norway, 'until the mooring cables are loosened. I'll go and make my farewell now.'

It took longer than he expected.

'How much did you give her?' asked Alan.

'Give her? Not a groat.' The idea shocked him.

Alan clucked with disapproval.

'Always leave something, boy. However small. It shows respect.'

'It was a transaction within the family,' Jamie replied curtly.

'I want a bath, maybe my last for weeks. Pour a bucket of water over me here on the deck.'

He loosened the belt that kept up his breeches and began to pull his shirt over his head.

'It will take more than a bucket of water to cool you, James. But, God, what's that mark on your shoulder, man?'

Alan looked at Stuart, his brow furrowed.

'That? Can't you read? That was made by a branding iron. Don't you know a galley slave when you see one?'

'A galley slave! For God's sake!'

'It happens to the best of people. Take my advice and keep away from the King of Spain's recruiters. Lower the bucket over the side, boy, and fill it for my bath.'

By the time Stuart was dry and clad once more, the anchor chain was rattling through the hawsehole. They had arrived.

Beside a little jetty was a hooded shed made of wood—a warehouse?—and close by were small wooden cottages, doll's houses set here and there on the irregular surface of the land as their unseen owners had found convenient.

Behind, above, beyond these trifling objects were the scornful mountains conveying a silent message—a threat? Under the sombre frown of nature, the wooden buildings shrank and shrivelled until it seemed that they were made of paper—the thinnest paper imaginable.

Alistair MacIan shook his head.

'Look at the hills,' he said. 'Man, what a barbarous country!'

Stuart turned to him in astonishment.

'From a cave-dwelling Highland robber, that's damned good!'

'Barbarous! Wild people live here.'

In the foreground of the scene, Stuart saw only one living figure, a solitary horseman, wearing a heavy riding cloak and mounted on a sturdy dun-coloured animal. He was watching the scene intently. When the first soldier scrambled up from the boat on to the jetty, this watcher turned his horse's head, touched its flank with his spurs and, in a moment, had disappeared into a dense belt of firs growing some feet above the water's edge.

Sinclair, frowning heavily, approached Stuart and, putting

his mouth close to Stuart's ear, spoke earnestly:

'Did you see that horseman?'

'The one who rode away?'

Sinclair nodded. 'He was watching for our coming, and he carried away the news that we had arrived. Maybe, after all, they are expecting us, James.' He nodded ponderously and moved away.

'There's one man on board that shouldn't come with us, James,' said Alistair MacIan suddenly.

'Go on.'

'His name is Jock Stevenson.'

'The man Dugald tried to murder.'

'A pity you stopped him, James.'

Alistair went on in his quiet way. 'He listens too much. He asks too many questions. Where are we going? Where are we landing? And nobody kens where he comes from or how he got here.'

'Like most of the others,' Jamie scoffed. 'Out of the nearest gaol.'

Alistair shook his head.

'I've met his kind before. They slide through the heather when the weather is warm. James, that one's a spy.'

'And what do you think he's going to do? What work is there for a spy in the wilds of Norway?'

'God kens. But this I'll tell you, man. He asks too many questions about you.'

'Does he, by God!'

Alistair smiled gently. 'James, I am thinking that Jock Stevenson might be the first casualty in this campaign.' His fingers fluttered for a second above the hilt of his claymore. 'War is too serious a business for risks to be taken,' he added and strolled away.

James gazed after him for a moment in amazement. Then he turned once more to the business on shore.

Moving at the double, musketeers from the ship's boat posted themselves at points on the land from which the jetty could be commanded. Soon the ship was warped alongside the jetty. Unloading began as soon as she was moored.

'The skipper wants to get out of here as quickly as he can,' remarked Alan Beaton. 'His next port is Bergen, which will be swarming with the King of Denmark's officials. When he gets there, the skipper wants to deny on his oath that he had part in landing foreign troops on Norwegian soil.'

'He has been seen already by a horseman,' said Jamie.

'The skipper has been well paid for his work,' Sinclair growled.

When the ship had put in at Dundee, Jamie had visited a gunsmith's booth where he had found a beautifully chased silver pistol.

'Once it was the property of a nobleman,' the smith had said in a confidential voice.

'What happened.'

'He died. Sudden-like.'

On the handle of the little weapon, James saw that an earl's coronet was engraved. Below it was the initial G.

'French work,' said the smith. 'Try it, my lord, try it.'

Jamie did. The trigger movement was as easy as a compliant woman.

'How much?'

He had been amazed to find that the pistol was so cheap.

Now, on the deck of that ship moored to a quay in Norway, he pulled out the little gun and snapped the trigger. Then he put his hand on the rail and leapt lightly ashore. Alan Beaton threw his sack of belongings after him.

'If you come to Copenhagen, James, be sure to ask for me at the Red Lion.'

Jamie grinned up at him.

'If you come to Moscow, Alan, ask for me at the Kremlin.'

He went to borrow a whetstone for his sword.

'Jamie the Limp'

At the end of the first day's march, Alistair MacIan, sitting at the fire they had lit, said casually to James, 'Funny thing.' James looked at him and said nothing. 'You may have noticed it yourself.'

'What the devil are you talking about, Alistair?'

'You remember that person I mentioned to you?'

'Jock Stevenson?'

Alistair kept his eyes fixed on the fire.

'He hasn't come with us, James. He didn't come ashore today. Funny.'

'Funny! You Highland devil!' said James quietly.

'I didn't lay a hand on him, James.'

'What happened, then?'

'My children tell me he wasn't seen on the ship all morning. He would have hidden. There were plenty of places to hide.'

'And now?'

'He will go to tell the King of Denmark's people about the road we will be taking. Where are you going to, James?'

'To have a word with Captain Sinclair.'

Sinclair listened; sneered. 'We'll be in Sweden before the King of Denmark can shake the drink out of his brains. Besides, he has no regular soldiers within a hundred miles of here. You're too nervous, Mr Stuart!'

When Jamie told Alistair MacIan, the Highlander said, 'Does Sinclair think it would need regulars to deal with this army of guttersnipes?' A contemptuous wave of his arm swept over the encampment.

And as it turned out, the journey took longer than Sinclair had expected.

They marched for seven days into the country, uphill most of the way, into wilder rocks, narrower passes and denser forests. At the end of the seventh day Stuart's ankle began to ache. When he looked at it, he saw a swelling there at the place where the fetters had left their mark. He would carry to the grave that memento of his life as a slave on the Spanish galley. He had been captured at sea by the Spanish Navy and had pulled an oar on one of their slave ships, chained by the ankle to his rowing bench. He had lived miserably for months as a convict until he was rescued by a Dutch ship in a fight at sea. The scar on his leg was one of two badges of his slavery. The other was, of course, the brand on his shoulder, the letters GAL burnt into his skin which he would carry all his life. But the damage to his ankle was more noticeable. One night he overheard one of the men speak of 'Jamie the Limp'. Another laughed. Stuart remembered that an officer should sometimes be deaf.

Among the trees there was no sound of bird-song. When he spoke of this to Sinclair, one evening as they bivouacked, Sinclair answered, 'Wait until you come to the real forest! There the birds sing, but not everyone likes their song. Not,' he added with a quick frown, 'that we are likely to hear it.'

Two days followed on which they could not march at all. The sky opened. The rain drew down a shining grey curtain between them and the mountains. They sheltered where they could, under trees, in brushwood shelters, in caves. When it ended, as suddenly as it had begun, the sun shone, a thousand rivulets sang, a million mosquitoes swarmed round them. In a few hours the land was as dry as if there had been no deluge.

All through those nine days of march from the coast they had not seen a human being. Only a stag breaking out of a thicket. The tracks of some heavy animal; Stuart thought it might be a bear. Hares, hawks and foxes galore. Once, at night, they heard a wolf howl.

But no men. And, for that matter, no women.

'Oblige me, young sir,' Sinclair had said one day before they landed, 'by keeping your hands off any girls you meet.

They can be beautiful. Like queens! Like goddesses! And I ken your weakness, Stuart. It's in the family. But be careful. They keep a pair of scissors at their belt to use on unmannerly strangers.'

But when they came to a farm, it stood silent and empty, although the ashes on its hearth were still warm. The uninvited guest must expect a cold shoulder.

'The peasants,' his father had told him long ago. 'They hate us soldiers. Do you blame them? We trample their crops, steal their chickens and set fire to their barns. Sometimes we do worse . . . Let me warn you, my son, the best behaved army in the world does more damage than a cloud of locusts . . .'

'See,' said Stuart to Alistair MacIan, 'we are driving them like chaff before us!' He waved his hand towards the hills emptied of their people.

MacIan, who seemed to grow more silent and introspective as the days passed, gave the lopsided grin which made his scarred cheek look more sinister than ever.

He prodded the air with his claymore in the direction of a man of his clan who was a few yards ahead of them.

'Dugald has the second sight,' he said, with a grin.

'Do you mean the half-witted one?' Stuart asked.

'Dugald is not half-witted, you unbelieving Saxon. He is greatly gifted. He lives in two worlds at the same time.'

'What does he see in his other world?'

'He will not tell me. But it is bad, bad.' By this time, Alistair was smiling broadly. 'I can tell that from his way of looking. Listen, James. Do you know what they call these mountains? The home of the gods! It's quite natural that the gods don't like foreigners coming into their country.'

'To the gods all men are foreigners,' Jamie pointed out.

'I have the idea that they particularly don't like us.'

They went on. Jamie in silence, MacIan humming some cheerful Highland tune. With a pensive smile he swung his broadsword idly from side to side, lopping the heads off the wayside bushes. All round them he was aware of unseen, threatening forces. Jamie, against his will, and in his different way, shared some of the feelings of his comrade.

The winding track they followed was little wider than a

bridle path. Even for men more used than Stuart was to wild scenery and desolate landscapes there was a daunting quality about these valleys which turned so quickly into ravines, these mountains which were so nearly cliffs.

A grim and magnificent country, naked in its armour above the line where the trees stopped growing; clothed only in resonant colours. A land for gods—and perhaps for heroes?

Like us? He cast sidelong glances at his companions. He did not think they were heroes.

After a few more days they changed direction and began to lose height. At one place they crossed a hurrying mountain torrent, as talkative as a peasant woman at a market. They were moving southwards—south by east to be exact—and were leaving the confused mass of peaks behind them. Before them was a valley, broad and fertile for the most part, but contracting here and there into a rocky defile with dense woods of pine and larch climbing up on their left while, on their right, the river flowed. In its noisy childhood they had crossed it. Now it was mature and spoke in a deeper voice.

Stuart noticed that Alistair spent some time sharpening his sword. Every now and then he would sniff in the air as if he were a hunting dog.

'Smoke,' he said once. 'Someone has a wood fire.'

For a moment Stuart thought that he glimpsed a small feather of pale blue smoke among the trees above them. Almost at once, it vanished. He could have been mistaken.

'They've smothered it with a blanket,' said the Highlander. 'It's a signal.'

'You're too nervous, MacIan,' said Stuart. 'Don't you know that peasants don't attack soldiers. Ask Sinclair.'

Alistair's chin jerked upwards.

'There are peasants and peasants,' he said with something like a snort. 'As for soldiers! Give me fifty good men and leave to pick my ground and I would sweep these soldiers of ours into the river!'

'You have been listening to Dugald,' said Stuart. 'What has he been telling you?'

MacIan rubbed his chin. 'He tells me nothing. That's what troubles me.'

26

Stuart made a contemptous noise with his lips, but without being aware of it pulled his sword an inch or two out of its scabbard.

'I wish you would stop whistling that tune,' said Alistair irritably.

'What tune?' But he knew what the Highlander meant. Alistair whistled it.

'That,' said Jamie, 'is a French song. A soldier's song. My father taught it me. Would you like to hear the words?'

'It's bad enough to hear the music.'

'An English comedian I met in Edinburgh had some good marching songs.' Stuart began to sing:

> Sweet violets, sweeter than the roses are
> Covered all over with marmalade
> Covered all over with—snow . . .

'There's another version but it's too vulgar for your refined ears. But what about this?'

> Molly's in the garden
> Lying on the cinders
> Lying on her back with—

He was going to stop there. But one of the men in the ranks ahead knew the words or improvised words of his own.

Alistair shook his head.

'You have a bad influence on this army,' he said. 'As if they needed one.'

'Maybe, but they're marching better. Look!'

It was perhaps his imagination.

He looked ahead along the straggling column of men before him. They were very close to the river here. It ran deep under the bank beside them and tumbled over stones on the far side. Not far ahead, a large wooded island divided the stream into two. The mountainside rose abruptly on their left hand in a slope on which ragged trees and bushes grew around huge blocks of weathered stone . . .

Yes, it would be easy enough to plan the destruction of this caterpillar. One did not need to be a military genius.

At this moment a big man, walking in the opposite direction

to the march, came up to him. Stuart recognised one of the recruits whom Sinclair had added to the party in the last days before they left a port in Caithness, in the North regions of Scotland.

'Mr Stuart? . . . Compliments of Captain Sinclair. A note from the captain, sir.'

Stuart unfolded the piece of paper.

The note read: 'Movements have been seen on the left flank in the last few minutes. Bearer will point to the place. Look at it more closely and report.'

'Where?' he asked. The messenger pointed up the slope of the hill.

Stuart could see nothing. Only trees; rocks; undergrowth. At one point on the bank that looked as if it had been levelled by man, there was a barn, or perhaps a storehouse of logs faded to a silver-grey with the years. It was roofed with turf on which grass was growing a foot high. It had an air of neglect and desertion. No signs of life. Nothing but the sound of a stream hurrying down the slope to meet the river.

While he scanned the landscape, once he thought he heard, far off and very frail, the sound of a man's shout snatched at by the wind. But he could not be sure. He needed a better view.

'Alistair,' he said, 'wait for me here with your people, under this tree. I'll be gone for a few minutes.'

'Don't make it too long,' said Alistair. This is where it will happen, James. Lots of signs for those who know how to use their eyes and ears. Be careful.'

The climb up the steep slope behind them was harder than he had expected and it was more than a few minutes before James heard the trumpet call and the confused sounds that followed it. Then he broke into a stumbling run downhill.

The Pipes Are Silent

At some point in that wild, downhill scramble, Jamie Stuart became aware of one silence which was more alarming than all the confusion of noise that he heard. The pipes were mute!

There were sounds of shots, first of all in short bursts and then in a sustained series of percussions. There were sounds like thunder in the hills, sounds that seemed to shake the earth. There was a high trembling vibration—men cheering? There were shouts of rage. There was the hard music of metal striking metal. There were—more dreadful than these—the screams of men—in agony or fear. Who was to say? Either way it was ominous.

But the pipers were no longer playing! There was a special chilling menace in that.

When he reached the level of the path that ran along the river, the path which he and his comrades had been following, Jamie plucked out his sword. For a moment he paused, drawing his finger along the edge. He was trying to make sense of what he saw, trying to relate it to the sounds he had heard. The expeditionary force which Captain Sinclair had brought over from Scotland had disintegrated. Where was it now? Knots of men, separated from each other and fighting against odds.

More than that, the whole riverside landscape immediately before him had changed. Large boulders were present, which had not been there before as he remembered it. Jamie suddenly understood what had happened.

An attacking force, suddenly appearing above the path in a

well-designed plan of action, had rolled the stones down upon the marchers and had broken up their order. Then they had charged down the slopes, through the trees, towards the vulnerable, unready men between them and the river. They had been armed with the crude, barbarous weapons that peasants have always at hand—scythes, forks, axes, above all axes—while marksmen hidden in a wooded island in the middle of the stream had kept up a fusillade. And the outcome had been what he grimly saw.

Some way ahead, a baggage waggon had come to a halt. The driver had dropped the reins and was looking round wildly. Men rushed forward reaching for the draught horses' heads. Men were shouting. Amid a great many words he could not understand, he heard the shrill yells of Highlandmen, uttering Gaelic incitements to fight, or run. A horse plunged and screamed. Suddenly someone drove a hayfork into its rump.

But Sinclair? Where was the commander of the Scots brigade? Not a sign of him. Nobody to lead, nobody to organise resistance to the tall, bronzed, blond-haired demons who had appeared from nowhere and now, with a butcher's tools, were busy at their butcher's work.

Where in God's name were his companions? What had happened? Ah, there at least was Alistair with his plaid wound about his left arm, crouching as he fought, holding off two assailants with savage sweeps of his claymore. Cramming his steel cap down on his brow, Stuart put his sword under his arm and pulled his pistol from his belt. He aimed and fired. Missed! He rushed towards Alistair.

The two attackers drew back a pace or two—paused—and then fell back. They were looking for support.

'After them! After them!' cried Jamie breathlessly, but Alistair caught his arm.

'I knew that pistol was no use,' he said. 'Now, wait a minute. See what's happening.'

'What's happening! God almighty, that's easy enough to see. We're being murdered, man. Where is Dugald?'

'Dead,' said Alistair. 'That was what he saw in his other world. Look at him!' He jerked his bloodstained claymore towards the ground.

Stuart looked, and looked away.

'Well, he's in it now. And your other friend?' he asked.

'The other member of my family fell to the first volley of shot from that island. But I put arrows into two of the bastards before we came to grips.'

'And where is Sinclair?'

'Tell me if you can see him,' said Alistair with a shrug. 'Damn me if I can!'

'Dead?'

'He might well be. And why not? Did he not bring us to this place?'

'What we should do is make for the upper ground,' he said. 'The hills, hills!'

Jamie waved his sword at something he saw ahead of them.

'We have no time to choose the battlefield, Alistair. It's here or nowhere.' It was here.

Five or six of the peasants, big, fair-haired men, wearing knitted caps, black breeches and scarlet stockings, were running towards them with uplifted weapons, axes for the most part. It would be an ugly way to die but the alternative was likely to be worse.

Lifting his sword, he broke into a run.

'Come on Scotland! En avant, l'Ecosse!'

He heard Alistair growling behind him. 'You French bastard, you!'

'Haven't I told you, my father was the bastard. Not me . . . God damn you!'

The last words were thrown at the men in front of them.

Now they were at sword length from the peasants. Alistair was shouting something in Gaelic beside him.

An axe is a dreadful weapon, dreadful and clumsy. When it swings and misses, a fraction of a second passes before it can be raised again for a fresh stroke. Jamie adopted his offensive style to this brutal warfare. He reckoned that he was younger, quicker and more cunning than the man in front. A high parry to delay the axe-stroke, a backward leap, then forward with a quick deep thrust under the axeman's arm.

A sunburnt face contorted in pain. A bellow of pain.

31

Someone had fallen. Then there came a warning shout from beside him.

'Look out, Jamie. To the left!'

At Alistair's cry, Jamie ducked. Somewhere ahead of him, close by, was a man. He butted hard, at the height where it was most likely to be useful. He heard a grunt. The steel cap was driven down over his eyes. He struck out with his sword while his hand went up to push away the helmet that prevented him seeing. His teeth seemed, for some reason, to be digging into his brain.

A sudden and tremendous clang that became unbearable pain at his temple. Blackness. Stones in his face. A taste of earth in his mouth. Earth to —

Jamie was smiling faintly when a deep, deep silence folded him in its arms . . .

He came at last out of the darkness and wanted urgently to return to it. But the pain dragged him insistently into life again.

He was looking at a dully gleaming surface which seemed to fill his whole field of vision. After a while, he realised that it was his steel cap which for some reason had a deep dent on one side. Strange. He could not remember it like that. He turned his head cautiously, only a fraction of an inch. A low soft voice in his ear said, 'Keep still, idiot.' The voice was familiar. He could not think why.

But what made him cease from movement was the shaft of intolerable pain which went through his head. He closed his eyes. Later he would have time to think it all out. Much later.

He moved his hand to touch his cheek. He found it incomprehensibly heavy. This again was something that must be thought about. Later. There would be plenty of time . . .

Now he was looking at a dark complicated pattern on a blue membrane that was stretched between him and the sky. No, it *was* the sky. And the pattern was made of leaves, branches, thorns.

He was lying on his back and over him those barbed canes were criss-crossed. He lifted his head an inch; then he thought better of it.

'You've wakened, have you?' It was Alistair.

'What happened?' he asked.

'Are you all right?'

'What happened?'

He thought he heard soft laughter.

These Highlanders had a perverted sense of humour.

The sound faded and, after a time, came back.

'What happened? They thought you were dead. I don't blame them. You looked dead enough. The helmet must have had good steel in it. Look at it.'

Jamie looked and grimaced. 'And what about you?'

'Me? I carried out a fighting retreat,' said Alistair.

'Meaning you ran away?'

Alistair shrugged. 'In war, it is best to be reasonable, James. Yes, I am good at running and good at hiding, too. We should never have been caught in that glen. Disgraceful.'

'So you keep on saying. What next?'

'After a bit, the man with the axe—terrible things, axes. Did I not say it was a barbarous country? Terrible! Anyway, the man with the axe made off. Then I came down and found you. Alive! A miracle. You must have a damned thick skull, James.'

'It feels like an eggshell.'

'You bled a lot. That would be the reason they thought you were dead.'

'I expect so.'

'There was a man prowling about looking for plunder. He was too near you for my liking. So—'

'You killed him?'

'What do you think? What's certain is he would have killed you. After that, I dragged you here. It's as good a hide as ever I saw. Clean-cut rock on either hand and a bramble bush growing over the top.'

'And now what do we do?'

'First, you'll get better. Then'—his face relaxed into an ironical smile. 'Experience has shown that it's a mistake to loiter on the scene of a massacre.'

'I'll be all right, Alistair.'

'You'll be all right. Given time. If you get it. But the massacre—a pretty story.'

33

'Go on.'

It seemed that the ambush had been prepared at a place well-chosen for that kind of attack. The Highlander admitted that he and his friends on one of their forays against an enemy's cattle could not have set a better trap. The bugle, the musket fire from the island, and then the torrent of rocks which broke the line of march—and, behind the rocks, the attacking force.

'It was a fight for a minute or two, no more; after that it was slaughter. They were big men for the most part. Like those fellows Sinclair brought out from the North, men of his own tribe for the most part. Remember?'

Stuart remembered. Gaunt, serious-looking men with shocks of blond hair. 'Tall men. About thirty of them. They brought their pipers and a priest.'

'He was no priest, Jamie. He was a minister of the kirk.'

'What happened to them?'

'I was too busy with things nearer hand to be sure. But those thirty made a ring. They had, maybe, a hundred of the enemy round them, mostly swinging axes. Next time I looked they had gone down, all thirty of them. Vanished. What happened? You can guess.'

'And the priest?'

'The *minister*. Last I saw of him he was waving a broadsword in a very Christian-like way. One thing I will say, Jamie. From that quarter of the battle there was no shouting—no cries of pain. They fought a very dignified action, as gentlemen should.'

'And Sinclair?'

'How the devil do I know! You know that yellow horse he found the day we landed? One minute I could see him at the head of the column—the horse had half turned as if he were trying to force it back, to rally the men maybe. Then, no more! He would be in the thick of his own people. It was a good fight they made . . .'

'Like Flodden.'

'Just. With the same result.'

'A massacre!'

'Just so, Jamie. I greatly fear that there is one Scottish

gentleman the fewer on this earth.'

Stuart thought for a minute in silence. Then he said, 'As a veteran of the wars, he would hate being killed by beginners.'

With infinite caution he raised himself to a sitting position. Now he could look around him.

The scene was one of derisive beauty. The dew had vanished from the leaves but the sunshine had not yet taken life from the leaves of the birch which—for it was the turn of the season—were beginning to change colour. He noticed that, where those trees grew higher up on the hills, they already had a silvery tint.

A rowan, first to signal a warning of winter, was clothed in tattered, blood-red drapings. In a few days, everything would be brilliantly different.

Below, he could hear the river. On the far side, the land swelled up to a distant ridge of mountains. In the clear sky birds circled. But they were not the kind of birds that sang.

With a sudden frown he turned.

'It is time to go, Alistair.'

'Go, yes. But where?'

Jamie pointed. 'Across the river.'

'Yes,' said Alistair. 'We passed a stretch of the river where there was a raft of logs. Foresters' work. Now, if we were to go back there, we would be able to cross. And I could keep this dry.' He touched the bow which he had slung over one shoulder.

But, as it chanced, some time passed before they crossed.

The Cymbals of the Birch

They stood on the summit of a bluff above the stream. They were still looking for the place where Alistair had seen the raft—a place among the reeds, he said, where the river made a wide swing and on one bank had thrown up a steep beach of pebbles on which purple wild flowers were growing.

'It is not far from where we are now,' Alistair said. 'Not far—'

And then he had stopped suddenly and the expression on his face had stiffened. With a hand he imposed silence on Jamie.

'People are coming. Don't you hear them?'

In a minute, Jamie did. By that time, the two were flat on the ground.

Peering cautiously through the tussocks of grass, Jamie saw a procession coming towards them. A knot of men on foot shouldering pikes or muskets—the victors in the fight. After them a farm sledge drawn by one of the yellow horses that seemed to be native to the region.

The track passed below the hiding place of the two men, a few yards distant.

Jamie pressed his face against the stones. Juniper needles scratched his brow. Listening, he heard the sledge come to a halt. It seemed that the men in the procession had been met by another group. They talked for a little, first in loud voices which seemed by their intonation to be asking a question, then more quietly with some laughter. One word was repeated, tantalising with its elusive familiarity.

A whip cracked. The sledge moved on again, creaking. He risked looking up and saw something on it, covered by a horse blanket.

'What was that word they kept saying?' he asked.

'Zinkler. Zinkler,' said Alistair.

Raising himself on one elbow, he jabbed with a finger in the direction of the retreating sledge.

'Sinclair.' James understood. 'They are carrying him off to the churchyard.'

But he looked in a puzzled way at the sledge.

'I wonder,' he said. 'I remember him as a fatter man.'

'Death has a mighty diminishing effect,' said Alistair. 'God rest his soul.'

For a moment, Stuart said nothing, then he struck his companion lightly on the shoulder.

'Alistair, my lad, we have a plain duty.'

MacIan questioned him with his eyes.

'To attend the funeral.'

Stuart scrambled to his feet and dusted his doublet.

The ceremony in the churchyard was brief. The grave was dug, not very deep, because spades were soon striking the underlying rock. Then the blanket-covered body was tilted from the sledge on to the ground. For a moment, the blanket fell away.

Stuart and MacIan, watching from the dry stone wall that surrounded the little enclosure, drew in their breaths and looked at one another. The body was put in the open grave.

A man in a black cassock read quickly from a prayer book. Then the spades were picked up again and the earth was thrown on top of the body. It was time for the two watchers to withdraw. Jamie went first. Alistair muttered some words and crossed himself before he crept away.

At a safe distance, Jamie asked, excitedly, 'You saw it— the body?'

Alistair nodded. 'I did. It was Ramsay they buried there. How were they to know?'

'And where is Sinclair?'

'Sinclair will be lying yonder under a heap of his people.'

'Who knows! We should go and find him, Alistair.'

MacIan looked at him in derision. 'Before the crows do? Don't be a fool, Jamie. Our duty is to stay alive.'

Stuart shrugged his shoulders. 'As long as we can,' he said, grimly. 'We have yet to find that raft.'

'Jesus,' said Alistair suddenly. 'Were we not slaughtered! Poor Dugald! I will write to his mother.'

'From Moscow?'

'It will be the first thing I do in that place—what do you call it, James?'

'The Kremlin.'

But Alistair, striding ahead, had not heard.

They set off together, downhill, towards the river.

An hour afterwards they came upon the raft of logs and, leaping from one log to the next, reached the other bank.

They headed south, walking at as fast a pace as Jamie's weak ankle would allow, and giving a wide berth to the farmhouses they came to—buildings made solidly of heavy logs painted a dark red. By nightfall, they were exhausted as well as famished. They fell asleep in their plaids.

When Jamie woke the sun was already high in the sky. He shivered for a minute and then was warm. Alistair had disappeared.

Jamie collected dry twigs which were lying in profusion under a nearby larch and with his tinder box made a fire. He was stooping over this task when a slight noise made him look up. Alistair was there with a brace of birds over his shoulder and an excited sparkle in his eye.

'These hills are alive with game,' he said. 'You have never seen anything like it. We're going to live like kings! Look! A golden plover and a ptarmigan—all got in half an hour's hunting.'

After eating a hunter's breakfast, Jamie stood up.

'Where would you say is the south?'

Alistair looked at the sun, looked at the way the shadows fell: 'There,' he said, at last, pointing.

'In that case, we go that way,' said Jamie, raising his arm in a direction somewhat to the left of Alistair's.

He remembered from his study of Sinclair's map that the

river valleys had run south-east by south.

'We should reach the Swedish border in three or four days. From there on it's a straight road.'

'Maybe. But where to?'

Jamie showed a row of teeth glistening in his sun-browned face like a Viking shield-wall.

'To the gleaming domes of the Kremlin.'

'Sometimes, James,' said Alistair severely, 'you are such a damned idiot I think you must belong to the House of Stewart after all.'

'Remember one thing. If we should have the misfortune to meet anybody, you are dumb and I speak only French.'

Throwing his cloak over one shoulder with a graceful gesture that did credit to the Academy in Paris, where his education had ended, Jamie flung his arm out dramatically towards the blue ridge of the mountains, far off to the south.

'Forward!'

By the third day, their faces were burnt by the sun and dried by the wind.

They were leaner than they had been when they landed from the Lubeck ship, leaner by two holes of Jamie's belt. But the hunting had prospered and one evening Jamie tempted a trout to swim an inch above his palm and, with a heave, threw it on the bank.

Then, on the third morning, it happened.

Alistair, who had been out on the search for game, came back to the fire with a pathetic tale. He had stalked a stag and hit it with an arrow which had gone behind the shoulder. The animal had fallen on its knees and risen. Alistair had waited for it to fall again and lie still. Instead, it had hobbled off. Now it must be found and dispatched. The stalker must put out of pain any animal he had hit.

A quarter of an hour later, the two stood on the edge of a shallow tilted valley drained by a fair-sized stream.

'It was here I hit him,' said Alistair. 'He ran uphill and then turned towards the stream. Will you search on this side, Jamie? I'll go across. Give me a call if you see him.'

But when it came, the call was Alistair's. Jamie, who had

seen neither hair nor hide of a stag, made towards the sound. When he halted it was because, simultaneously, his senses had become aware of two facts—the sound of a shot, and the sight of men. He dropped behind a rise in the ground where rock and low bushes combined to hide him. When he peered through the branches, he could see two men walking slowly towards him. Each had a fowling piece under his arm. Between them trotted a black and white dog of a breed he knew. If they said the word, it would point at him.

Jamie scrambled as fast as he could, covering the ground crablike. In two minutes he was in a wholly different part of the glen and was working his way into a copse thicker than the rest.

He heard two reports. They had the leisurely sound of shot aimed away from him.

The light changes when the clouds pass. The shadows fall differently as the day advances. One hill, or wood, is very like another. The same hill, or wood, changes its aspect utterly when it is looked at from a new angle. Jamie lay low for a while and then, alarmed by the silence, moved on cautiously. In an hour he was lost. He did not go far that day but when he lay down among the trees to rest, famished, sleep fell upon him like a footpad, although by that time his ankle was aching damnably. He woke once during that night and looked for a fire. He was sure that Alistair would light one. He saw nothing.

At first light he set off, pulling his belt in one more hole. He was walking, he thought, towards the south. For two days he lived on berries which stained his face but did not satisfy his belly. Far off and above the tree line he saw a group of log houses. A farm. He made to go to it. He would steal if he could; beg if he had to.

Half an hour later, he saw that a broad river, deep and smooth, flowed between him and the farm. Some distance away, above him as the river flowed, was a fall, dark green like the glass of wine bottles.

He went on.

On the bank, walking towards him, was a man with a

musket on his shoulder.

It was no time to stay. No moment for inquiry. Time to go, quickly. And only one place to go.

Behind him was the steep bank with the river ten or twenty feet below. The man with a musket, only a few yards away, was about to fire. Jamie plucked off his steel cap and threw. Stepping backwards, crouching as he went, he felt the ground give way behind him. At that moment, he heard the report of the musket.

He went down in a slithering fall, his face torn by roots and stones. Brought up sharply, he found that he was standing on a tree which jutted out of the bank above the water. Cat-like, he made his way along the trunk, slippery with moss. Suddenly it began to crack as its roots pulled out of the earth.

He jumped free, his nose pinched between his fingers.

Now he was in an ice-cold, pale-green world, the tug of a powerful current taking possession of his body. His feet touched bottom. He kicked out strongly and stayed below the surface until his lungs were bursting.

When he opened his eyes again, the river had carried him far from the point at which he had entered it. He breathed deeply and plunged below the water once more, swimming slowly, saving his strength.

When he put up his head again, the other bank was near at hand. A larch trailed its long green branches in the water. He pulled himself up, dripping, breathing raucously.

After many hours, Stuart's ankle was making him limp badly. On this bank of the river, the ground was less steep. The forest—rowans and stunted oaks among pine—thinned out.

At last he came to an open space where the tufted trees had halted on the verge of lichen-covered rocks which lay about in great crustacean slabs. Between them, the ground sank into deep green coolnesses where sphagnum moss was quilted over bog.

He could hear somewhere—probably in the midst of a cluster of white chivalric plumes carried by some reedy plant—a small rill of water talking to itself on its way to the river. He would go no farther.

He began to peel off his clothes—doublet, shirt, shoes, stockings, breeches, drawers—and laid them out to dry. He unfastened the leather bag he wore round his neck and looked at the folded sheet inside. His passport. He put it on a stone, weighing it with another stone.

Before him was a flat dome of rock, half-shaded from the sun by a young birch. He found a place where a round pillow of sphagnum moss rose on the grey belly of the stone.

He collapsed on his feet, hearing the numberless cymbals of the birch. Then with a faint smile he turned over.

In a minute, he was asleep.

Lady Anstruther Looks for a Maid

The midday sun was shining weakly into a first-floor room in the High Street of Edinburgh. A gauntly handsome woman with greying fair hair was busy at the stove watched by a beautiful young girl. There was an obvious family likeness between them.

'I don't ken which of the two of them is the worse,' exclaimed Mrs Beaton, making a clatter with pans and ladles which adequately conveyed the notion that her son Alan was a scatterbrain, that her daughter Mary was deceitful and as for this boy James Stuart—if ever she had set eyes on a wastrel, he was one! It was like Mary to have become involved with the young man who had appeared in Edinburgh from nowhere in particular and was, from what she could gather, looked on with deep suspicion by the authorities; and now he had left for foreign parts—for Russia no less! Was there ever such nonsense! 'Going off like that, God knows where—and doing what I'd like to ken!'

'Well, Mother,' said Mary, 'here are the letters, one from each of them, answering all your questions.'

'What do they say? No, no! I want to hear none of their nonsense. Going to Moscow, did ever you—'

'It's Mr Stuart who is going to Moscow, Mother. He has gone with Captain Sinclair who is a most respectable soldier. As for Alan, he is going to Copenhagen. Alan is going to Copenhagen on business.'

'And what kind of business—no, don't tell me! It's better I should not know what mischief my son is up to. As if things

43

weren't bad enough here without that! Where are you off to, girl?'

Mary had risen and smoothed her skirt.

'To fetch the sheets from the laundry, of course. Which reminds me, Jamie says—'

'Oh, it's Jamie now, is it? A while ago it was Mr Stuart. Why don't you call him *King* Jamie and be done with it?'

'That's what Alistair says he should be.'

'Alistair! A false-spoken Highlandman like the rest of them.'

'But so handsome, Mother mine! With a long beautiful scar on his cheek.'

Mrs Beaton sniffed with irritation.

Smiling, Mary went on, 'Jamie says in his letter that he will keep your shirt to wear at a banquet in the Kremlin.'

'Kremlin! If ever he gets there . . .'

'He'll be lucky, ma'am!' They turned toward the hoarse, rusty voice.

The door to the passage had been quietly opened and there stood a red-bearded, red-eyed, red-nosed man. Out of his little eyes peered all the wickedness of the fallen world. A caddy. One of the members of the Edinburgh underworld whom respectable people sometimes found useful. This one was called Gregory and he had been in the service of Jamie Stuart during that young man's visit to Scotland not long before.

'Gregory!' said Mary. 'Who'll be lucky?'

'The man you were talking about, ma'am. They call him James Stuart, which is part of his trouble, poor gentleman.'

'What have you heard?'

'Oh, nothing—nothing to speak of.' Gregory scraped his cheek noisily with his thumb. 'But some persons have heard that Mr Stuart has gone walking through the mountains of Norway. And some persons have the notion that Mr Stuart might have an accident. Yes . . . He is a lucky young gentleman, ma'am. He'll need to be.'

His little eyes wandered round the room.

'How did they come to think he had gone to Norway, Gregory?' Mary asked.

'Maybe they had a spy on board, young lady. And maybe another spy reached Norway before the ship did. Is there a town over there called Bergen?'

The two women looked at him sharply.

'And is that all?' asked Mrs Beaton. 'Is that what you came to tell us?'

Gregory, cringing in the doorway, nodded and shook his head all at once.

'Just so. That and something else. It might be those persons I mentioned had an idea . . .'

'Those persons . . .?'

'Weesht, weesht! For God's sake!'

'Speak what's in your mind, Gregory,' said Mary impatiently.

'They purpose to harm friends of Mr Stuart.'

'Meaning?'

'It's obvious what he means, Mother. They want to harm us.'

'You, young lady, you!' said Gregory, jabbing at the air in her direction.

'What an idea!' exclaimed Mrs Beaton. 'A body would think there was no law in Scotland. No judges.'

'I wouldn't count on them too much,' said Gregory. 'These are matters of state, ma'am.'

'So what do I do?' said Mary. 'Wait here till they march me off to the tolbooth?'

The caddy leant forward and spoke quickly. His eyes darted about, but bright now, evasive no more. The whisky on his breath made the two women draw their chins back an inch or two.

'The Lady Anstruther leaves in a few days to join her man, Sir Ralph. She might be wanting a lassie to go with her.'

'A lady's maid?'

'Call it a lady-in-waiting, ma'am.'

'And I might be the lady?' asked Mary.

'What for no'?' said Gregory eagerly.

'Sir Ralph Anstruther. What is he?'

'He's the king's ambassador in Copenhagen, ma'am.'

A grin slowly widened on his lips, mirroring Mary's grow-

45

ing smile as the ingenuity, the neatness, the humour of the proposal dawned on her. While the king's emissaries looked for her in Edinburgh, she would be snugly in the king's service in Copenhagen.

'And now if you'll excuse me, ladies,' said the caddy, 'I have other business.'

A last smirk, a last bow, a last whiff of spirits, and he was gone.

'Lady Anstruther—'

'Gregory knows that she is looking for a maid, Mother. I'll find out where she is and go to see her at once.'

'We'll both go,' said Mrs Beaton firmly. Already she was untying her apron.

'Devil Take You, I Can't Kill You'

Jamie had been dreaming of a strange woman, neither young nor old, plump nor thin, loving nor cold. He awoke to find her standing between him and the sun.

Gradually she came into focus and he understood that, after all, she belonged to the world of reality. She was no longer a girl, but not very old. She was not friendly at all. She held a naked sword an inch or two from his throat.

It was his own sword, thrown down beside him when he collapsed on the rock. As it moved slightly in her grasp, the sun danced along the blade.

Her face was stern, with lips compressed, a deep frown drawn between her eyebrows. He eyes were a colour between grey and blue.

She seemed—but it was an effect of the light, of the sky behind her and her place above him on the rock—taller than any woman he had ever seen.

He lay still for a moment, his eyes roaming over her—bare feet, a black skirt of coarse woollen fabric which fell below her knees, a sleeveless scarlet tunic with small silver buttons. The sleeves of her smock were rolled above the elbows. Braids of blonde hair, from which the dry mountain air had snatched some of the brightness, were coiled round her head like new cords on a ship. He thought that, with a different expression, she would be beautiful.

It was hard to say, and not very important during what were likely to be the last few seconds of his life. For, of course, she would kill him. His chief anxiety was that she would make a swift, clean job of it. But he doubted if she would. He had been brought up to believe that women could not be trusted with any weapon bigger than a dagger, which they kept in their garter to deal with importunate suitors.

'Father was right,' he said in French. 'A woman would bring me bad luck in the end.'

She said nothing, but went on looking at him. If anything, the frown on her brow deepened.

'What are you waiting for?' he asked.

She answered in words which he could not understand, words which seemed to have a sob in them as if they were a mixture of fury and despair.

What she said—using the local dialect which would have been as incomprehensible at the court in Copenhagen as it was to Stuart—was 'Why the devil can't I drive this sword through your breast?'

But it was a long time before he found out what she said in that first moment.

'One rib farther down,' he said, 'and an inch more to the left. Otherwise you are going to bungle it.'

As she realised something that had escaped her until then her expression changed. A surprised curiosity came to soften enmity. Can one say that steel softens into bronze, or stone into marble? A marble made golden by the sun.

There was a brief but perceptible pause.

'Are you French?' she asked.

To his astonishment she was speaking in French. A faltering French spoken with an accent which she had never heard before. It had the effect of making her seem younger—and more appealing.

'I was born in France. My mother was French, my father was—something else.'

He would have liked to ask her how she came to have some knowledge of the tongue of his childhood. But with the sword an inch from his heart—no, it was hardly the moment.

He moved his hands slightly, making the first outline of a gesture. At once, the sword touched his breastbone. The face above him lost the warmth of marble, the gold.

'French? What are you doing here?'

48

'I came with friends. We lost our way.'

'I know,' she said, angrily. 'You came with others. I have heard of your friends. The bandits from Scotland. You have no right to be here, Monsieur le Français.'

He grimaced. The matter could be discussed. But not now. Not with that sword, sharpened a few days before by his own hands, and now poised above him, ready to be plunged into his breast by that strong and, by God! beautiful arm.

'Very well,' he said, with feeling. 'Either you will kill me or take me to the people who have massacred my friends. They will blow my brains out. I understand. But let me ask you one thing. Do you mean to take me there without my clothes on?'

His head jerked in the direction of the bush where his garments hung.

'You are safer as you are,' she said.

'I don't feel very safe.' He drew a finger across his throat.

This time the sword point did not move. There was a remote cell of intelligence within him which noted that fact—the failure of the sword to move.

'Besides,' he went on, 'I am not used to receiving ladies as if I were Adam in the Garden of Eden.'

The expression on her face had softened again. If he did not delude himself, she was a younger woman than he had thought. But her voice when she spoke had still the edge of anger.

'They'll cut your throat. I only wish I could! How do you think that we should welcome robbers who break in? How would you treat us'—she tapped her breast—'if we came to Scotland?'

'Scotland?'

'That is the country where you come from, isn't it—although you speak French?'

'Scotland?' He seized on the word. 'It is another country where I'm hunted as if I were a wolf.'

'Wolf! We have wolves here. We don't need to import them.'

Then suddenly it was over. She stamped her foot and threw the sword clattering down on the rocks.

49

'Go,' she cried, 'and devil take you! I can't kill you.'

The sternness in her face had broken into something else. Sorrow? Tenderness? And something else. She was, at that moment, a woman of awe-inspiring—no!—heart-rending beauty.

Jamie rose and went over to where his clothes were spread on the junipers. When he turned again, she was crying. He ran over and put his arms gently round her. But, shaking her head in anger—with herself, or with him? Who could say?— and sobbing as she did so, she pushed him away. Not understanding, he spoke words of comfort.

'Do not weep. Do not weep—Ne pleurez pas.' he said, turning to his first tongue. 'Je vous prie.'

'Go away,' she said in her own language. 'You should never have come. Go!'

Even without her gestures of dismissal he would have understood. As he went over once more to where his clothes were spread out, he saw his sword where she had thrown it down on the rock. He stepped back, picked it up and offered it to her, holding the hilt towards her. But she shook her head, refusing.

He continued dressing in haste.

Opening his mouth, he pointed with one finger to his throat. How many hours was it since he had eaten?

'Faim,' he said.

'Sulten?' she said in her language. He nodded. He took out the purse which he had kept hidden in his doublet.

Her answer blasted him with its fury: she did not belong to a race that were so poor that they came thieving in other people's gardens. They gave charity to beggars. They did not take money from bandits.

He thought her magnificent.

'The truth is, chère madame, I am fainting from hunger. Faim! Sulten!'

After a minute she said 'Come', and began to walk away.

He picked up his sword and followed, a few paces behind her, through woods dappled by the afternoon sun, along the borders of fields of rye and barley and oats which would need another month of autumn weather before they ripened. The path grew steeper as they went on.

At length, she brought him to a group of low, wooden buildings which had weathered to a soft silver grey. A rough wooden fence, made of upright posts crossed diagonally by boards which had been crudely trimmed, enclosed a small meadow. A few cows were grazing it. Beyond was an orchard with apple trees and black cherries. A dog ran towards them, barking wildly.

'It is an English hound,' she said curtly. The dog was a well-bred black and white pointer, a hunter's dog.

As they came closer, he saw that the house was made of heavy logs, squared by the axe and raised on piles of stone so that it was clear of the ground. Grey moss had been used to caulk the gaps between the layers of timber. At each corner the logs were keyed into one another so that no upright post was needed. On the roof, grass was growing, cropped by a tethered goat.

Jamie wiped his shoes on the mat of fresh juniper twigs spread out in a fan shape in front of the threshold.

To the Sea

She watched him eat, sitting in his shirt-sleeves at the big, rough table in her mountain cabin.

When he apologised for his ravenousness, she looked at him out of her soft grey eyes above which fine brows had risen imperceptibly. He noticed how well the colour of her eyes accorded with the tan of her cheeks. But she said nothing.

He told her about the march from the coast and the slaughter beside the river. They had not thought to be attacked . . . Her eyes flashed at that.

'What did you expect? To walk through our country as if it was your own?'

'But this is a time of peace, madame.'

'Then why do you come here armed?'

As he could think of no good answer, he went on to tell her of the flight down the great valley, of his parting from Alistair.

'He has a dreadful scar on one cheek but women find him attractive.'

'We women have strange tastes,' she said tartly.

'Do not hold that against him, please.'

He told her how he swam the river to escape from the musket man and lay down to dry himself and his clothes on the rock where she had found him. She asked him about the river. 'They must be very near,' she said.

Telling snatches of his story, he heard snatches of hers. She was a widow. Her husband had been called up for the militia and had been killed in some border clash which, so far as he could understand, had been hardly more than a misunderstanding between patrols. There had not even been a war at the time. 'Like now,' she said, with a flash.

She looked after the farm which had been her husband's. How long that would last? . . . she finished with a shrug.

'Do you live here alone—and do the work?'

She told him that this place in the mountains was no more than a summer pasture to which she brought the cows when the grass was sweet. Down below, in the valley, was the farm itself, to which she would be returning soon.

How did it happen that she spoke French so well?

She did not speak French well at all. But when she was a young girl, living in the town, a Frenchman had come to stay there, a watchmaker, a refugee from the wars of religion. Yes (she nodded), a Huguenot. From him, she had picked up what she knew.

'He taught you to speak with a good accent,' he told her.

At this point, Jamie rose from the table where he had been eating.

'I came here as a beggar,' he said. 'You treat me like a guest. Let me introduce myself. James Stuart.'

He bowed, although more stiffly than M. de Pluvinel had taught him. She surprised him by the grace of her answering curtsey.

'Jeems Stuart,' she said.

He nodded. It was near enough. 'May I ask your name? Or is that a secret between you and the mountains?'

She frowned quickly and smiled reluctantly.

'Ingrid Sigurdsdottir,' she said. When he wrinkled his brows over the name, she found a pen and wrote it down.

'Sigurd. My father.'

Ingrid, the daughter of Sigurd.

He took up the quill and wrote his own name below hers. Her eyebrows rose.

'Ah!' she exclaimed. 'La reine! Maria!'

Even on this wild mountain, the name was known. The dead Queen of Scots, who had been his father's half-sister; but beyond all doubt was born on the right side of the blanket.

'The same surname,' he said, 'but a different family.'

53

She did not inquire how he was, apparently, both French and Scots and how he came to be invading her country. On that question he thought he knew how her mind was working. The less she knew about him, the easier would be her conscience. From time to time, she gave him a quick, sharp glance. Once she said, 'That is a beautiful shirt.'

'Yes,' he said. 'And it has been beautifully mended.'

'So I see. A lady has worked on it.'

'A lady,' he agreed.

Once or twice he caught her glance returning to the shirt with the faintest ghost of a question. She had seen the crown which a girl had once mischievously embroidered above his initials.

Soon she said that it was time for her to go. She had the animals to see to.

'Then I must leave,' he said, rising. 'Never did a sad adventure have a happier ending—if it is an ending.'

She opened her eyes. 'But you are not leaving now? The sun will soon be down. You will only lose your way again. Tomorrow I will lead the herd down to the lower country. Summer is over. If you come with me, I will show you the sea. But you must promise me one thing.'

'Yes?'

'You will not go to Sweden. To Scotland—yes.'

He laughed. 'If I go to Scotland, I shall end on the gallows. Will you allow me to go to Denmark instead?'

She said something quickly in her own language. He decided, later, that she had probably said he would end on the gallows anyhow.

I must go. Tonight, he told himself. If I stay here, they will come to look—and that will be trouble for two people.

He heard her moving about in an outhouse. There was music of many bells, the half-dulled sound of cowbells.

He went into the clear, thin air.

Quite suddenly, the light had faded. The sun had sunk below the mountain. Already a chill had fallen on the air. A wind had sprung up.

The woods round the house brandished their spears. In a little, the stars would be visible. He needed only one, which, on a clear night like this, he would easily find, to guide him on the way.

Eastwards, eastwards!

That probably meant crossing the river again, if his sense of direction did not deceive him.

More important it was to put as many miles as possible between himself and the men who would be looking for fugitives. If he were lucky he would find a pass leading into the next valley. Matters might be quieter there . . . He would be a Frenchman, an officer in the Danish army . . .

She came and spoke earnestly, her hand held up in a gesture of restraint, or warning. Then she pointed up at the sky.

'Mirk! Nuit!'

Yes, it would soon be night. The sooner he started the better.

She took him by the arm and, leading him to the door, she pointed to a small log hut which stood a few yards away.

'Come.' She led him over to it and unlocked the door— which stood a clear foot above the ground. Inside, it was dark and cool and filled with inviting smells. Her storehouse. She pointed to a heap of empty corn sacks. He would be comfortable sleeping there.

Some time later he fell asleep.

Once that night he heard horses outside, or dreamt that he did so. A dog barking. Voices. Later, a heavy body moving on the turf roof above him. Some night bird—an owl perhaps? Later, cowbells and a woman singing.

At last he woke. Between the logs of the wall, blades of light dissected the gloom of the storehouse. Outside, it would be brilliant sunshine. After a while there were steps outside. A key turned and the door was opened.

She looked smaller, shyer and happier than she had done before. The sunlight fell across her cheeks. A strand of rye-coloured hair had fallen over her forehead. She blew it out of her eyes in embarrassment.

He kissed her hand, smelling of milk.

It had rained once during the night. The light sparkled on the leaves of the birches.

She told him men had come, and gone. Whether they would come back—that seemed to be uncertain. They had given a horrifying account of the ambush. A massacre! An execution by the axe!

Stuart was gripped by the guilty chill of the survivor. Bad conscience, an uneasy sense of fate postponed—muddled emotions against which reason fought in vain.

The name 'Zinkler' kept recurring.

'Yes? Sinclair? Is he alive?' he asked.

It would be a miracle. But no. By the sharp, darting of her finger towards the ground, it was clear that 'Zinkler' was dead. So died professionals in his trade. The lucky ones.

'They asked for you,' she said suddenly.

'For me? By name?'

'Yes. For James Stuart. They said it many times. I could not be mistaken. You are a man they greatly want to find. I pretended not to understand them. I may have done wrong. But—I do not give a man shelter one night and give him up to his executioners before dawn.'

'I am a wanted criminal, an escaped convict. You have seen the brand.'

'I do not know what you have done.'

'I am not one of the saints, Ingrid, but the crime for which I am hunted, the crime that brings me here, is to have the name I bear—James Stuart.'

She lifted her hands and let them fall, as if in complete bewilderment or dismay.

'It's the name my father gave me. Sons have the right to take their father's name, haven't they?'

She answered, speaking slowly. 'I do not think you are a criminal, Jeems.'

The blood rushed to his head.

'For some things one cannot say Thank you. One can only . . . Now I will go.'

'No,' she said, calmly. 'No, you will not go, not alone. You will come with me, to the sea.'

There could be no refusing her.

All was ready for their journey. An old woman would come to lock everything up after they were gone. If he would keep out of her sight, all would be well. But they must be on their way quickly. They could eat on the road. And, to hide his foreign-looking clothes, he must wear an old cloak she had found for him.

Ten minutes later, they set out in the wake of the tinkling herd.

A God Enters the Room

They walked all that day, following the herd, resting once when a huge, shrouded larch sheltered them from the heat of the sun. Towards evening they came to smoother, low-lying country. Between the dark, green woods were fields where grain was ripening. They passed beside stretches of water which might be lakes or inlets of the sea.

Once a grassy mound about fifty feet high rose not far from the path. There was an area of lichen-grown rocks round it, on which grew rows of juniper bushes. Ingrid pointed to it.

'That is the tomb of a warrior lady,' she said.

'There are stories like that in every country,' he said.

Her eyes flashed. 'Do you not believe me? In our family we do not remember lies.'

'Ah, you are descended from this lady.'

'What do you think! There is a spell on this howe. Many people will not pass here, at night. They hear music. They are afraid.'

'Have you heard the music?'

'The lady would not harm one of her own people,' she said.

The journey ended at a collection of wooden buildings set in a disorderly oblong round a yard. Trees, a dark-green tide, frothed up to the entrance of the yard.

He watched while a rush of women, with a clatter of peasant voices, emerged from the main house of the group. There were cries of joy, curtseys and kissings of the hand. In a minute or two Ingrid beckoned him to come forward. He found himself in a circle of curious eyes and sunburnt smiles. A middle-aged woman said something and others laughed.

'Excuse them,' said Ingrid. 'They think you are too fair for a Frenchman. They wonder if your mother had a blond lover?'

'Tell them my father had.'

Shaved, washed and combed, he came out into a low chamber which seemed to be the central room of the house. He looked round curiously.

The wooden walls were hung with peasant tapestries. He recognised one of the Queen of Sheba meeting Solomon.

In one corner, a long table of massive timber stood near the wall. In another was a big fireplace of brick, covered with cement and whitewashed. It held the dull embers of a fire, which very quickly could be blown into life with the bellows lying handy.

It was some time before Ingrid came in and, in the interval, the room was invaded by delicious smells from the kitchen. She blew the ashes until suddenly the big fireplace was alive with soft explosions and sharp cracklings.

She brushed ash from her hands and, with a flaming twig, lit more candles set in sconces round the walls. She wore a small cap of black embroidered velvet and, at the breast of her bodice, a gold brooch made of gold coins linked together by small wire rings twinkled in the light.

'You have done something to your hair,' he remarked. He might have gone further, but a woman must not be over-praised.

'And you have done something to your face. You look very handsome,' she said, tartly. 'Now we are going to eat.'

She clapped her hands and, in a moment, a sturdy peasant woman entered, carrying a flat, oval dish that was twice as wide as she was. She put it down on the heavy table. A dish of grilled mackerel, prepared as it should be, with deep incisions stuffed with parsley.

'Do you have the sea close to you here?'

She laughed as she beckoned him to sit down.

'In Norway, what we have most of is sea. In daytime you can see it from this room, glittering through the trees. At

59

night, if you listen, you can hear it lapping against the rocks.'

'And the mermaids—can I hear them singing?'

She held up a finger. 'To hear them brings bad luck. You must close your ears.'

For a time he closed his ears. He was incredibly hungry and blamed it on the nearness of the sea. The fish was excellent and the flat, crisp bread went well with it.

The room grew warm.

He took off his doublet and sat in his elegant shirt. On the crimson light from the fireplace, the gently vibrant light of the candles threw orange-coloured shadows.

Her face became a dusky golden colour; her hair was silver-gilt; her eyes larger and darker than they had been in daylight.

It was strange that she had been allowed to remain a widow for so long—a year as far as he could reckon. That she would be hard to please he could believe.

'All this is yours?' It was half a question, half sheer pleasure at the soft beauty of the room.

'Most of it was Erik's,' she told him. 'Some of it was my father's. Now, for the moment, it is mine.'

She went on to explain. By law, she, the widow and heiress, could be challenged in a local court composed of the neighbouring peasants. They might think she did not farm the land well enough. Farming was a man's job and they were men.

'And they might have an eye on the land for themselves—or on the woman who farms it?'

'They will be bound by custom. Besides, I have a bailiff,' she said, with a shrug.

'And you do not trust him.'

'I would not want him to see you, James.'

'But I shall soon be gone. Soon, Ingrid, you will be troubled no more by the man you saved! I shall slip away into the trees and disappear.'

'But not to Sweden!'

'No. I shall go to Russia, or Denmark. To Copenhagen. I have a friend there.'

'It is a long swim, James. You had better take a boat.'

'Find me a boat, then! I will sail right out of your life, leaving not a ripple behind.'

'I shall have all the more time to bring in the harvest.'

Suddenly serious, he said, 'You must marry, Ingrid.'

She sent him a curious glance across the table.

'First, I must love,' she said softly. 'This time I must love.'

For a minute they looked into one another's eyes, glowing, dilated in the light of the candles.

A god had entered the room.

'Love,' he said at last. *'That* is important.

'Everything,' she said.

'It may be mistaken. It may be mad!'

'It is always mad,' she told him. 'It is never a mistake.'

In the silence, he heard again the frail, pulsating sound that came from outside. Small waves, one after another, were lapping a beach. By chance, they kept time with the rise and fall of her bosom.

'You must go,' she said. 'You have been here too long already. They are looking for you, James. They know what you are like. Tall, blond, ugly—'

'Do they say ugly?'

'You limp—'

'Not much.'

'And you have a mark on your shoulder. I have seen it. They know about it.'

'Do you know what that mark means, Ingrid? Listen.'

He told her how he had pulled an oar in a Spanish galley.

I think you are mad, James. But I didn't think you were a slave.'

He rose. He had an idea.

'Ingrid, the sea is near us . . . I can hear it. Let us go and find a boat.'

She called out something to the moman who had brought their food to the table. Then they walked out into the warmth of the night. From the kitchen came a clatter of pans. A lewd gush of women's laughter spilled out.

At some distance from the house they climbed on to a naked platform of rock sloping down towards darkness. A wild smell summoned up a world of images and ideas. Wet rocks and drying weeds. Lonely diligent birds with white bodies and orange beaks keeping watch over long expanses of sand.

Dampness that clung and excited.

The sea.

She walked confidently ahead, he following cautiously, feeling with his feet the uneven surface of the rocks.

There was a milky sky and phosphorescence on the water. He was aware of dark presences of land, quite near, across the water which they were approaching.

At the edge he lay down, and dipped his arm in the water. It was like a milder, more clinging kind of air.

She sat down and pointed out to sea.

'You asked the way to Denmark. Can you read the stars, James?'

'I can find the North Star.'

'Turn your back on it. Sail south, due south for eighteen miles and you will see the Skaw over the bow.'

'Eighteen miles! That is very near.'

'Our miles are longer than yours, James. For you, it will be a hundred.'

'South for a hundred miles. That should not be difficult.'

'But there are hundreds of little islands on the way, skerries, rocks, hidden reefs and only one lighthouse.'

'Come with me, Ingrid, show me the way.'

Her laughter was as warm as the night.

She rose. 'I will show you the way to your house, James.' She held out her hand and pulled him to his feet.

The hut was sheltered by a wall of rock which had been cut out to cover it from the wind. It looked over an expanse of dark-grey sea on which, far off, the light of a ship was flashing.

She stooped and picked something from under a stone.

'Here!' she said. 'This is the key. You will find a lamp inside and a bed.'

It began to rain.

The Ship Named Glory

James woke early—how early he did not know—in a room flooded with golden light. He threw off the sheet that had covered him and went out. It had rained heavily during the night. A mist was lifting from the sea but here, in the small clearing that had been made for the hut behind the rampart of rock, the morning sun was already making the trees into a jewellery of jade and emeralds.

He could hear a dozen swollen brooks as they hurried, as if panic-stricken, downhill to pour their burden of lament into the sea.

Within him, a commanding voice sounded and he obeyed it. He strode forward, barefoot, into the embrace of the trees and within a minute was lost.

After a time, he came to a sudden rocky hill, lifting itself clear of the trees. But he was not prepared for the sight that silenced him when at last he stood upright on the small rocky summit.

The morning haze had cleared from the water. From the faint, pink line of clouds above the distant coastline that was the furthest point of his vision, to the summits of the trees immediately beneath his feet, he could see the wide expanse with an extraordinary clarity.

In front of him was a channel opening into a wider channel. Tree-covered islands—maybe a dozen in all—were set in the water at different distances. He could guess that they were separated by small seaways which he could not see.

Silence, stillness, peace under the blue dome of heaven. A

sea like a polished golden shield. No living thing in sight except a row of white seabirds drawn up along a stone jetty below him.

Below the surface of the water, he could discern a slow pulsing. A shape was moving there.

Translucent white frills round a pale pink core veined with crimson threads were opening and closing in a languorous rhythm like the hands of a ballerina dancing. At one moment a small rosy ball was thrusting upwards to the surface; at the next it weakly opened and became a white flower with eight petals and a vermilion heart. The jellyfish was swimming in its sleep.

The warmth of the sun grew from minute to minute. Soon it would be the full heat of day. A thin scent of thyme came to his nostrils, rising in the still air from a strip of wheat which grew below him, between the trees and the rocks. More robust and nearer was the smell of the pines with its undertone of tar.

A faint breath of wind ran a finger over the wheat. A bee shot across his face, like a twanged string.

It was over.

The pause in time was ended. Jamie was about to turn away when something happened that transfixed him to the spot.

In the bay beneath him where, a minute before, the water had moved languidly to the beach in loops that were barely perceptible creases in its surface, there was now a sudden agitation. In an instant, the whole surface was boiling. Hundreds of small silver streaks were visible. Fish raced upwards and shot into the air. Jamie realised what was happening.

A school of mackerel had surprised a shoal of small herring and were hunting them into the shallow water. The gulls had seen it, too. They were immobile no longer. Soaring into the air above the bay they launched themselves, screaming, again and again, striking the water furiously and climbing once more with frantically beating wings and fish in their beaks.

Then, as suddenly as it had begun, it was all over. The herring had reached water too shallow for the mackerel to follow. The mackerel had fled from the gulls.

But now the scene had changed once more. Round the headland which screened the bay from the sea beyond, a ship glided slowly into sight. Her style was ancient. Stuart could remember when he was a child seeing veterans of this type lying in muddy backwaters of the Dutch canals behind Flushing. Already they were hopelessly out of date. But this old crone . . . Age should confer some dignity. This was a disgrace to the seven seas.

The soot-coloured sails were patched in black, brown and shades of grey. The paint on its black hull was streaked with rust from anchor chains and with nameless drippings which had dried on the wood. Ropes dangled from the deck into the water. A solitary man was leaning over the rail. He was as dirty and ill-kempt as his vessel.

Another man appeared at the rail and tipped overboard a bucket of some dark liquid. A flurry of gulls screamed above him. On a warm day, thought Jamie, I should not care to be moored to leeward of that.

The two men on the ship exchanged words and looked intently in Jamie's direction. Perhaps they had seen him.

The ship passed across the stretch of water in front of him and disappeared slowly behind the outcrop of rock under which the hut nestled. He climbed down from the summit.

He was still out of sight of the hut when he saw Ingrid among the trees.

'Have you seen the ship?' she asked.

He nodded.

'Who are they?'

She told him: ships like that were a plague on that coast as highwaymen and footpads were on the roads in England and France. They were not quite pirates—not brave enough! —but only honest when they had to be. They were of many nationalities—escaped convicts, wanted criminals, deserters. They lived, pilfering, begging, drinking, stealing, burning the hayricks of those they did not like, maiming the cattle and annoying any woman they met.

'So far they have not dropped anchor. They may pass farther. They may come back and my bailiff has disappeared.

He has gone to have a horse shoed. Perhaps he knew they were coming. Perhaps he asked them to come!'

'Why should he?'

'Because my bailiff would be quite glad to see me driven from the farm. Other men in the district are conspiring with him. They will say, if these ruffians plunder the farm, that it is too hard a task for a woman—that it is a job for a man! The council will believe them. The governor in his castle in Christiania will believe the council.'

'And beyond him is there no appeal?'

'Oh yes. To the king in Copenhagen. But will he listen to a poor woman in a country parish in Norway?'

Jamie thought for a minute. 'Have you a good riding horse?' She nodded. 'Ride it to the nearest friends you can trust. How long would it take?'

'Two hours of hard riding. He is a cousin. A good man.'

'Ask him to send help. At once.'

'James, you must not be seen,' she said. 'This will mean men coming to the farm.'

'I will go to the rocks and see what is happening.'

When he came to a place commanding a view over the sea, he sat down.

The ship lay there, idly swinging, with the movements of wind and water.

A man came to her rail and gave Jamie a long, sharp stare. Others joined him, talking and pointing until one man came forward and parted the chatterers roughly.

Jamie had seen him before when he looked down from the peak of the rock. Now he saw him better.

He wore a dark woollen sea cap and no shirt; a jacket that had once been orange and now was bleached to a streaky grey. Over one shoulder was a broad belt from which hung a scimitar of Turkish pattern.

He was tall, red-bearded, with a hanging nose and tufted black eyebrows. One of his eyes twitched all the time.

He turned to the others and spoke in French. A dinghy that the ship had been towing was pulled forward to the waist. In a few minutes the boat was being rowed towards the shore. Within hailing distance, the oarsman feathered. Redbeard rose in the stern of the boat.

He looked intently at Jamie from under his frowning eyebrows. Then he pulled a knife from his sash and ran his finger along the blade.

Jamie, without rising, casually drew his sword and began to play a tattoo with it on the rock.

For a minute, the two men watched one another in silence and stillness. Then Redbeard made a signal to his rower and the boat moved back, stern first, to the ship. In a few minutes, a sail was set and it moved slowly up the channel.

On the stern in letters that had once been gilded Jamie read its name: *La Gloire.* He slipped his sword back into its scabbard and rose.

At least they would know one another again, he and Redbeard. He went back to the rocky peak which he had climbed in the morning.

The afternoon was well advanced when Ingrid joined him.

'Listen! He is coming. My cousin. I will go to meet him. You will stay here, James. They have gone with their ship. You saw him, yes? The man with the knife. That's what we call him here.'

'I saw him. He is French. Did you know that?'

She nodded. 'I will send Ragnhild with something for you to eat. Later . . . we'll meet . . . Listen!'

He could hear horses in the distance. Then voices. She left him.

By the time she came back, it was dark. She told him that her cousin had arrived and had gone again.

'Below here in the bay is a sandy beach. There we must light a fire. Oh, a big fire. Something they can see far out at sea.'

'And then?'

'Among these islands,' she said, 'there are many people who do not always obey the law. Some of them are better than others . . . Tonight, there will be no moon. It is the best kind of night for business, some kinds of business. A friend of mine sometimes passes along the fjord, outside the islands, on his way to fish. I should not be surprised if he passes tonight. Then he may see the fire and then—'

'And then!' Jamie understood. A smuggler, very likely.

She built the fire so expertly that he could see she had done it many times before. It was necessary to build it as near the waterline as possible for, although there was only a light breeze and it blew offshore, hundreds of trees grew around, and thousands of dead branches strewed the ground. They would burn like tinder. And the wind might change.

When the fire was kindled, it flared up at once. The scene was changed suddenly in an extraordinary way. Where there had been darkness and mystery, now there was a livid, leaping, barbaric dance of crimson trunks and shrill green branches.

Ingrid sat down where the woods ended and the shore began. She was looking out to sea.

An hour passed. Two hours. Many times they built up the fire.

At last, 'There it is,' she cried, pointing.

Jamie saw a light wink several times far out in the darkness.

'We need put no more branches on the fire,' she said. 'He knows where to come.'

In half an hour there was the crash of a sail coming down and the crunch of a boat's keel against the stones. A man waded ashore, keeping his face well hidden in the collar of his boat-cloak. Ingrid went forward to meet him. They talked for a long time. At last, she came back to where James was sitting in the red glow of the fading fire.

'He will take you. Farther than the Skaw. He will put you ashore on a beach a day's march from the city. He understands. Farewell, James.'

He went to her. Suddenly, stormily, torrentially, she was weeping.

'Ingrid—'

But imperiously she had shaken her head and was crying no more.

'Go. Please,' she commanded.

He walked into the water, and pulled himself aboard the boat. At once the thrust from an oar brought her into deeper water.

It was some time before James saw the red embers of the

fire swallowed by the blackness of the night.

Later, the wind died and the boat lay all night becalmed, on a sea like grey oil. When daylight came, a breeze sprang up. They tacked slowly along the coast passing island after island. Pink smooth rocks; low spruce growing along clefts where a few spoonfuls of soil had settled; here and there a grey fisher's cottage; brown nets drying on the rocks. A chain of enchanted islands in the morning light.

At last there was a lonely white beacon on a rock and the boat took the swell of the open sea.

But it was some time before he shook off the spell that had fallen on him when he woke, naked, on a Norwegian mountain.

'Monsieur Jacques. Escrime'

Stuart sat at one of the tables in a garden behind a small inn. It was just inside the crumbling wall of the King of Denmark's capital city, which he had reached that morning on foot.

In the early dawn hours of the previous day, he had been put ashore on a sandy beach many miles to the north.

It is never difficult to find the way to a metropolis. As you go, the roads grow broader and they bear more traffic.

He had walked through rolling country where there were fine beech woods. There had been reed-fringed lakes, with red-brick manors beside them.

There had been a vast fortress, set squarely by the sea, with a row of cannon on its bastions commanding a narrow channel. Ships hove to and lowered their colours, as if asking permission to pass.

At last, after a night spent none too comfortably curled up at the foot of a beech, he had seen the city—the tall, thin spires of its churches, beyond a wall: a castle, a compact maze of turrets and towers and bulbous roofs; in the background, a cool grey sea, on which he could see many ships of a type he remembered from his boyhood. Easterlings.

He had passed through the gates, ready to show his French passport. But it had not been asked for.

First, he had searched the streets for an inn called the Red Lion. When, at last, he found it, he had asked in French for Alan Beaton. He had been answered at some length by an ostler, whose face had lit up for a moment on hearing Alan's name. Apparently, Jamie had come to the right place. But, so far as he could understand, Alan had left the town on a journey.

When would he be coming back? The ostler held up the fingers of both hands. Ten. But ten days—or ten weeks? He could not tell. At the same time he held up a letter which had already been waiting for Mr Beaton for some days. Jamie noticed the seal which seemed to have the impress of a flower of some kind. But he could not be sure.

The only thing Jamie could do was to come back on another day. He decided that he would not look for a lodging in the Red Lion. It seemed to be a resort of skippers and merchants from Scotland. Jamie thought it prudent to keep away from his fellow-countrymen for a time.

He found a third-floor room over a tailor's shop in the centre of the town. It was cheap and almost clean. After that, he had gone out to look at Copenhagen—the streets, the shops, the people, especially the people; and, in a little, had settled down in this garden to ponder the problems of life.

Soon he was engaged in earnest conversation, with himself, for he could not speak the language of the country, and in a low voice.

'Besides,' as he remarked encouragingly to himself, 'Jamie, my dear fellow, I find your company congenial. There is not a man in the world—and not many women—I would rather talk to than you. And now the moment has come when I must consult you.

'Outwardly, our situation appears to be excellent. We are in good health. It is a beautiful day. And this is a strange town with unknown possibilities of adventure. The inhabitants appear to be friendly. The women have that indulgent look which I like in their sex.

'However, there is another side to all this; it is a beautiful day—but autumn approaches. The town is excitingly strange—but at any moment the Watch may begin to make inquiries. The women are attractive—but I can't talk to them. The friend we came to find is absent, no doubt on business. When he will return is doubtful. Above all, our purse is in urgent need of nourishment. What, in short, are we to do?'

Looking up, he caught the eye of a girl who had been serving him. Oyster-grey, a colour they seemed to favour in these parts. Healthy skin. Hair that seen the curling-tongs too recently and too enthusiastically and that was not fair enough to be fair. A firm mouth and, unless he was much mistaken, a firm pair of breasts.

All in all, just the sort of girl for whom, had circumstances been otherwise, he would gladly have unmasked his batteries. Especially as those grey eyes had an expression which pleasingly combined softness and challenge.

It was just his luck! Always when it was impossible for him to seize it, opportunity cast itself in his path.

He smiled at the girl, in a way which, he thought, tactfully suggested the conflicting ideas of friendship and regret.

She sighed as she looked at him. He was confirmed in his opinion that she was one of those sentimental girls with whom, in different circumstances, it would have been interesting to dally.

James made her a series of signals which she seemed to have no difficulty in understanding. Vaguely, James remembered being told by someone—his father, probably—about the Danish gift for foreign languages.

Waiting for his mug to be replenished with the excellent beer of the country, he cast an eye over his neighbours. Dignified men. Comfortable women. Inclined to run to flesh, although not on the scale he had grown accustomed to when he lived in Holland. And children playing at their parents' feet, active but not too noisy. Those two little boys, for instance, imitating with wooden swords and cardboard bucklers the bloody doings of their elders. And doing it clumsily and innocently.

At this moment the serving girl returned with a foaming mug in her hand. She giggled as she put it down before him. A kindly girl whose cheeks blushed with wind and sun. What she found to giggle about was hard to say, unless it was the sight of a young man apparently still possessed of his senses, talking to himself in a foreign language.

'Greta. Maria. Anna. Ulrica,' he said.

She shook her head.

72

'Sofie,' she said.

'Sofie, of course! Listen to me with due respect, for what you are hearing is the language of Ronsard. Tell me, my darling, what you would do if you found yourself in a strange town with only a handful of ducats in your pocket? No. Do not tell me. You would have one resource between you and the ultimate extremity. Sofie, it is not open to me.'

James was aware that already he was feeling less oppressed by life. It was an effect which, in the past, had often coincided with the presence of a good-natured young woman. But, on this occasion, he thought there was an additional reason.

Sofie, eyes big, mouth open, looked at him in perplexed silence.

'Go on talking,' he told her encouragingly. 'Your thoughts are passing by magic channels into my mind. And your advice is excellent. You say, become the best-dressed man in Copenhagen. Easy! Remember, the wearer makes the clothes. So I shall spend a few ducats on a new hat. I shall wear it with an ease, an elegance, a panache, unmatched at the court of king . . . What is the monarch's name, by the way? I must remember to ask.

'Further, Sofie, you tell me to go into the most fashionable quarter of the city and mix with my own class. Admirable advice! The nobility, Sofie! Coronets, empty heads and heavy purses! Once I am there—yes, by God! '—he brought his fist down on the table in a sudden excitement—'the game is as good as won. I know exactly what I am going to do! Sofie, you marvellous girl! While I have been listening to you and watching the children play on the gravel, inspiration has visited me. You have been present at a turning point in my life.'

James emptied his mug, slid a coin across the table to the girl, rose buoyantly to his feet and kissed her on the cheek. Her eyes, wider than ever, followed him as he went.

Jamie was on his way to find a sign-writer's workshop.

It was those small boys playing at soldiers outside the beer-shop who had given him the idea. At that moment, he remembered how the fencing master at his academy in Paris had begged him to stay on as an assistant. The sight and the memory fused instantly into a thought which had the simplicity of genius. There was, of course, the problem of his immediate need of working capital. He would have to borrow the money for a little while, until the fees began to come in.

But, as it turned out, that had not been necessary.

The sign which Jamie had composed, and which an experienced artist had executed in an elegant script, was hung out in an alley, in the old town only a few hundred yards from where, between the city and the sea, the royal palace rose above the crowded red roofs of the houses.

It was an irregular but impressive building which had as its culmination a fretted mass of ornate work in copper covering a massive tower. Over all was a spire on which three golden crowns were transfixed, one above the other. Within sight of it Jamie set up his business, in what had been a carpenter's workshop.

The sign said: *Monsieur Jacques. Escrime.* That was all; it was enough. There was, it implied, a French gentleman, a master of the sword and rapier, who could be persuaded for a respectable fee to instruct young gentlemen of the court in the elements of the noble art of defence.

For two days James tightened his belt and avoided meeting the eye of his landlord who, it was clear, was beginning to wonder whether he had done right to let a room to this plausible young foreigner, on the strength of a smooth flow of French and a new hat of the best Russian beaver, encircled by a brilliant crimson ostrich feather.

Concealing any anxiety that may have gnawed at him, James spent his last few coins in frugal eating-places in the best streets of the town. He liked, in particular, the shops on the fish quay, a lively, noisy street running alongside a waterway which encircled the palace.

Below, the fishing boats were moored as they came in. Above, on the street, the booths were laid out, watched over by women wearing white kerchiefs and gifted with tongues as quick and salty as the fish they sold. Among the old houses that lined the quay—three steps up to the merchant's counting house, three steps down to the shop or the tavern—were ship's chandlers' stores, tattooing artists' premises, a brothel or two, and other by-products of man's traffic with the sea.

74

There was also this eating place, Den Guldene Krebs, The Golden Crayfish, with its bracing smell of fresh fish. From its kitchen there came, from time to time, the subtler aromas of cooking. As he breathed in, Jamie found the prospect of starvation becoming less oppressive. It was easy to believe that food would, somehow, always be at hand. There would be a sentimental woman who would not be too busy in her kitchen to—No, he thought that he would not need to steal.

In one of these moments of spiritual comfort, Jamie found himself looking at a face that was familiar to him and yet could not immediately be identified. It belonged to a pink-cheeked, portly young man.

The face expressed, with the greatest eloquence in the world, dismay, consternation, a general anticipation of disaster. It was plump, round as a cheese, with a small button nose, a mouth like a cherry and eyes round and glistening like sloes.

The young man's hair grew on his forehead in a perfect widow's peak. His black eyebrows, almost an inch and a half apart, drooped on either side of his face so that they seemed about to fall off altogether. Two inches below them and exactly parallel, his moustache sagged down on either side of his mouth.

After a second, Jamie's memory played. He was looking at an old school friend from Paris.

'François,' he cried, advancing on the young man whom he remembered as the laziest pupil in Antoine de Pluvinel's Academy in the Rue St Honoré. François Carbon de Castel Jaloux, scion of an ancient threadbare line of Gascon squires.

At that moment François was engaged in earnest conversation with a woman who was apparently employed by the tavern. She had the moist, over-heated look of one who spent a great deal of time in the kitchen.

François turned towards Jamie as if he were being rudely brought back from an ideal world to one less beautiful.

'Stuart!' he remarked, without the faintest sign of surprise.

'Call me Jacques.'

François shook his head gloomily.

'You have come at a painful moment. I was telling madame how to cook a bourride. The fish can be got easily enough.

75

But—you will hardly believe it!—garlic is hard to come by here. Garlic! What a country!'

'I shall wait until you have finished.'

'Thank you very much.' François went on talking gravely to the cook for several minutes in a language which Jamie supposed to be a kind of kitchen Danish. At last, with an exchange of nods and emphatic waggings of the fingers, he dismissed her and turned to James.

'You will find the food here quite good,' he said sombrely. 'The Danes are simple people. Peasants. But they are willing to learn. Also, they have grasped the first principle of the kitchen.'

'Which is?'

'To put enough on the plate. Tell me, Jacques,' he added, reluctantly turning to a less interesting topic, 'what are you doing in this town?'

'Looking for customers. And you, François?'

'I am in our embassy.'

'A diplomat! Well! I always thought you would end in the dragoons.'

François shook his head with gloomy dignity. 'They would not have me.'

'Ah! Don't say you were too heavy?'

'Good heavens, no. They said, damn them, I was not clever enough. So there was only one thing to do. Diplomacy. The Career!'

'And how do you like it?'

'Not bad. With one exception. In that school we went to in Paris, they neglected two subjects—cookery and spelling. I have taught myself to cook. But spelling! No, that is really asking too much of a man.'

'You might be worse off. At least you can count.'

'Of course I can count.'

'You are taking too much for granted, François. The world is divided into those who learn to spell before they can count and those who—'

'There are also those who never learn to spell. Like me. But,' and here his manner became noticeably more cautious, 'you said something about customers?'

76

'Yes. I am broke but full of confidence. Two days ago I opened a fencing school,' said Jamie.

François's eyes grew even rounder in astonishment.

'Here? You are wasting your time, my poor friend! This is the most peace-loving city in Europe. They will scarcely fight even when they're drunk—too drunk to fence. I wish you had asked me first.'

'The truth is I had to find something to do in a hurry.'

François understood. 'There are moments when one has to act quickly. I had to leave Paris like that! —it broke my heart.'

'A question of money?'

'Money! I had an understanding with two of the best cooks in the Marais. Unhappily, each woman found out about the other. I have often wondered which of my friends betrayed me. May he perish of hunger!'

'It wasn't me, François. But I'm going to perish of hunger very soon at the present rate. Or find work'

'Pardon! Did you say "work"?' The round moon face was creased with pain. 'This is a serious subject, Jacques. One shouldn't be flippant.'

'Flippant? Far from it! What do you suggest, then?'

François's face, which had been almost devoid of expression before, now seemed to retreat into realms in which any mental process was impossible. When he spoke it was in a voice choked, not with emotion, but with solemnity.

'Tell me, Jacques, what are you—Aries, Sagittarius, Gemini —what?'

Jamie looked at him, amazed.

'As a matter of fact, I'm a Leo,' he said irritably. 'Why?'

'Ah, Leo. I must think about this—il faut réfléchir.'

'Yes. But not for too long. Time is running short.'

François knitted his brow.

'Give me until tonight. I have a friend, a nice woman,' he said. 'Baroness Caroline Gyldenstierne. She receives this evening. Shall I introduce you—you are a Scottish nobleman, aren't you? They are very comme il faut, the Gyldenstiernes.'

'This time, I am travelling incognito, as a Frenchman. A commoner. Of good family, of course. But there are reasons why I cannot fly my true colours.'

77

François might have been about to ask him to explain that but a more important matter came into his head.

'Excuse me,' he said, with a sudden frown. 'I forgot to tell her to put a bayleaf into the court-bouillon.'

The Gyldenstiernes lived in a little palace—in Paris it would have been called an hotel—overlooking the harbour, which at that point, at that hour of the evening, was a confused mass of jostling ships and shouting sailors.

Looking along the quay on which the house stood, Jamie could see a stretch of grey water and a low coastline about twelve miles away. On an island, nearer the quay, was a battery of cannon pointing seawards. Between the guns were neat little pyramids of cannon balls. But no gunners were in sight. Apparently no early attack was expected.

As he sauntered at the side of François along the quay with the sun behind him, Jamie looked forward with curiosity to the evening. He had dressed for the occasion. On his hands were a pair of scented gloves which he had persuaded the glove-maker to sell him on credit. At his wrists were lace cuffs, a new fashion, fresh from Paris, which the mercer wished to launch in the town. James, he had agreed, was just the man to do it.

His boots had not been worn before and were damnably uncomfortable. He had been able to borrow them from the bootmaker on condition that he helped to make them easier for the owner when they were delivered.

If only he had a warmer cloak—but he was confident that somehow he would acquire one soon. The sooner the better. Already there was a nip in the wind.

'This friend of yours?' he asked François.

'Caroline? She keeps an excellent table. Clever woman. She engaged a fellow countryman of mine who had left Paris owing to—well, a question of religion . . . When one thinks of the number of artists—great artists—France has lost through those absurd quarrels! Shocking. About Caroline? She has a gift—but you will see for yourself. Incidentally, her husband—'

'There is a husband?'

François touched his moustache at each corner of his mouth.

'There is always a husband,' he said, firmly. 'He shoots, he hunts and he drinks. They say he is a good soldier. He doesn't leave his estates often.'

Jamie thought he understood. In imagination he could see the baroness—tall, heavy, red-faced, fond of food and drink, with the suspicion of a moustache. A grenadier married to a dragoon.

They turned off the street through a doorway over which, carved in sandstone and painted, was a shield—a gold star on a blue ground. The door led into a courtyard.

'By the way,' said François, 'I've been doing some work on your behalf in the last few hours. You are a Leo. Well, be very cautious this evening. This is a day of exceptional opportunity for you—and of great danger! If you fail to grasp the opportunity, it may never come again. But the danger is serious. You must at all costs avoid it. Otherwise . . .'

'And how the devil am I to tell the opportunity from the danger?'

'The stars do not go into details like that, James,' said François severely. 'The point is, do you believe in freewill or predestination? Are you a Calvinist, by any chance?'

'My father was. But what has that got to do with it?' he asked, irritably.

'Everything,' said François. 'By the way,' he went on with a change of tone, 'I have been wondering as we walked along, how the devil do you manage to look so presentable, after all those barbarous adventures?'

'Easily enough.' He drew himself up. 'The wearer makes the clothes.'

François nodded in grave approval.

'As the pheasant makes the terrine,' he said.

The stairs were shallow and wide. Ascent was gradual and was meant to be dignified. At the top, a footman took hats and gloves and passed them to a colleague.

A major-domo approached them, smiling, and led them to the hostess.

Jamie owed François an apology.

The Baroness Caroline, far from being a grenadier, was

small and vivacious, with hair of that tawny tint which gave the last mistress of Henry IV her sobriquet, 'The Lioness'. But this was no man-eater. At most, a cat, a playful cat.

As Jamie bowed over her hand, a new respect for François had already come to life in his mind. The laziest pupil in that Academy in Paris had not, it seemed, been wasting his time. And the frozen North was not, he was certain, always frozen.

At the same time, by some subtle quirk of logic, James felt a wave of confidence in his own fate sweep over him. This— the sweet smell from the wood burning in the white stove, the perfume of the women's bodies, the jewels which suggested wealth, the sound of silk rustling against silk, which suggested something else besides the idea of clothes—this was a game of which he knew the rules.

'Madame la baronne,' he said, in a voice unnecessarily low, excessively respectful, as if in apology for the impudence of his gaze.

During a fraction of a second their eyes—hers a deep brown —lingered in one another with a complete understanding.

'Monsieur—Jacques?' she said, with the faintest shadow of a question after the name. 'My sister-in-law, Leonora, Countess Rosenkrantz.'

Jamie looked from the baroness to her neighbour.

Once or twice in his life Jamie had felt these small vibrations, like the ringing of tiny bells somewhere, warning bells. Bells that meant danger. Why the devil had he never learnt to heed them?

Until a second ago the room had been filled, agreeably filled, with guests, mostly young; some footmen; a chamberlain. Now it was empty. Save for one person.

And suddenly Jamie was no longer confident about his fate.

She was a slight pillar of black satin. Pale. Indeed, a dead white complexion—that white which is, in fact, a very pale and glowing pink. Tumbling about her face a mass of lustrous raven curls in which there were purple lights.

A particularly magnificent wig, a masterpiece of its kind? No. Not with that gloss upon it.

Not often in his life had Jamie seen hair of such splendour. And he remembered the last time had been in a painting, the portrait of a boy, hanging on the wall of a house in Scotland.

Her eyes were enormous, dark, and might have been tragic were it not for their expression. But that seemed to belong to the first act of the drama and not to the dénouement, when we know the worst. The fury was still suppressed.

She was a woman who had played many parts. Versatile.

Bowing, he had the opportunity to admire her hand—small, white, with long tapering fingers—her rings, and her taste. With her colouring, diamonds were the only wear. A woman of a different temperament would have worn fewer.

'Grevinne,' he said. 'Countess.' It was as far as his Danish went.

A cool voice answered, rather lower in the register than he had expected and speaking a French which came from the South, perhaps from beyond the Alps. Or the Pyrenees.

'You are Monsieur Jacques—not by any chance the fencing master who has just opened a school here?'

Jamie shrugged.

'You look very much as I expected,' said the Countess Leonora.

What he thought was disparagement in her voice might only be indifference.

'And you are the one I have been warned against,' he said.

'Warned! By whom?'

'By my own eyes.'

'Don't believe all you see, monsieur.'

'I am sorry I look as you expected I should. I had hoped to be a surprise,' he said.

'A surprise? Tell me why.'

'I'd like nothing better. At another time.'

For a moment there was silence. Then, as if with an effort, she spoke more briskly. 'I have a proposal to make, monsieur, which you may find rather strange. If so, please say so.'

'I can't imagine that. But the answer is, I accept.'

'Will you give me lessons in fencing?'

'I should be delighted, of course. But don't you think that a woman who is endangered by her beauty is best defended by her wit.'

'But what if she wants to attack?' Something flickered in

her eyes.

'Then she should employ an assassin. In a lady, it would be permissible.'

She shook her head angrily.

'No.'

'I am not offering my services.'

'And I am not sure that I would trust you, Monsieur Jacques.'

'I am not sure I would trust myself. But fencing lessons—that is something quite different. Perhaps one day soon? May I call on you?'

She glanced at him with something that was stronger than resentment; as if he had mortally insulted her. Then, without more ado, she left him to join a group in another part of the room. Through the rustle of her satin he heard her say, 'I shall call on you. One morning. Perhaps tomorrow.'

He followed her with his eyes as she walked away from him.

Her body had very musical movements. Beyond the Pyrenees, it said, but the voice came from beyond the Alps, he decided.

At his elbow a voice—a man's—said quietly: 'Mr James Stuart?'

Jamie turned quickly. 'You are mistaken. I am called Monsieur Jacques.'

'No,' said the Englishman.

Drunk Men and Little Children

'You and I are not going to quarrel about names, I hope, when there are so many things we can agree on.'

This Englishman with the cool voice was about ten years older than Jamie and about two inches shorter. He had the brown hair and the small bones that so many of his nation have. His expression was whimsical and sardonic. But pleasant.

Jamie thought that the touch of eccentricity in his appearance was probably due to the set of his eyes, one of which was almost imperceptibly higher than the other. But, with the English, one could never be sure.

'We can hardly quarrel about names when you are mistaken about mine and I don't know yours.'

'Carey,' said the Englishman politely. 'Edward Carey.'

'Mr Carey. Delighted. And now perhaps you'll excuse me.'

'What else can I do? Here we are on neutral ground, more or less. But no doubt we shall have other opportunities to talk, and plenty to say. By the way,' said Carey, stroking his beard, 'how is your wound? I mean the scar on your ankle, not the bruise on your head.'

'Neither prevents me from defending myself.'

As Jamie turned away, he thought he heard a murmur: 'I advise you to keep in practice.'

Jamie, after a quick glance, passed on towards a little knot of men discussing something with passion. He heard one word repeated, 'ducats, ducats, ducats'.

'It is the same in every country,' he said to François. 'Wherever conversation is lively, people are talking about one of two things. Money. Or food.'

François smirked with approval. 'There are serious people everywhere,' he said.

'This Englishman, Carey. Who is he?'

François looked and shrugged. 'A spy. From their embassy.'

'You're sure?'

'One should assume that all Englishmen are spies. It is the first principle we learn in the Career.'

'And Leonora? Countess something.'

'Be careful, Jacques. Be careful!' François spoke behind his hand.

'It's a little late to tell me that now,' said Jamie, indignantly.

François glanced anxiously at his old schoolfriend.

'Pluvinel used to say you were good in attack but too damned hasty in reconnaissance.'

'I remember he said you would make the best commissariat officer in Europe if only you didn't eat so much. But tell me, is Leonora a spy, too?'

François scowled.

'If it were only as simple as that!' he said.

By this time they were close to a table in a corner of the room where four elderly people were playing cards while three younger people looked on.

There was a woman who, from her protruding eyes and swelling chin, looked like a good-natured frog. Beside her at the table sat a woman whom life and time had inclined sideways. One of the men was big and paunchy, looking at his cards out of pale blue eyes with a calm stare. The other man was almost bald, with a fringe of light-coloured hair. Four old folk, half-forgotten by the rest, collecting a little dust in a corner of the room.

'One of them is the wife of a man in the embassy—*that* woman,' François whispered. 'So none of your sarcasm, if you please.'

'Sarcasm?' Jamie said, as he paused to watch the fall of cards.

'By the way, Hélène,' remarked the bald man, as he put down the king of hearts. 'You have been keeping something from me.'

'Such as?' The lady who was like a frog had a contralto voice, her accent probably came from Touraine.

'Yes. Your King Henri has married beneath him. Why should I have to depend on my banker to tell me?'

'Perhaps because the King of France has married his banker's daughter,' said the second woman—the slanting one —speaking the kind of French which Jamie had often heard when he lived in the Netherlands. Ah, he thought, so Henri Quatre has at last married Marie de' Medici, whose family had lent him millions.

'The king has married for money.' The Frenchwoman put down the ace of hearts. 'Wise men do.'

'Ah, you had the ace!' exclaimed her partner. 'And now what?'

'The latest from London. The Queen of England has trouble with her lover,' she said, looking quizzically at her cards. 'They say he is wildly beautiful.'

She laid the knave of diamonds on the table.

'Milord Essex? Has she locked him in the Tower? That was a story I heard a day or two ago.'

'Not yet, but after deserting his post as Viceroy of Ireland he is under arrest. It is not too tragic. Milord is guarded in his own house.'

The man sitting beside her flicked the queen of diamonds on to the table.

'Thank you, partner,' he said, as he scooped up the cards.

'It is lucky for some people,' said the woman who spoke in clouded French, 'that old Philip of Spain is dead. He would not miss such a chance of making trouble for the queen.'

'My lead?' The man who had taken the trick put down the ace of spades with an air of modest triumph.

'But I have a trump. The last, I believe,' said the bald man as, with a gesture of triumph, he swept the cards into a heap.

'It is high time we were dealt a new hand,' said Hélène.

'We shall be! We shall be! Tsar Boris will see to that. He sits in the Kremlin planning new troubles for Europe.'

'Boris Godunov!' A heavily-built, heavily-bearded young man, who had been moodily watching the game, uttered the name contemptuously. 'Tsar Boris, as you call him, will have troubles enough of his own to handle.'

He was dressed in a long coat trimmed with sable and having a great deal of gold and brocade about it. In a sash he wore a curved dagger with a jewelled hilt. The French he spoke could have been used for chopping wood.

The card-players looked up at him.

'You are thinking of Sweden, Dmitri? Will the Swedes march on Moscow, do you think?'

The tall young man scowled. 'No. But Boris will have problems nearer home—wait and see! My country has many troubles to come.' He spoke with satisfaction.

'I don't think we have time for another rubber tonight,' said the woman with the Flemish accent. 'I am fainting with hunger.'

The four players pushed back their chairs and rose from the table. As they straightened their legs, the twinges of rheumatism showed in their faces.

'The queen . . .'

'They say this Carey is a distant cousin of the queen's.'

'Yes, through her mother, Anne Boleyn.'

'Who was a whore.'

The sloping woman held up her hand in protest. 'Oh, Hélène! How uncharitable people can be!'

'See, he is going over to talk to Leonora. What do you suppose?'

'She hates the queen—and with reason!'

'She loathes Essex—for a better reason.'

'What is certain,' said the man with the bulging, pale blue eyes, 'is that Leonora has letters from England every few days.'

'How one would like to read—"

'They are said to be in cypher.'

'No cypher exists that can't be broken!' said the bald man.

'Did I mention that I was hungry?' said the Flemish lady.

Jamie saw François approaching. 'Why does the Countess Leonora detest Queen Elizabeth?' he asked.

François frowned. He spoke quickly. 'There are many things about that lady which are puzzling. When you meet a man named Giovanni, you will see what is most puzzling of all.'

'Giovanni?'

'He is her servant. But . . . another time . . . Meanwhile, something else—you are bidden to supper,' he said. 'Caroline would like you to stay. By the way, I advise you to go lightly on the smørrebrod.'

'The what?'

'The smørrebrod. You will see.'

But when the time came, François ate twice as much as Jamie.

Baroness Caroline kept an excellent table. Not only was it loaded with exotic dishes—black fish eggs from Russia, reindeer tongues brought from beyond the Arctic Circle, seven kinds of ham, a variety of fish, sea and river, fresh and cured, a culinary orchestra where all the notes were sharp, but there was also a procession of wines, Rhenish for the most part, interrupted by small glasses filled with a kind of alcohol that caught Jamie by the throat before it soared upwards to riot in his head.

There was music. Leonora Rosenkrantz, when pressed, sang to the lute, frowning at first, if one can frown without a shadow appearing on the brow. Her voice was a stream of dark velvet flowing through a night of stars.

François remembered that Jamie had a voice and Caroline insisted that he should sing. He remembered a song he had learned at Pluvinel's Academy, where music had been, after fencing and equitation, the most important subject.

The Russian named Dmitri gathered about him the quilted, fur-edged coat which fell to his heels and sang, unaccompanied, in a soul-searching bass, a song so gloomy and wonderful that everybody wept openly and François consoled himself with another slice of ham.

After a while something strange seemed to happen to the evening so far as Jamie was concerned. Time changed its nature, lost its continuity, and turned into a succession of unrelated images with inexplicable gaps between them.

Perhaps, said Jamie to himself, after thinking it over, I have eaten something that has disagreed with me. I shall close my eyes for a few minutes. After that, I shall feel much better.

He closed his eyes but the effect was so alarming that, with a superhuman effort, he forced them open again. There was only one thing to do: sit quietly, ignore these foolish people who were trying to engage him in conversation and in due course go back to his lodgings. He sat quietly.

At one point Countess Leonora said, 'Ten o'clock one morning?' and he said, 'Make it eleven.' He did not know whether she had heard or not.

By the time the footman loomed up before him, holding out hat and gloves, Jamie felt well enough to go down the Gyldenstiernes' staircase without reaching for the handrail.

With him walked François, and behind came the Russian, singing sorrowfully. He is drunk, Jamie thought.

Outside, on the quay, a wet night wind was blowing in from the sea. 'Let us have a drink,' said Dmitri.

'Nonsense, nonsense.'

'I insist.'

'Bed for me,' said François.

'Bed! What cowardly talk is this? Look, here is a little place! Just three steps down—one, two, three! Easy!'

'Yes,' said François, 'but one, two, three, up! Not so easy.'

In the low, brick-vaulted cellar which they entered a few sailors were drinking. Dmitri filled the place with his tremendous voice as he shouted something in Russian. Whether they understood or not, the waiters brought drink—beer.

With a gesture of disgust, Dmitri swept it to the floor. They brought glasses and a bottle containing a colourless liquid. Dmitri greeted it with enthusiasm. 'Vodka!' he bellowed. 'The tsar of drinks. Try it, my friends, try it.'

Jamie smelt and shuddered. After that he pretended to drink and emptied his glass furtively on the floor. François drank cautiously. Dmitri sang, made a passionate speech in Russian and suddenly rose to his feet. He threw a handful of money to the cringing waiters and dived for the door. He struck his head against the lintel with a force that would have felled most men. Dmitri bellowed with rage and plunged on.

'Let the imbecile go,' said François.

'He'll fall into the harbour.'

'Drunk men and little children—' François began. But they followed the Russian up the steps on to the quay.

The clouds had divided. A half-moon rode high. Points of light sparkled here and there on the roof of the king's palace. In the harbour, the water had risen high, inky black and agitated. The air smelt of salt and tar.

Dmitri ran across the cobbles towards the water. 'Stop him!' shouted Jamie.

'Drunk men and —' François began.

The Russian stopped hard on the brink of the water. There he began to perform an extraordinary dance, crossing his arms on his chest and kicking out with one leg and then the other over the water. He ended with a loud smack of his hands and a laugh that woke up some seabirds asleep on a buoy in the middle of the harbour.

Jamie sat on a bollard. His borrowed boots were hurting. He took them off with some difficulty.

'You think that's clever?' he asked the Russian. 'Now watch this.' He took off his hat, his gloves, unbuckled his sword and slipped out of his doublet.

'No, Jamie, no!' François pleaded.

'Shut up! Watch, both of you.'

In an instant he was standing on his hands and was advancing slowly towards the edge of the quay. Then, with a spring, he whirled round in the air and was standing with his feet where his hands had been.

Dmitri shouted something in Russian. 'Wait, wait.' said Jamie. This time he turned a complete circle backwards, landing where he began. 'Voilà!' he cried.

Now Dmitri was pulling off his coat, revealing a long, embroidered shirt of cloth of gold, François was shouting, 'Enough, enough!' Then it happened.

Jamie suddenly became aware of a trio of men who were walking slowly towards them along the quay. Two tall men in uniform, shouldering halberds, walked on either side of a third man. He was the most striking figure of the three.

His legs were bare, and criss-crossed by the thongs of his shoes. His wrists were in chains and he in rags. Uncombed, unshaven, filthy, he strode along with composure, even with a swagger. One of his cheeks was horribly disfigured by a scar. Seeing him, Jamie's face lit up with joy.

'Alistair!' he shouted.

Alistair MacIan looked towards Jamie with eyes suddenly open. He ran forward. His two warders, taken by surprise, hesitated for a second, then they made after him with levelled halberds. Dmitri drew his scimitar and with the roar of a bull, advanced on the halberd men. Alistair darted away into the darkness.

Jamie took a step forward, the butt of a halberd struck him in the chest. He staggered, slipped; his heel went back—back and into nothing! He swayed for an instant on the brink of the quay. Then he fell backwards.

He thought he heard somewhere the cry of a curlew.

Then the cold, fishy water of Copenhagen harbour closed over him.

A Very Big Game

'It is, perhaps, just as well,' Jamie said, putting down the shaving brush and picking up the razor.

'Just as well, what?' asked François, frowning and smoothing his moustache down with thumb and forefinger. Under the soap, Jamie's cheek twitched with irritation.

'Just as well I didn't have my boots on at the time. They are not mine anyway.'

'It's just as well you couldn't interfere with those policemen.'

'And now I need not. Alistair has escaped, you say. He is free, somewhere.'

'He has disappeared. That's the only thing that's certain.'

'You don't know Alistair,' said Jamie. 'At least the boots did not get wet.'

'James, I beg of you. No more follies! No more risks! It needs only one slip by you and —'

'I know. I know. I agree with you entirely.'

'And no women! Above all, not *one* woman!'

'Leonora? Damn it, she's my first pupil! On what day she'll turn up, I don't know. But I have an idea that it will be today.'

'For God's sake be careful!' said François.

He went out, shaking his head, but buoyed up by the thought of the excellent breakfast he would soon be eating at the Golden Crayfish.

Jamie, alone in his bare little room above the roofs of Copenhagen, shaving in the grey light of a Baltic morning, read himself a lecture on caution. It was, he decided, a sober, unlovely virtue, despised by too many and only revealing its true worth to the man in danger of his life. Caution, that grey-clad, prim-lipped bodyguard—caution would now be his inseparable companion!

Chivalry would not tempt him—a beguiling sentiment, no doubt, but in his present circumstances merely suicidal. And is not suicide a sin? If ten girls as beautiful as, say, that girl he had known in Edinburgh, Mary Beaton, were attacked by ten scoundrels, he would walk on, saddened but irrevocably dedicated to self-preservation. If ten countesses as enticing as Leonora were to tempt him—but to what?—he would remain immovable, impervious, a rock of circumspection and rectitude.

Pleased at finding himself to be such a resolutely prudent young man, Jamie relaxed his guard a little. He completed his toilet, putting on the breeches he had borrowed from the tailor downstairs in place of the pair that were still wet with harbour water. Feeling his self-confidence flow back, he allowed a hint of jauntiness to show in his gait as he went downstairs. Passing through the tailor's shop, he gave the cheerful wave of a man whose intentions towards his creditors were unimpeachably benevolent.

At the thought that, within an hour, he might be teaching the Countess Leonora Rosenkrantz to fence, he said, with a slight smile, 'Careful, James, careful.' Then he began to hum a childish air as he sauntered towards the pastrycook's shop where he would eat a roll and a sausage before opening his fencing school for the day.

He had bought the equipment on credit, two fencing suits and two foils. If his own hand was not as steady this morning as it should be, that was something a novice—above all, a woman—would be unlikely to notice.

The bells of the town churches had not finished striking eleven when the door of the warehouse which Jamie had hired as his fencing school was flung open.

A long black cloak swept in. A hat was pulled well down over a pale face. The cloak was thrown off. The hat sailed across the room.

'My God,' he exclaimed. 'You are dressed for the part!'

The Countess Leonora Rosenkrantz had the hips—and the

hose—of a boy.

'You did not think I was going to learn fencing in a skirt, did you?' she said. 'Besides, it might embarrass you if a woman were seen coming into your school.'

'I am only embarrassed if the women who visit me are not beautiful. In that case, I kill them.' He smiled.

'Naturally. And if, by chance, they are beautiful, are they allowed to kill you?'

By daylight she had a faint flush of carmine in her cheeks which he had not noticed the night before.

'Unnecessary. I am dead already,' he said.

'I heard that you had been drowned. A strange, blond Frenchman, quite mad, fell into the harbour. I thought it must be you.'

'You didn't deny it, I hope.'

She shook her curls. 'There was another man. He escaped. They are looking for him.'

'An outlaw I know.'

'He is hiding—somewhere.'

'Good. They will not find him easily.'

'We shall see, Jamie.'

'Jacques.'

'The English name seems more natural.'

She tore off her doublet. She wore a shirt made of some heavy silk material. He thought it had probably come from China. It was beautiful.

'Where are the foils? What! Only two!'

'Yes. One each. It is quite usual. But there are padded jackets as well.'

She tried the foil and waved away the jacket.

'Surely I shall not need that for the first lesson,' she said. She was smiling in that curious sullen way.

'As you like. First of all, I will show you the on-guard position.'

'Let us have one or two passes first. So that I can become accustomed to holding the foil.'

At the fourth pass she was inside his guard and touched him on the chest. He looked at her coldly.

'Your eye is not so quick this morning,' she said.

'No,' he agreed. 'Now, tell me where you learned to handle a foil like that? After that we shall try again.'

'At a school in Padua. Signor Orlando. You've heard of him?'

'Who hasn't!' She was speaking of a great maestro.

'He taught me.'

'That explains it.'

'But you have a second question, I think.'

'I have a dozen. But first, let us have another bout,' said Jamie. 'And this time put your jacket on, please. My eye is quicker now.'

But it needed ten minutes, in which all his cunning and experience were brought into play, before he could claim to have beaten her.

'Would you like to go again, M. Jacques?' she asked.

'Another time.' he said, taking the foil from her. 'And now, Madame la Comtesse—or should I say contessa?'

'The title is Danish.'

'But the woman is not. You did not come here to learn fencing.'

Her face became a mask of haughtiness and insolence.

'No. I wanted to find out what kind of man you are. You puzzle me. I am not content to stay puzzled.'

'I am sure of that.'

'You speak French,' she said. 'You may *be* French. You have good manners, but you think it more amusing to have bad ones. You are in trouble of some kind. Probably you've been in gaol.'

He laughed. 'I've been in worse.'

'You have good nerves, and you need them. You fence beautifully—and you are apt to underrate an opponent.'

'You haven't seen my somersaults. Watch!'

When he alighted, hands outspread, she said coolly: 'If I were engaging a troupe of acrobats . . . But —'

'I didn't think you were. You are looking for an assassin. Wrong address, Countess.'

She shook her curls. 'No,' she said. 'I am looking for —'

She came nearer to him, close enough for him to recognise that the perfume she was using was one he had never encountered before. Then, deliberately, almost slowly, she kissed him on the lips.

'A special kind of man,' she murmured.

He thought he knew the kind. We all make these mistakes.

'We shall meet again,' she said. 'At Caroline's. And perhaps, some evening you will call on me.'

'For the second lesson?' He put her cloak round her shoulders.

'For the first.' she said.

Someone was knocking at the door of Monsieur Jacques's fencing school.

'My next pupil,' he told her.

He opened the door. Outside stood a red-cheeked, heavy young man dressed for hunting.

'You teach fencing, monsieur?'

'I teach fencing,' said Jamie. 'Other arts I am learning.'

By the middle of the afternoon, Jamie had collected enough money in fees to pay the debt to his landlord and buy something to eat. He looked confidently into the future. Soon he would take better premises and engage an assistant. If only François were not so fat. If only Alistair would turn up.

'Someone,' he remarked to François when he saw him in the Golden Crayfish, 'has been telling people I am the best swordsman in Europe. Who would it be, do you think?'

François rolled his small round eyes. His mouth was an O of solemnity rather than surprise. His widow's peak, black and gleaming, emphasised the pink rotundity of his face.

He put one finger to his lips. In his other hand he held his watch.

'S'sh!'

'What on earth for?'

'Because I am listening for the first bubbles of the gravy. It is all a question of timing. Ah, there it is! . . . You asked who has been spreading rumours about you. The answer is, nobody. Men and women have nothing to do with matters like this! It is the stars! Didn't I tell you —'

'You said it was a day of great danger.'

'And you fell into the harbour, didn't you? Also I spoke of opportunity—well! Now today, James, today is very important

95

for you. I have taken the trouble to look at your horoscope. Sagittarius is in Leo! I needn't tell you what that means. The commercial situation is still promising but—*but*—in affairs of the heart, trouble looms. Trouble! You will have to be very careful, more than careful! If you meet a woman today, run, James, run! That reminds me. You have seen the Countess Leonora. How was that?'

'Very dangerous indeed. If she had taken the button off her foil she could have killed me.'

'Didn't I warn you!'

'You didn't tell me she is one of the best fencers between here and Naples! Man or woman! All you said was that she is dangerous. Every beautiful woman is dangerous. What did you mean, François? Who is the Countess Leonora?'

'I know only what everybody knows. She is an Italian.'

'Not a Borgia by any chance?'

François shook his head impassively.

'From Venice, I believe. She was in England, at the Court, in the train of a noble lady. Then she became the mistress of some lord, a friend of the queen's. That is the story.'

'A friend of the queen's! Dangerous indeed!'

François's shoulders moved a fraction of an inch.

'Suddenly she went to Court no more. It is said the queen dismissed her. Then she married young Rosenkrantz who had arrived in London with a Danish embassy. And here she is!'

'Rosenkrantz. What sort of man is he?'

'A calf. Rich. Stupid.'

'Not the husband for Leonora.'

'On the contrary, Jacques. Just the husband for Leonora.'

'Of course. And that's all you know?'

François leant across the table, anxiety lifting his eyebrows even higher than normal.

'The rest I can guess. Can't you, James? Don't you feel in your bones that she is an agent?'

'For you, everyone is an agent. But an agent for whom?'

'Perhaps for the Catholic king,' said François, in that ecclesiastical voice he had learnt in the Career.

'His Majesty of Spain?'

'Who knows?' François sniffed. 'Now you'll excuse me,

96

Jacques, for a moment. I must look in the kitchen. I told her I wanted a daube—à la mode d'Avignon. But—without garlic in the town! Who is to say? It may be a tragedy! Pray for us, Jacques. Pray!'

In the kitchen, consultations went on for some time. The smells grew steadily stronger and more appetising.

'It will be eatable,' said François, emerging at last. 'I can't say more.' He was still anxious.

'Have you any news of Alistair?' Jamie asked. 'The man in the chains?'

'They will have picked him up. He will be in a cell by this time.'

'I don't believe it.'

'With those chains!'

'Chains? To Alistair, nothing! And the Russian —'

'Prince Dmitri.'

'Prince!'

'All Russians are princes. I thought everybody knew that. They arrested him. It took six of them. This morning they released him. Politically, Dmitri is important. God, doesn't this climate give you an appetite?'

'It's the sea air. Last night you said he was mad!'

'He *is* mad. But important all the same.'

'For so big a man, he is damned light on his feet.'

At that moment the kitchen door was kicked open and the daube entered.

'It doesn't smell so badly, does it,' said François.

As dinner drew to its close, Jamie remembered something.

'Dmitri—why does he matter?'

François reluctantly interrupted something he was doing to the gravy with a piece of bread.

'It's a long story and probably most of it is lies,' he said. 'But Tsar Ivan—the one they call the Terrible—had two sons. One went mad. The other was murdered.'

'So?'

'He was called Dmitri,' said François. 'But some people believe that he was not murdered, that he left Russia.'

'And is living in Denmark,' said Jamie.

'The world is full of pretenders,' said François.

At the Countess Gyldenstierne's little palace that evening, Jamie was persuaded to do acrobatic tricks. 'Show us what you did on the quay.' Women crowded round him, anxious to know where he had learnt this art. An air of mystery surrounded him.

'I belong to a family of Transylvanian gypsies,' he said sadly. 'We are the only fair-haired gypsies in the world. Nobody knows where we came from originally . . . No, madame, I must not tell you our family name. It is a deadly secret. If I were only to breathe it, you would be horrified.'

He refused to tell fortunes—'too serious a matter for a charming social occasion like this.'

After a time François left and Jamie stayed on talking to Caroline who, as he rose to make his farewells, insisted that he should wear a magnificent sealskin cloak which had belonged to her father. A whaling boat had brought the skins from Greenland.

'It is a cold night,' she said, putting it round his shoulders. 'Winter is at hand.'

'You do not seem to be cold, Caroline.'

She laughed and came closer.

He found her extraordinarily easy to lift.

'No! Put me down, Jacques!'

When, at last, he found his way through the empty streets, a clock struck three. Was it the hour bell or the three-quarters?

A few flakes of snow were drifting down; innocent and questioning, they whirled along: suspended for a moment in the deep blue air, then afflicted with a sudden burst of panic and charging furiously forward.

Tomorrow it will be too cold for anyone to want to fence, he told himself.

He was wrong.

The news had spread through the town that he was a gypsy nobleman, exiled after a fatal duel; that he was a magician, a necromancer, a wizard—in short, a figure of infinite appeal. His fencing school was busy all day and, by the time the door closed, he had taken enough in fees to buy a new doublet.

When he went to hand Caroline back the sealskin cloak, she

said, 'Aren't we friends any more, Jacques? Or is winter over so soon? Somehow, I must make sure than Leonora hears that you have it. Although she will probably kill you.'

'I thought that François might do that.'

'François! My dear Jacques, he is very happy with that plump little cook at the Golden Crayfish.'

Jamie kept the cloak.

It was a morning like a fallen soufflé.

After a few skirmishes winter had brought up its main force and settled down to a relentless siege of the town.

Jamie looked out of his window on a brown sky on which copper roofs and spires burned like livid green flames, on the edges of which, here and there, were sparks of gold.

The streets were covered with trodden snow. The harbour slept under a thin blanket of ice. There, nothing moved apart from the pale blue columns of smoke rising slowly into the air from boats' galley-fires. It seemed that there was nothing in the world so heavy as smoke.

Along the rim of silence ran a small tinkling. The bells of a sleigh.

Suddenly there came before his eyes the picture of a morning in the Norwegian mountains; a milk herd going to the sea. The scents and the sounds.

He wrapped Caroline's cloak about his shoulders and went downstairs. 'A letter for you, sir.' One of the apprentices in the tailor's shop held out a small, sealed packet. He thought that he had seen the seal before. Some sort of flower. Perhaps a rose. He could not remember where.

Under a coronet, 'Gaolbird,' the note said. 'Why do you not visit this nest? Say, at six.

'But perhaps you have no need of a nest now that you wear these splendid furs.'

'Ask the sentry at the drawbridge. He will direct you. L.'

The sentry at the drawbridge? He spoke to the tailor. 'The Countess Rosenkrantz,' he asked. 'Where do I find her?'

From what he could understand of the reply, she lived in the palace—the king's palace, that vast, irresolute heap of architecture huddled under its spire with the three golden crowns.

Jamie walked thoughtfully over the crisp snow to his fencing school.

When he reached the door, he saw in front of his door a gaily painted sleigh drawn by a fine, black horse.

'May I have three words of conversation with you?'

The light, assured voice sounded suddenly at his elbow. Edward Carey was standing beside him.

Jamie looked at the Englishman and said nothing.

'Can we go in, perhaps?' Carey said, pointing a glove at the school door. 'You are five minutes later in arriving than you usually are. It is a damnably cold morning to be standing in the open.'

Jamie opened the door and stood back to let the Englishman go in first.

'This time you're sure that you haven't mistaken my identity?'

Carey laughed pleasantly. 'Quite sure,' he said.

'I'm sorry I've kept you waiting in the cold. If only I had known to expect you! The fact is that I was detained reading a letter. And, if it's a question of fencing lessons, the answer is No. My appointment book is already full. So, with a thousand regrets—'

'Of course! The whole town has heard of your success. But I am a man of peace. What I would like to speak of is something different.'

'Oh? You'll forgive me if I light the wood in this stove of mine, Mr Carey.'

'Please do!' Carey continued with a barely imperceptible increase of emphasis in his voice. 'I must give you a warning, Stuart.' He paused for a moment. 'The hounds are on your trail. You were followed to Norway. There the scent was lost. Now it has been picked up again. In the Red Lion, of all places. Very soon, the whole town will be searched for you. How long do you think you can stay at large?'

James, frowning, looked down at the sticks kindling in the stove.

'How did all this fairy tale come to your ears?'

Carey smiled. 'But surely you have been told about our

marvellous English Secret Service. We hear most things, Stuart.'

'So what am I to do, assuming for a moment my name is Stuart, which it isn't?'

'You could leave the town without warning. A ship could be found. Passage money? No problem!'

'Very kind. But why would the English Secret Service take such pains?'

'Simple. You know someone does not wish you well. You know why? Perhaps we could help you against him.'

'We?'

'Yes, we. England.'

'You are talking about a very big game, Carey.'

The Englishman leant forward and spoke in an urgent whisper. 'But already you are being drawn into a big game, bigger than you imagine. It would not surprise me if somebody—before the day is finished—*somebody* whispered in your ear a proposal which will sound very attractive.'

'I can't wait to hear it.'

'Especially when it is whispered in that particular voice. My advice is, don't listen. It is not so bad being taken as a knight. But it would be depressing to be sacrificed as a pawn.'

The wood crackled in the stove. Jamie stood up, rubbing the shavings from his hands.

'I think it will burn now,' he said. Then, with a smile, 'I am quite comfortable here, thank you. An occupation. Good friends and good advice.'

'Yes. It looks as if it has really taken,' said Carey. 'You will be able to take off that cloak soon. Good morning, M. Jacques.' He broke off with a little humorous grimace and turned to the door.

'One minute,' said Jamie. 'You spoke of somebody who wishes me no good.'

Carey raised his eyebrows. 'Don't brood over it, my dear fellow.'

'Thank you,' said Jamie. 'What do you suggest I do about it?'

Carey produced a charming smile. 'Come over to the other side of the street,' he said.

Opening the door, he left. In a moment Jamie heard the trembling rhythmic sound of sleighbells dying in the distance.

Thirty-Six Black Pearls

The King of Denmark's palace was built on an island separated from the city by a broad channel crossed by a bridge. The buildings were grouped round a massive square tower surmounted by a bulbous lantern above which soared an irregular copper spire.

At the approach to the bridge was a gatehouse outside which stood a sentry who wore a bearskin cap and cape. His well-padded breeches were striped in scarlet and yellow and his stockings were striped in the same colours. He leant on a halberd eight feet long with a blue and white tassle where the blade met the shaft.

Jamie approached him, uttering a name. It seemed that no mental activity went on behind the guard's glazed, bright blue eyes. But that, apparently, would have been too hasty a judgement. At least he knew where the Countess Leonora was to be found. He pointed to a vaulted gate that led into a courtyard.

The countess lived in a suite in the palace to which her husband had a right as a lord of the bedchamber to H.M. Christian IV, King of Denmark, Norway, the Vandals, the Goths, etc.

Jamie crossed the courtyard and entered a stately doorway. Then he was directed by a chamberlain along a darkly magnificent stone corridor hung with tapestries. At the end was a staircase. He went up and another official, hearing the name he murmured, indicated a door.

Jamie knocked and was admitted by a major-domo in livery.

A gaunt man with piercing eyes and a sombre expression. A dark-skinned woman wearing black—Italian? he wondered—who had been busy with some needlework, scurried away as he entered.

The rooms were small, the ceilings low and the walls panelled in heavily carved wood, boldly coloured. Candles burned in splendid silver sconces. On the floor was a white bearskin.

A powerful aromatic perfume stole towards him from a door in the corner of the room. From the same quarter came a sound of singing: a woman's voice; an Italian song. He went across and tapped on the door.

'I am in my bath,' said Leonora . . .

'So I see,' he said.

'Jacques!'

'Yes. To look at a lady in her bath—vulgarity! Not to look—foolishness!'

'Now your doublet is soaked, Jacques . . .'

'It will dry in a few minutes at the fire. May I kiss your toe—I assume you are not the pope, Leonora?'

Her lips curled contemptuously. 'Oh! Don't tell me you are a Protestant! . . . Now, Jacques, I am going to get up from here. Throw me the towel and, while Lucrezia dresses me, sing one of those indecent songs you learnt in Paris.'

He had been surprised by something he saw and, as usual, his mind worked more rapidly.

'And after that?'

'We shall eat, of course; then we may talk business.'

'If there is time,' he said.

'There will be time.'

'And if there is business.'

'There is always business, Jacques.'

He watched her dressing. It was always worthwhile to see a woman of fashion deciding what she would wear with what—the weather, the mood, the style of hair, the necklace, the frock, the rings.

She wore no rouge; no whitening powder. Nature had made her skin like that, almost without colour, lustrous. She wore many rings. He had noticed that when they first met at

Caroline Gyldenstierne's house.

Now a small gold case was tilted up and the rings spilled out over the dressing table. She put on one, two, three—at last five—and held up her hand in the candlelight with fingers outspread.

'That black pearl alone—that's it,' he told her.

She whipped round on her tabouret; her eyes were alight. It was the first time he had surprised any real emotion in her face.

'Why did you say that?' she asked.

'Why? Because a black pearl is just what your skin needs tonight. And that one is a beauty.'

She stripped her fingers of the other rings with fierce, clawing movements of her hands.

'What these silly women say about you is right, after all,' she said. 'You are a mind-reader.'

'But you know I am the only blond gypsy from Transylvania,' he reminded her.

'Liar. But I should like to know why you chose the black pearl.' She was frowning.

'Because it came into my mind out of infinite space. And because, when you held it up on your finger, I could see nothing else.'

'Gypsy!' she sneered.

'When I want to tempt you, Leonora, I shall know what to offer.'

For a moment, her thoughts were far away.

'Black pearls. A necklace of black pearls.'

She shook the reverie out of her eyes.

'Now help me to choose a frock for tonight,' she said briskly, and added, in Italian—'Lucrezia, open the wardrobe to the signore!'

The old woman appeared silently from nowhere and threw open a door behind which was arrayed a treasury of dresses. For an instant, Jamie's eye caught hers. It was bright, vigilant but not unfriendly.

In the end, he chose a pale, sulky pink which displayed her shoulders.

'The queen receives at midnight,' she said. 'I shall do very well for that.'

During the next hour he recalled something François had said. It was true. She had the best cook in Denmark.

A single footman waited on them. The man had opened the door to Jamie, who now noticed that the livery he wore was not the King of Denmark's. He had a nose like a sickle and lively green eyes. He was probably a Spaniard, or an Italian.

'Giovanni has been with me a long time,' she said at a moment when the servant had left the room. 'As a waiter, he is beyond price.'

'I know what you mean,' he said. 'My father used to say that a waiter had four virtues. To be as silent as the soup. As discreet as the sauce. As blind as the oysters. And as invisible as the bouquet that floats above the wine. Has Giovanni all four of these?'

He had some thoughts about Giovanni which he kept to himself.

Leonora nodded gravely. 'Your father forgot one virtue,' she said. 'A waiter must be deaf to everything but the summons to bring the next course.'

'Yes,' Jamie agreed. 'Deaf as a fish who hears only the voices of other fish.'

'Giovanni only hears fish if they talk in Italian. Speaking of that, what do you think of the wine?'

It was a white wine which he did not recognise. It seemed that it came from the hills somewhere north of Venice.

'Not far from where I lived as a child,' she told him.

'You have travelled since then!'

'Good wine and bad women—both of them travel,' she said, with a shrug so imperceptible that he would not have noticed it had not the light rippled faintly at that moment on her bare shoulders.

'Bad women! You might add poor men.'

She looked at him without much interest, but as if she had suddenly remembered his existence. She spoke after a pause.

'You remind me of a man I knew. He had something of your colour and something of your impertinence, too. Otherwise, he was different.'

'He was rich?' he asked.

'Yes, rich. And beautiful. But something else, too. Women loved him. Men loved him. But he loved himself. Only himself. Not like you, Jacques. He was an Englishman. I met him when I was in London.'

'London. Tell me, Leonora.'

Across the table he took her hand, the hand with the black pearl ring on one of the fingers. She did not seem to have noticed, although her voice warmed a little as she talked. Her face remained the pale mask of—no, not passivity—simmering rebellion.

'You have never been there? But, of course not. You are French, aren't you . . . London—you should go there. It is a city for an adventurous man.'

'Or woman?'

She shook her head. 'London is a man's city,' she said. 'The life in the streets. The theatres. Above all, the theatres. And the river. The ships. The English are all pirates.'

'It sounds just the place for me.'

'Yes. Would you like to go there?'

'Alone?'

'Maybe not alone.'

His heart beat faster at this sudden change in the mood of their conversation, although it was accompanied by no change of her expression.

'Tonight? I have been warned that tonight danger will be near. That's what the stars say.'

'Do you believe in the stars, or in your star?'

'I am dedicated to caution,' he said.

'Yes. I can see that. Well, the danger might be considerable. Otherwise, I shouldn't have troubled to mention it.'

'He might kill me, might he?'

'He—who are you talking about?' A little line had appeared above one eyebrow.

'The man you are talking about,' he said. 'The beautiful one.'

For the first time he saw something like a smile, a smile as it might be taught to the daughters of some ancient, decadent court, about to form on her lips. And die away instead.

'No.' she said. 'By that time, the beautiful one will probably be dead.'

'Are you so fond of him, Leonora?' he murmured.

Two teeth showed for a flash. 'Fond of him? You mean love him?'

It did not last for more than a fraction of a second. Then, as suddenly as it had come, it was gone. The white, sullen, lovely surface seemed never to have been disturbed.

He had seen something of her that he had not known. Now he knew less about her than he did before.

Love him . . . It could be read in so many ways.

'Love,' she said, with the slightest curl of her lip, 'that illusion!'

'Of course! But an illusion based on reality,' he suggested.

'And reality—what is that? Only a special kind of illusion.'

'Love,' he said, watching her closely. 'What is it?'

'The religion of sceptics,' she said, 'the folly of the worldly-wise.'

'On the contrary,' said James, cheerfully. 'It is the wisdom of the foolish.'

She shrugged.

'A tale told by an idiot,' she said.

'To another idiot.'

'We have had too much of this wine,' she said.

His eyes did not leave hers while he reached for the flagon and filled her glass to the brim with the white wine which came from somewhere north of Venice.

'One thing at least is certain,' he said. 'It is a game without rules.'

Her eyes opened, looking into his.

'But not without forfeits, Jacques. Jacques—promise me . . .'

The husky voice reached out to him over the table. It reached for his heart like a pickpocket reaching for a purse. He would have liked to tell her so, but he had the good sense not to. Women should not be told when their tactics are succeeding.

'Promise you? Nothing. Ever.'

'Promise me that if ever I should ask you to go to London

for me, you will not go.'

'You ask me to do something and tell me I must not do it,' he said. 'A bribe and a challenge! Incidentally, is he so beautiful, this man in London, beautiful as I am ugly?'

'You look worse than you are,' she said. 'He doesn't.'

'You ought to see Alistair,' he told her.

'Alistair?'

'He is a Scotsman I know. When Alistair and I are together, I am beautiful.'

'Then certainly I'd like to meet him.'

'Probably you shall. I should think at this moment he is somewhere in the town . . . But the beautiful one—do I have to go to London and kill him?'

'But I have told you already. You would be too late, Jacques.'

A tap came at the door. The footman appeared and whispered a name over Leonora's shoulder. While his lips moved, his glance moved restlessly about Jamie's face.

For some reason, this reptile has decided he does not love me, Jamie thought.

'Show him in, Giovanni,' she said. 'This is a gentleman I have been waiting for,' she explained to Jamie.

A dark-skinned, weather-beaten man stamped into the warm little room, with a jingle and a clatter. He was clad for riding and, to judge from the state of his boots, had ridden far.

He had a big, bony nose, battered by time and hard living, and, under frowning, eloquent eyebrows, two quick-moving and suspicious brown eyes. He had the look of one who had never worried where his next meal was coming from—or how. It came, one way or another.

From a glance at him, Jamie thought he knew what trade the newcomer followed. Very much the same as his own. Whatever that may be! Tinker, tailor, soldier . . .

This one belonged to a special type. Not so gentle as the Highlandmen he had met in Scotland. And more intelligent than the Irish. A variation on the same theme.

'Captain Morgan,' said Leonora. She held out the hand on which the big pearl gleamed darkly. The captain fell on it like a famished wolf.

'My lady! '

'The captain and I will talk in English,' Leonora went on. 'That accent you hear is Welsh, Jacques. Many soldiers are Welsh.'

'Ours is a poor country,' said Morgan.

'Monsieur Jacques is a Frenchman.'

'But I warn you that I understand English.'

Jamie rose to his feet, but Leonora waved him to sit down.

'When the captain and I have something very secret to say, we shall go into another room. Won't we, Captain?'

Captain Morgan shot at Jamie a glance of sulphurous distrust as he sat down at the table.

'As you wish,' he said.

'Monsieur Jacques teaches fencing. Captain Morgan is a famous duellist, with God knows how many victims on his conscience.'

'Not my conscience, ma'am,' Morgan protested.

'Obviously, we must avoid one another,' said Jamie.

'If we can.' Morgan's smile was full of teeth. His hand, as if by accident, fell on the hilt of his rapier.

'A glass of wine, Captain Morgan,' said Leonora. 'And now, tell us about your journey.'

'The weather is as you see, my lady. The roads are worse than that. All the way from Hamburg to here—sheets of ice, drifts of snow! '

'Ah, Hamburg,' Jamie broke in.

'You know Hamburg, monsieur?' Morgan looked at him sharply.

'I have a friend there—at least I think I have.'

'It is best to be sure where your friends are,' said Morgan.

'And who they are,' said Jamie grinning.

'That is usually easy enough.'

'The news,' Leonora broke in. 'The latest news from— there! —you know where I mean. England! Good? Bad? What is it?'

Morgan shrugged. 'That depends on how you look at it. According to the last packet that came in by sea, our friend in London has been freed and not freed.'

'The lady is clever,' said Leonora. 'He is allowed to live

in his own house. But to leave it?—no! That is forbidden. The house—by the river—you remember?—is crowded with his friends—and infested with her spies.'

'*Her* spies? You are sure they are *her* spies?'

'I am sure of nothing. But whose spies could they be?'

'Do you think he has only one enemy?'

'You are speaking of a certain little toad,' said Morgan.

'Little. Misshapen. But subtle. He is the nearest thing England has to an Italian. Cecil . . . Our friend—has he seen the lady?'

'Not once. Half the time he swears he will not see her, not for all the gold of the Indies. The other half—' He broke off with a grimace.

'Yes?'

'He pours out letters to her like the poems of a lovesick boy.'

'To an old hag of seventy!'

'Begging to be taken back into her love.'

'Love! Coming from him, that is good! In all his life, he has loved only one being.'

'They said that his sister—' Morgan broke off, frowning and embarrassed.

Leonora tossed her head. 'I never believed that story. No. My lord of Essex is madly, besottedly in love with the beautiful image he sees when he looks in the mirror . . . These letters he writes—what are they? Only the whines of wounded vanity. The power and the glory have been snatched away from him. And he has not summoned up the energy or the courage to snatch it back for himself.'

'Not yet, Countess.'

'Will he? Will he ever? I know him better than you do, Captain Morgan. He will shout his defiance to heaven—and come fawning when she calls.'

'You see him with the prejudice of love,' he said.

Her eyes were pools of black fire. 'I see him with something that sees more deeply than love does. What is it that comes after love?'

'You should not ask an old soldier a question like that. Ask somebody else. This Frenchman, for instance. He might know.

Or is he too young?'

'The French learn quickly,' Jamie pointed out.

'I don't think he is too young,' said Leonora.

'It depends,' said Jamie, 'on how love died. Perhaps it was killed.'

Morgan gave him an unfriendly glance. 'And perhaps it is not dead,' he said.

'Dead. Dead. Of course it's dead,' she said bitterly.

Morgan leant forward and spoke vehemently. 'Then why do you go to all this trouble to help him? All this web you have spun! Without you, there would be nothing. Why have you done it?'

She spoke coldly now, her face as expressionless as it always was.

'Why? Because a woman can act from contempt as well as love. It's a kind of revenge, Captain.'

'And that's all, would you say?'

'No. By no means all.'

'There is someone else in your mind?'

'Yes. Someone else. Not only my lord of Essex—'

Morgan drew his bushy eyebrows together and struck the table sharply. '*Her*. Herself? By God, you aim high, madam!'

'Enough! Enough! M. Jacques will think we are talking treason. But go on. Tell me more, Captain . . . What has happened in Hamburg?'

'Your friend the Scotsman—'

'The red-haired one?'

Jamie looked up sharply. 'With pale blue eyes and a hot temper?' he asked.

'You know him?'

'I know one of the kind. His name is Alan Beaton. He traffics in arms.'

'Already you know too much,' said Morgan sourly.

'Go on, Captain,' she said. 'We can trust M. Jacques.'

After a moment's hesitation, Morgan resumed. 'Beaton has a ship,' he said. 'German. A flyboat. Perfect for work like this. Muskets he has, by the hundred. Corslets. Helmets. And five lasts of powder. All ready to be shipped.'

'Have they been paid for?' she asked.

'Countess, you have given a great deal already whether out of love or something else. So have others. Now more is needed. Much more.'

She smiled. 'Lord Essex means to bring his friends down in ruin.'

'Great deeds of state are costly, ma'am. You have the credit. You can raise money in the market. He counts on you.'

'Yes, he counts on me, as he counted on me once before when he threw me over because that lady had banned me from her palace. Now, I have to give and give again, so that one day he may seize power in England if he can at last screw up his courage to do it. The price of love is high, Captain Morgan, but it seems to me that the price of contempt is higher. The answer to you is No. I have done all I am going to do. Given all I am going to give. When I read that he has become regent of England I shall weep with joy. Until then, my eyes will be dry and—'

'And your purse will be closed,' said Morgan. 'And nobody will have a word of reproach for you. Least of all my lord! You say he does not love you—'

'He loves—'

'Himself only. That is what you say. It may not be true, Countess. A man's heart is a battleground of impulses—love, ambition, greed. I need not tell you. Now this man whom once you loved is broken, a prisoner of his defeated dreams more than of the queen's guards. He may fear to strike, so you say. I am more afraid that he will be goaded into striking before all is ready. He may overrate the power against him. He underrates its cunning. The cunning of Cecil. The cunning of the queen.'

Morgan paused for a moment. 'What is certain is that in his despair he remembers you. He thinks of love.'

'Oh, love!' she scoffed.

'He sends me this to give to you.' Morgan laid on the table a small packet elaborately sealed. 'What is in it, I know not.'

She thought for a moment before speaking:

'Yes. He may strike when he should not. Remember! His image in the mirror grows a little older every time he looks at it. They say he has already seen a white hair in his beard.

113

Love cannot wait for ever . . . What is in that packet, Morgan?'

He pushed it across the table to her.

Quickly she broke the seals and cut the cords and the threads that sewed the canvas covering together. At last, under a layer of wool, she found a letter, folded, unsealed. She looked at it.

'His writing,' she said. Then she read:

'Leonora. My mother had this. Now it is yours to keep in remembrance of Robin.'

'Robin?' Jamie spoke in the silence.

'Robert Devereux, Earl of Essex,' she said, impatiently.

She raised the lid of a black case of morocco leather and sprang to her feet.

'Jesu!'

On the velvet lining of the case was displayed a necklace—black pearls perfectly matched, each the size of a grape, twenty, thirty—Jamie counted—thirty-six in all, laid out in three rows. Between each pair a large diamond sparkled on a golden chain. He was looking at one of the great jewels of the world.

'Black pearls!' Jamie pointed to her ring.

Morgan's eyes glowed. His voice was hushed with wonder.

'A necklace for a queen,' he said.

She glanced at him. Her eyes flashed. A faint wash of colour had come into her cheeks..

'Better than that!' she said. 'A queen's necklace! Look at them! The size! The matching! It took the jewellers years of search to find them. The merchants of half Asia were enlisted in the hunt. And look at the setting in diamonds and gold.'

'Elizabeth's?' asked Morgan.

She shook her head.

'Elizabeth Tudor bought it when the man who stole it wished to sell it. She bought it cheaply. Then, one day she sold it. She needed to buy cannon. An Italian woman, a queen too, had seen it and wanted it. Catherine de' Medici. Elizabeth would not sell. Not to her. A jeweller got it, who sold it to Lady Essex. But the necklace belongs forever to the queen who had it first—from whom it was stolen—'

'I know! I know!' cried Jamie.

'The Queen of Scots.'

'Mary Stuart,' said Morgan in a whisper.

'Given her by a French king—which of them, God knows,' said Jamie. 'My father used to speak of this necklace.'

She had lifted it from its velvet nest and undid the clasp. He helped her fasten it behind her neck.

'Lucrezia! A mirror! Quickly!'

On the gleaming expanse of her shoulders, the pearls looked incomparably magnificent and sinister.

The old woman came in and threw up her hands.

'Contessa mia! Que bellezza!'

Leonora stood, the mirror in her hand, turning her head this way and that, a strange smile on her lips, watching the dusky light play softly on the pearls. A solar system of darkly glowing planets seemed to revolve round the white column of her neck.

'Cunning devil! He knew I would rather have this than the crown of England itself. Oh, that I could wear it before Queen Jezebel!'

'But tonight,' said Jamie, 'you can show it to the Queen of Denmark.'

She shook her head. 'No. Not tonight. But perhaps I shall borrow it for the night of the masked ball.'

Morgan broke in vehemently.

'Borrow it! One does not borrow a gift, Countess.'

'Gifts must be paid for, Morgan. They are the dearest commodity of all. But it was astute of him to remember my passion for these pearls.'

'It was love, ma'am.'

But she shook her head, interrupting for a moment the slow movement of her head from side to side before the mirror.

'Love? No. What he hopes to buy from me is something else. He knows I despise him. He has never been happy about that. Now he thinks he can buy—not love, Captain—but esteem, forgiveness, gratitude. As if they were worth having! My lord is not a passionate man, but he is a sensitive one. And stupid, too.'

'Stupid?'

'Oh, stupid and cunning! This letter. The shortest I have ever had from him. Do I not detect in it the sad music of the passing bell? It is farewell. Is he in danger, Morgan?'

'In deadly danger, ma'am. He has friends, many friends. But he has not many arms.'

'And not enough courage. Your eagle is only a peacock, Morgan.'

'It is easier to be an eagle when you have talons, ma'am.'

'Arms!' she said. 'We must think of a way to pay for them. How much do you reckon will be needed?'

Morgan grimaced and said nothing.

'Jacques, the necklace. What do you think of it?'

'There are shoulders that need no pearls, Leonora.'

'Liar! Flatterer! Cut his throat, Morgan!'

'A pleasure, ma'am.'

She unfastened the necklace quickly.

'Giovanni,' she called. The servant entered. 'Take this necklace. Here is the box. Lock it in the coffer, the one you know of.' The servant looked at them. His eyes seemed suddenly to dilate with some powerful emotion.

'You have the key yourself,' he said.

The Italian he spoke was easy to understand; the surliness in his voice was a universal language. Leonora said something quickly under her breath. She brushed past Giovanni and left the room. The footman followed her.

Morgan watched them go out. Then he leant forward across the table. His red-veined eyes under their bushy brows were fixed on Jamie's. They had a quality of stony impassivity. He kept his voice down as he spoke.

'Giovanni . . . A servant? . . . Don't be too sure.'

'What is he, then?'

The eyebrows rose.

'They have been together a long time, these two. In London, some people thought he was her brother.'

'And what do you think?'

'Not her brother,' said the Welshman. 'Brothers do not have that power.'

'Then who have it, Morgan? And why do they have it?'

116

'If you want to know the answer—but why do you?—you should ask the old woman, Lucrezia.'

'She knows?'

'She knows everything.'

The silence lasted a minute, then Jamie asked, 'What does he want, my lord Essex?'

'What do you think, Frenchie?'

'To see Cecil's head fall into the basket?'

Morgan shook his head. 'More than that. To reign as regent for a little. Then to rule as king.'

Jamie raised his eyebrows. 'And what of the King of Scots?'

Morgan laughed cynically. 'He belongs to an unlucky family.'

Death of a Spy

The snow came down like a blanket, deadening the palace chimes. It was time for Leonora to make her curtsey to the queen. Morgan, with a deep bow to her and a hard nod to Jamie, had gone his way.

'Your friend, Beaton, will be here one of these days,' he said.

Jamie kissed her hand. Then he eased his shoulders into the fur cloak Giovanni had put round them and went out along the shadowy corridor, down the staircase and out into the courtyard.

By this time there were no chamberlains about. No guards. No sound of voices came from behind the oaken doors of the apartments. On his way to the door leading to the open air, he caught sight of only one living creature. A dwarf in royal livery scuttled past him, without uttering a word, but with a look as cold and malignant as a viper's.

As Jamie crossed the courtyard the snow creaked under his boots.

One problem was worrying at his mind. When Leonora rose from the bath, and reached for her towel, he had caught a glimpse of something which had astounded him.

Her back bore the bruises of a beating. There could be no mistake. He had seen too many stigmata of this kind during the time when he had pulled an oar for the King of Spain. Leonora had been beaten, and not many days before!

But why? And by whom?

There was some mystery about her, he knew. And probably

a vice. But, surely, not *that* one. What then could be the explanation?

For some reason, he found that into his mind came the image of her footman, Giovanni.

An Italian like her. A Venetian probably, with that dark skin and big, imposing nose. And more than a footman. Morgan was surely right.

How much more? A spy? An accomplice? A—what?

Man of confidence? One who was to his mistress what Rizzio had been to Mary Stuart, whatever that had been? He recalled his father. 'My poor sister. She made mistakes— but Rizzio was not one of them.' The meaning of that remark was obscure. And his father would never enlarge on it.

Giovanni and Leonora . . . What was certain was that, as Morgan said, they had been a long time together, these two . . . adventurers. All this was based on nothing, except a remark of Morgan's—and a certain tingling of the nerves when the man helped him into the fur cloak. And the bruises of a beating.

Halfway across the palace yard, he paused. From the gate-house came a bellow of command, followed by the clash of steel. Through the archway rode a knot of horsemen. The man in the lead was a giant, in height and girth alike. As the horseman came into the flickering light of the lanterns at the gate, Jamie made out ruddy cheeks and a blond beard; an appearance of brutal good nature; an air of command. The rider wore a long hunting coat cut from some hide—elkskin? Under a fine lace ruff twinkled a jewelled order of some kind.

As he neared Jamie, he raised his arm and gave a jovial growl. By this time, Jamie had noticed the resemblance to engravings he had seen in the town.

'Majesté!' His ostrich plume swept to the snow. He counted ten as M. de Pluvinel had told him to do. Then he straightened.

By that time the cavalcade had passed. Grooms were rushing to the horses' heads. Torches appeared. The baying of a hound echoed dismally along a corridor of the palace.

He was turning to go when he heard a shout, 'Hoi!' The big man, who must be King Christian, was beckoning him to approach. Hat in hand, James went over. The king said something he could not understand.

'I am French, your majesty.'

The king went on in French, 'Haven't we met before, somewhere?'

'I think not, your majesty. I arrived here only a few days ago.'

The king bent on him a sharp, prolonged gaze.

'That's damned strange. Your face is familiar. French, eh? What do you do?'

'I am a fencing master.'

'Ah—ha! Let us have a bout one day. In the meantime, I shall try to think where I have seen your face before. What is your name?'

'Jacques, sire.' He bowed again as, with a last puzzled look, the King of Denmark turned towards the state entrance to his palace.

Jamie shook the snow from his ostrich plume. When he had reached the gatehouse, the main doors were shut and bolted. A sergeant of the guard let him out by a postern.

He may not be the greatest sovereign in Christendom, he thought, but he is probably the biggest. I wonder why he thinks we have met before. My father—no, he was never here. Besides, he was not in the least like me . . .

When he came to the drawbridge, Jamie found himself suddenly in the middle of the town. He had only to walk across and there he was, among the shops, the taverns, the barrows all ready stacked for the market which would open at dawn.

On his right the channel which served as the castle moat opened into the harbour. There, lights moved on the water. Men shouted. A boat was coming to the quay.

Somewhere along the wharf, yellow light spilled out as a door was kicked open among the shops on the waterfront.

Sailors, tramping in their sea boots, poured on to the cobbles, bellowing songs. Somebody slipped and fell heavily. A woman shrieked something, probably an insult.

Nearer him was a sentry box before which a brazier was burning. The guardsman on duty came to the salute with a smack of his palm on the staff of his halberd. Jamie touched the brim of his hat and passed on over the bridge.

'Good night,' he said.

He walked maybe a dozen steps farther, his chin well tucked into the collar of the sealskin cloak, his thoughts busy with what Leonora had told him and what she had failed to tell.

He had—on another plane—come to an important decision. In a town like this, in a climate like this, a felt hat was no headgear for a man of sense. What he needed was a fur cap like the sentry, with ear flaps if possible. First thing in the morning! As a man who was received at court, he had no reason to be anxious about his credit with the haberdashers.

At that moment, two events snatched at his mind.

He heard, or thought he heard—but it was impossible—the cry of a curlew. Where did it come from? He looked round, startled, alert—

There was not a soul in sight. Only the sailors staggering along the quay, their bawling subdued by the cold into grumbled curses. And the sentry motionless beside his brazier.

He put his head down and went on. Just at this point, the east wind, blowing along the snow-covered quay, had an edge like a razor.

Again, wavering but clear, the curlew's cry. Jamie swung round in the direction to which his quickened senses led him, but as he did so, his attention was arrested by something else even more startling.

In front of him, at a distance of maybe thirty yards, a narrow alley opened off the quayside street. At its corner, a lamp hung from an iron bracket, throwing a splash of light on the snow. A man was walking towards him along this street, when from the shadows on either side two cloaked figures darted out simultaneously and with sinister speed. Arms rose and fell. There was a thud of blows, the glint of a knife. The man gave a choking groan and fell forward on his knees.

For a second the other two watched him, crouching over him, one on either side. He stumbled to his feet, his hands thrown out, groping in the thick air above the snow for something that was not there. One of the assailants pounced forward and struck again. The man fell forward and lay still, his cheek in the snow.

By the time Jamie, his sword drawn, had come up to him, the two assailants had vanished soundlessly into the darkness along the street.

But as he ran, Jamie noticed that, before they disappeared, one of them, the one who had dealt the final blow, stopped for an instant above the fallen man and snatched something from him. It could have been a purse.

The whole incident had lasted no longer than five seconds.

Jamie pulled up, hesitant, his mind working fast. A simple case of manslaughter—murder perhaps—and robbery. No doubt. But it was the only simple aspect of the affair.

If he were mixed in it too far, he would have to speak to the Watch, who would ask questions and would not be easily satisfied with his answers. He was a wanted man.

Jamie bent over the man who lay very still. Dead? For sure. That hand thrown out dramatically with the fingers curled. That foot turned the wrong way. And that dark patch on the snow. By daylight it would look like a gaudy sweet to tempt children at a fair.

He turned the body over cautiously and peered down at the face. As if he had been stung, Jamie leapt upright . . .

Boots crunched on the snow. He swung round in alarm. A soldier with a bearskin cape and a halberd stood before him.

'Jamie,' said the sentry in his soft voice. 'I thought it might be you. Did you not hear me?'

'Alistair!'

'I'll explain this get-up in a minute,' said Alistair MacIan. 'What has happened to this poor devil?'

'Look!' Jamie whispered. 'Look!'

Alistair bent over the face, the grey and yellow beard, the pallor, green in the lamplight, the eyes staring at nothing.

'By God, I'd know that whey face anywhere.'

'Now you can toll the bell for him, Alistair.'

The Highlander crossed himself. Then he spoke urgently. 'Toll the bell for all of us, if we are not careful. Jamie, you disappear along the quay. Fast. I'll go back and turn out the guard.'

Both of them looked round at that moment in a sudden panic. But there were lights at none of the windows. Signs of life in none of the doorways.

'There's just one thing, Alistair.'

'What's that?'

'Are you sure that this is—who you thought it was?'

Alistair's eyes questioned Jamie's before he answered:

'I am indeed not. I could not swear that I had seen the man before. What is in your mind, James?'

Jamie opened his sealskin cloak at the collar and, with some difficulty, pulled out the small leather bag he wore there. He opened it and between his fingers held a small folded parchment with a seal.

'The scoundrels who robbed this man took away every clue to his name. Except this.' He tore a corner off the parchment. 'It seems to be in Latin and it speaks of somebody called Jacobus Stuart. Now, if I were to put it on his body—so—where the thieves have torn his doublet open, maybe it would be found.'

'It might be, James.' Alistair's face lit up with understanding.

'It would be a pity to waste men's time looking for a person already dead.'

'Sinful,' said Alistair.

'So, good night, Alistair. Oh, and make sure that there's somebody about who can read Latin.'

'Good night. Tomorrow we'll meet. The Red Lion. At noon.'

He walked back towards the sentry box.

Before leaving, James looked down once more at the staring eyes in the dead face of Jock Stevenson, the spy.

'Little Frog, Say Your Prayers'

'For God's sake, keep your voice down, Alistair! There are too many Scotsmen here. I am not in the mood to trust them. So oblige me. When one of the waiters is hovering about, speak French.'

They were dining at the Red Lion.

'French I can't be doing,' said Alistair.

'Gaelic then. Anything so long as it's not English. Go on with what you were saying. But in a whisper . . . What makes you think they are looking for me?'

'They are looking for a young man named James Stuart. Tall. Blond. Wanted for murder in Scotland.'

James considered it in silence for a moment. Then, Jamie nodded thoughtfully. It was true that during his stay in Edinburgh a man had been killed. It was also true that he, Jamie Stuart, was accused of the murder—falsely accused. And certainly he had joined Sinclair, that old mercenary captain, in a journey across Norway which was planned to end in the Swedish Army occupying Russia. All that was true enough.

'The news gets around fast,' said Stuart.

He remembered the day, not so long ago, when walls in Edinburgh were covered with placards denouncing him for a murder. He had not committed the murder but it suited the authorities in Scotland to fasten the crime on him. It was one of the reasons he had left the country in a hurry.

'It does,' said Alistair. 'Very fast. Also this Stuart is thought to have gone to Norway in the company of Captain George

124

Sinclair.'

'And, therefore, been slaughtered with all the rest of Sinclair's force,' said Stuart. 'That was the end of Jamie Stuart, poor devil.'

Alistair agreed.

'Yes, indeed, man. It was a terrible tragedy. The only weakness is that not everybody believes it. And Jock Stevenson, God rest his soul, was one of them.'

'Why should he care, one way or the other?'

'Money, James, money,' said Alistair, with distaste. 'He was a spy, he was going to be well-paid. At the very moment he was killed, he was on his way to the palace with some news. News about you.'

'How did you hear all this?'

'In the Bodyguard we hear a great deal. And one of my cousins has been in the corps for some time. I had lost sight of him for years and there, all of a sudden, he was! Roderick tells me things as one Highland gentleman to another.'

'Perhaps you'll tell me one thing, Alistair. What happened to you after I fell into the harbour?'

'I lay low. And next morning I went to a blacksmith and asked him to take the chains off!'

'And he did?'

Alistair nodded vigorously.

'I was most polite. I explained it all to him in Gaelic and in English. Both of them, mind you. So what else could he do as a Christian?'

James could think of several things. He mentioned one of them.

'Take you to the police.'

'That is just what he wanted to do, of course. But I said, "No, boy. Take me to the barracks, instead. I want to 'list for a soldier." He couldn't understand me at first. Yes. It took a long time to persuade him. I believe he thought I was mad.'

'And he couldn't understand what you were saying anyway.'

Alistair nodded emphatically. 'Oh, he understood. In the end he understood, James. It's surprising what these foreigners can understand when you speak the Language to them slowly.

Although, when you come to think of it, it's natural enough seeing that it was the language they spoke in Eden.'

'You mean Hebrew.'

'A Sassenach lie!'

Jamie laughed. 'So now you're a soldier.'

'Soldier! I'm a guardsman! Were it not for the likes of me, the King of Denmark, God save His Majesty, would not be able to sleep at night for worry. James, you should join. The uniform would suit you.'

James shook his head.

'Think it over,' said Alistair earnestly. 'Come, let's have another glass of this poison. God, what would I not give for a gill of whisky! Do you know that my flask'—he held it up and shook it—'has been empty since that day I lost you up yonder in the mountains!'

He made signals to the serving man.

'You must tell me what happened after that,' said James.

'After that—a lot happened after that.'

It turned out to be a long story and it might have been longer still if Alistair, in a moment of imprudence, had not entered a village and stolen bread in a baker's shop . . . 'Man, I thought they would murder me on the spot. But mostly I was anxious about you, Jamie—' he went on.

'The devil you were!'

'Yes, I thought either he will die of hunger, poor handless fellow, or—he'll meet a woman. That was your only hope, I thought. Did you, James? . . . What was she like?'

'Like a queen,' he said.

Alistair gave him a long, questioning look.

'Either you are a damned liar, or you're luckier than you deserve to be,' he said.

The drinks came. The waiting man, a sandy-haired immigrant from across the North Sea, put the glasses down on the table; he spoke English with a finicking Edinburgh accent.

'Would any of you gentlemen have heard of a man, James Stuart?'

James sat silent. Overcoming his distaste for the waiter's accent, Alistair replied, 'Heard of him! Would he be a Scotsman? Like yourself.'

'He might be,' said the waiter, looking from one to the other.

'Then he's dead. Why do you ask?'

'There's a letter waiting for him here.'

'Give it to me,' said Alistair, brusquely. 'I'll see that it reaches the family. Hurry up, man. I haven't all day to wait.'

When the waiter brought the letter a few minutes later, he peered at them inquisitively from beneath his yellow eyebrows. 'You'll give me a receipt for the letter,' he said to Alistair. 'Just in case, like.'

Alistair gave him a haughty glance. 'Receipt,' he said. 'Are you suggesting I'm not a gentleman?'

'God forbid, sir.'

'Well, then!'

When the waiter had left, Alistair passed the letter to Jamie.

'You are better at the Sassenach than I am, Jamie. Besides, it's your letter.'

James broke the seal.

'It's from Alan Beaton. He has heard that I am here. How the devil has the news reached Hamburg? That's where he is!'

'Is that all?'

'No. he says this. "They're hunting you, James." My God, that's news! "Look out," he says. He goes on to speak about some business that keeps him in Hamburg. But he'll be here soon. I'm to leave word for him at this inn. "Try to keep your head on your shoulders, James! A ploy is afoot that will dazzle you with its splendour. Yellow boys in heaps for all of us."'

Alistair's face twisted into a hideous grin. His eyes shone. 'Yellow boys' was English slang that he understood.

'Yellow boys!' he said softly, rubbing his thumb against his fingers. 'What kind of ploy will he have in mind?'

Jamie shrugged his shoulders. 'God knows,' he said. 'But if I know anything about Alan there will be weapons in the business somewhere. And somewhere will be on the far side of the law.'

Alistair clucked in pious disapproval. 'You don't say! The far side of the law! Terrible!'

'Yes. The trouble is, I'm on that side myself.'

127

'Yes, James. It would never do for you to be caught. Grow a beard.'

'I had a better plan than that,' said James, with a flash of white teeth. 'I'm Monsieur Jacques. I'm French. I teach young noblemen to fence. I am invisible.'

Alistair reached out his hand across the table.

'Some people will never learn sense,' he said joyfully.

By the time James had made his way through the snow to the Golden Crayfish, François was in the middle of the third course. He listened to the story without interrupting the stately rhythm of his meal.

'At present,' he said, 'you have nothing to fear. Today and tomorrow are very favourable for Leo. My own case is very different. You'll notice I have eaten no shellfish. The reason? Simple.' His voice fell to a mournful mumble. 'Sagittarius is threatened by Pisces. And the influence of the Crab could be dangerous. I am taking no risks.'

'Perhaps the stars will tell you something else,' said James, irritably. 'Why am I being hunted like this?'

François looked at him with surprise. 'For a clever man, you're stupid at times.'

'I come from a stupid family.'

'It's simple,' and François, while he chewed steadily. 'The King of Scotland believes that you are dangerous. He has always thought so. And something happened in Edinburgh not so long ago that has made him think so even more. Something about a marriage. I don't understand it altogether.'

'When I have a minute to spare, I'll explain it, François. Go on.'

It was no moment to burden François's digestion with the evidence, such as it was, that James Stuart's father might, after all, have been the legitimate son of King James V of Scotland. In which case, Jamie would have a respectable claim to the Scottish throne.

François took another mouthful and resumed.

'The King of Scotland expects to be King of England one day soon. He does not want the prize to be snatched from him at the last minute.'

James was impressed by François's flow of information.

'How do you come to know all this?'

'Because I see intelligence reports. Every embassy in the town knows it. King James has given orders to have you found and removed, one way or another! He believed you were in Norway, then Sweden. Now he thinks you are here. However, you are safe for the moment, as I have explained.'

James looked resentfully at his old schoolfriend, who now resumed eating industriously.

'You have heard that a man named Jock Stevenson was murdered last night?'

'I have heard that a man, unknown, was found dead in the streets with his pockets picked. I hadn't heard his name. What did you say it was?'

'Stevenson.'

'Stevenson . . .' François suddenly spoke more cautiously. 'Did you kill him, Jacques?' he asked.

'Why do you ask that?'

'Oh. I only wondered. It's high time you ordered your dinner. First things first. She has a good plaice that was caught early this morning. A Leo can risk it,' said François with a sigh.

James leant forward and spoke vehemently. 'I did not kill Stevenson,' he said.

François with a wave of his hand indicated that the matter was of the greatest triviality. 'My dear boy,' he said. 'If you did, I am sure you had a good reason. If you didn't, there is no need to worry, is there?'

'What is more, I don't know who killed Stevenson. And I don't even know why he was killed.'

'No, no, Jacques, of course not. But probably it was a good thing for you that he *was* killed. Now, be sensible. Order your dinner.'

'François,' said James, suddenly solemn, with sparkling eyes, 'a ploy is afoot. What it is, I don't know. But—a ploy! Understand?'

But in French, however he tried to say it, the idea did not sound so exciting. And François remained quite unresponsive . . .

Jamie changed the subject.

'Leonora Rosenkrantz,' he said, 'What do your people in the Embassy know about her servant Giovanni?'

François frowned. 'Not much. They say about him what they say about anybody who puzzles them.'

'And what's that?'

'That he's a Jesuit, of course.'

James was not convinced.

Walking thoughtfully back to his lodgings, over the trampled snow, he passed the King of Denmark's galleons, drawn up in rows at anchor, dismasted, with black canvas awnings stretched over their decks. After that, he reached the quays where the merchantmen were unloading.

Out at sea, there were patches of yellow faintly showing beneath the grey. Sandbanks—shoals. Treacherous waters for ships that had no experienced pilots. Far off, on another coast, the late sun caught a stretch of white dunes.

When he arrived at the tailor's shop where he lodged there was some excitement. An armed man wearing the royal livery had arrived from the palace bringing a sealed missive.

Prison? A lettre de cachet? He broke the seal and read.

The Chevalier Jacques, a Frenchman of noble birth, was—was what? He peered at the document in perplexity.

It was written in French but in a hand so elegant and tortured that he could not understand it. Jamie was forced to ask the tailor to tell him what some of the written images represented . . .

It seemed that His Majesty was holding a feast—a masked ball in the palace—and that he commanded the presence of the said Chevalier.

Leonora has done this, he told himself. It could be nobody else.

The snow had half melted and frozen again. James, with his new fur cap pulled over his ears, went to the Red Lion. A waiter whom he had seen before said, 'Somebody has been looking for you, sir. That friend of yours in the Guard.'

'Did he leave a message? No? Would you say it was good news or bad, boy?'

The waiter rubbed his chin. 'With you, all news is good, sir.'

After a long look into the man's eyes, James decided that he was being warned. He went to look for François, in his usual eating place.

François gave him a careworn look. 'Have you read the stars today, Jacques?'

'To hell with them! Have you seen Alistair?'

'The mad Scotsman? No. But let me tell you one thing. In spite of what the stars say, you should be careful tonight. Very careful.'

'I prefer to believe what the stars say.' And with a nod in the direction of the kitchen—'What has she for us tonight?'

At that moment, the fat woman came in with a wave of cooking smells behind her.

'Oh it's you,' she said to Jamie, in the French that François had taught her. 'Now why have I been thinking of you today?'

Jamie bowed over her hand.

'Because it's my lucky day, beautiful,' he said.

'No, she said, frowning.

'Tonight,' said François nervously, 'we might eat in the kitchen. It is quieter there. What do you say, Jacques?'

'The kitchen will do very well.'

Afterwards François said, 'Tonight I will take you somewhere you have never visited. By the way, you have no valuables with you, I hope—money, jewels?'

'Only this sealskin coat of Caroline's.'

'Do not take it off, Jacques, even if the room gets warm. It is that kind of place.'

François led the way. In a few minutes, Jamie sensed from the clammy chill of the air that they were nearing the open sea. They went through a low porch, into a cobbled yard at the far end of which a yellow light shone murkily through glass. Down steps, François pushed a door open.

Music, stormy as a hunt in full cry, struck their ears—wild strings, throbbing drums, and a wailing voice.

'Gypsies,' said François. 'They are the same everywhere. These ones come from Poland.'

The gypsy girls had lithe tawny shoulders, glistening black

hair and eyes which were too lustrous for nature alone.

The cellar in which Jamie had arrived had rough tables set between barrels. In the middle an open brick floor. Sitting around, he was aware of men wearing long coats and pointed fur caps. There seemed to be a good deal of gold thread about.

'Who are they?' he whispered.

'These?' said François. 'They are Polaks, Russians, Hungarians and God knows what else. Boyars! All fur, dirt and jewels! I hope you don't mind lice, Jacques?'

'I do not appeal to them.'

'They have a wine here from Hungary. Drinkable.'

'Why have you brought me here, François?'

'Because the Watch don't often come here.'

Looking round, Jamie could believe that.

'Too many of them got hurt. And tonight,' François went on, 'I don't want the police to set eyes on you.'

He sat down, and struck the table with his fist. 'And the girls. Be careful, Jacques. Sometimes they are virtuous. Sometimes they have a jealous lover. Always, they are thieves.'

Jamie raised a finger. 'Caution,' he said solemnly. 'The queen of virtues.'

Wine came. Whether white or red he could not tell in the half-darkness. He disliked it so much that he drank it down quickly.

The music dragged itself into sudden tantrums. In Moscow, he thought, it would be like this all the time. Perhaps it would have been better if . . . Someone had filled his glass.

Caution—all very well in its place, but one must not allow it to be a tyrant in one's life. He looked around benevolently.

A girl came and sat on the table in front of him. He noticed how impudently, how beautifully, her face was painted. She came closer and threw an arm round his shoulder. There was a shimmer of frail sound from a shower of gold bangles that fell to her wrist. She would be about eighteen, he thought—but girls of her kind looked older than they were. This was not one of the virtuous ones. But there would be a lover not far away.

She pointed to the glass and said something. He filled it and put it to her lips. She drank, her eyes in his. Disturbingly, they

132

reminded him of other eyes, eyes of a different colour but with the same animal half asleep in them . . . Leonora? No. Before Leonora. In another country . . . She brought her lips near his. She used a heavy perfume which he ought to find unpleasant.

'I know you have a dagger in your garter,' he murmured.

Her eyes became at once awake.

'You are French! A French boy! But I have no garter. No stockings. See!'

He saw.

'But a dagger, yes' he said. 'I can feel it. Here.'

Her lips, painted a dark orange, swayed forward and touched him.

'Your eyes make me think of someone.'

'Eyes?' She had not understood.

'Jacques, watch your money,' said François out of the corner of his mouth.

But at that moment Jamie was watching something else. His eyes had become accustomed to the smoky yellow light of the cellar. Not far away a party of Russians or Poles, huge men with extravagant moustaches—blond for the most part— sprawled at a table, throwing dice and arguing noisily. All of a sudden, one of them rose to his feet, swaying slightly, and made a gesture of command to the gypsy musician.

'See who it is?' asked Jamie.

François nodded. 'Dmitri.'

Without any preliminary, the Russian began to sing in that darkly resplendent voice of his, filling the cellar with a torrent of passionate music. Meanwhile, the gypsy strings kept up a threatening murmur, barely audible, like the sound of a city about to break out in revolt.

Before it was over the gypsy girl had slipped from the table on to Jamie's knee. He could feel her hard little body quivering against him.

'What a voice!' he said at the end.

'What a man!' she said, but he did not know whom she was talking about.

For a moment or two the cellar was silent, crushed it seemed under the assault of the Russian's voice. The pause ended when Dmitri caught sight of Jamie.

133

'The acrobat!' he bellowed. He lurched towards Jamie. 'You'll drink a glass with me,' he commanded.

Jamie shook his head, pointing to the glass before him.

'Drink, idiot!' muttered François.

Dmitri staggered across with a glass in his hand. He was very drunk. His other hand rested on the curved dagger at his belt. His eyes were tiny and shone wickedly. Jamie took the glass from him and touched it with his lips, smiling. The Russian watched him closely.

'Drink,' he said thickly.

Jamie, still smiling, handed the glass back. In an instant the temper of the scene changed. Dmitri leant forward, swaying.

'You insult me, you French pig,' he growled. 'You will not drink with me. Very well. You will, perhaps, fight me.'

Jamie pushed the gypsy girl from his knee.

'No,' he said, with a shrug. 'I am only a fencing master. I don't fight with princes.'

Dmitri made a contemptuous sound with his lips.

'What does rank matter? We are men, aren't we? Come on! You aren't frightened, are you?'

He leant forward and grabbed James by his doublet at the neck.

'Don't do that, prince,' said Jamie coldly. 'Don't do that, I beg of you.'

'Prince! What the devil do you mean? Don't you know that I am the rightful tsar? Dmitri, Grand Duke of Moscow and Tsar of all the Russias!'

'If it comes to that, I am the rightful King of Scotland.'

'Two pretenders! We're equal then! There's no reason in the world why we shouldn't fight. Come on!'

With a bellow of laughter, the Russian pulled Jamie's doublet.

Now Stuart was on his feet. He threw his coat to François and thoughtfully drew his sword.

The cellar had become very quiet. Talk had stopped. Feet no longer shuffled on the stone floor. Stillness reigned. The gypsies had stopped playing and sat watching with glittering eyes.

Dmitri threw off his long, fur-trimmed coat and stood in a

loose white shirt stitched with gold thread. He had drawn his scimitar and thrown it across the room to his friends, shouting something in Russian.

From somewhere a heavy sabre appeared. Dmitri took it, one hand on the hilt, the other feeling the edge of the blade. It was a long and generously curved weapon which would have looked right on a mounted dragoon. In Dmitri's hands, it seemed a weapon for a schoolboy.

'Now little frog, say your prayers,' he growled, looming over Jamie.

This animal is very drunk, Jamie thought, but how do I avoid killing him?

The two swords met with a shudder of steel. In a moment, Jamie began to think that he had, perhaps, asked the wrong question.

The Russian was enormous, but light on his feet. He was drunk, but his hand was steady. He might be an animal, but he was dangerous. And he was exceptionally strong.

After a few cautious parries, Jamie said to himself: At this rate, I shall have to kill him.

The passes became faster: after all, it may not be so easy to kill him!

Dmitri lunged forward, using his vast reach with effect so that Jamie, stepping back smartly to take the Russian's blade close to the hilt of his, thought: If I don't look out, he will kill *me*. He was in acute danger—but he was suddenly completely cool, supremely confident, fighting a defensive battle with a subtlety which he knew the Russian could not match, carrying out the passata sotto—ducking below Dmitri's sabre aimed at his heart—but refraining from the counter-riposte which would have laid Dmitri on the flagstones of the cellar.

How it was going to end—that was another matter.

I will not disarm him, he decided. If I were to do that, I should have all of them on me. And if I don't disarm him? What?

Patience. Patience!

Two minutes later, he was aware of noises somewhere outside. A blast of cold air made the candles quail. Tables were pushed back, chairs overturned. A woman screamed, as women do in that kind of place on that kind of occasion. And suddenly the cellar was full of halberdiers in uniform blinking in the murky light. Two of them carried smoking torches.

One shouted a command in Danish. Someone—it was François—bawled the translation, 'Messieurs, messieurs! A bas les armes!'

The Chief Mourner

Considering that the pillow was stuffed with old, smelly straw and that the bed consisted of three planks without a mattress, Jamie had slept pretty well. Considering that he was charged with drunken brawling in a public place, he woke up feeling reasonably fresh.

Shivering a little, it was true, and more stiff than usual but that was hardly surprising since the cell he had occupied had no heating and, in place of a window, a small unglazed opening high up in the wall crossed by heavy iron bars.

The smell had been the normal prison smell, made even worse by the fact that this was the wing reserved for drunks.

But, in all fairness, as prisons went, Jamie had been in worse.

The night before, which he remembered in vivid flashes between obscurer intervals, had ended better than might have been expected. Dmitri had regarded the incursion of the police as a personal—even a national—affront justifying an abrupt switch of alliances.

Roaring like a bull, he had hurled himself on the men with the halberds, shouting to Jamie to join him in the battle. And Jamie, against all his natural instincts of caution, had obeyed the call.

He had, however, fought a retreating action and had been at some pains not to injure any of the policemen. At length, Dmitri had been disarmed, pinioned by three men and dragged kicking and cursing to the floor. Jamie had then surrendered and he and Dmitri were marched off through the snow to the city gaol.

Dmitri, handcuffed and pushed roughly along, had shouted in Russian all the way, a harangue which sounded like a string of ferocious threats and blasphemies. Locked in a cell, a long time passed before he stopped hammering on the door.

Jamie had gone more quietly.

The two had been detained to appear before a magistrate in the morning . . .

Yes, it might have turned out much worse. He might well have committed manslaughter. He might even, through some momentary failure in vigilance, have lost his life.

In fact, all things considered, the evening had ended reasonably well, if only—and at this alarming thought Jamie sprang from his pallet in alarm—if only he had not lost Caroline's fur cloak!

He looked round. It was not to be seen hanging in the cell. But then, in the normal course of things, it would not be. The police, acting as their regulations dictated, would have impounded it, to be held as security against his fine.

So long as that little gypsy slut—and at the sudden recollection of her his face darkened with anxiety—her shoulders, her slanting eyes, her gypsy odour—so long as she had not made off with it! He remembered the warnings François had given him.

He was looking round in haggard anxiety when he heard the scratching of a key in the lock. The executioner!

But this was no executioner. Instead, at the door stood a gaoler with a huge ring of keys fastened to his belt. Beyond him, Jamie caught sight of François. His schoolfriend looked, he thought, even graver than usual.

The gaoler entered the cell and, with a murmur of deferential words, motioned him out.

'Mon Dieu,' said François, 'I've been worried about you . . . Yes. That man who was found dead in the snow. You were mistaken about his name. He had the same name as you, Jacques. So for a while, I was worried. The stars—'

'He was an imposter,' said Jamie.

'Apparently. Anyhow, now it's all right. You are under the protection of the Most Christian King, my sovereign,' said

François. 'By the way, you will find it rather cold outside.'

He handed him Caroline's fur cloak.

'Thank God,' cried Jamie.

'On the contrary, you can thank that gitane. She defended it for you. For some reason, Jacques, the girl seems to have taken a liking for you.'

'Gitane! It's years since I've heard that word,' said Jamie.

'I expect it's years since you've met one.'

'She will be rewarded suitably.'

From behind the door of one of the neighbouring cells came a rhythmic rumbling noise, as if thunder had become the music of an underground orchestra.

The warder, with a nervous grin, muttered something in Danish.

'He says that his highness is still sleeping,' François explained. 'He also says that two of the policemen are still unconscious. But it is thought they will recover.'

'Dmitri is a good fighter. For a moment he had me worried. I must have another bout with him one day, but with buttons on the foils next time. François, have you any money? Let me have a few pennies.'

With a grunt, François handed him a coin which Jamie pressed into the warder's palm.

'You keep a clean, comfortable place here,' he said graciously.

The warder bowed. 'Thank you very much, sir.'

'Why did you do that?' asked François.

'One can never tell,' said Jamie. 'One of us might be back here some day. It is best to leave a pleasant memory behind.'

'The stars have been very kind to you this week,' said François gloomily. 'If you had not spent last night in that place, you would probably be executed by now.'

Jamie's eyes opened wide.

'Explain,' he said.

'By order of the king, the whole town was combed—combed! —for a dangerous criminal, a Scotsman named James Stuart. A cruel-looking man, it seems, with red hair.'

'Cruel, yes. But red hair, no. In any case, Stuart is dead. Didn't they know he had been murdered?'

'They had not heard that then. Scores of men were employed in the search. Every house was examined. They even had the bad manners to ask questions at the Embassy!'

François gulped at the indignity of it.

'The king had given orders to hunt this man down and hound him out of the country. Or worse. As you know, the king is a brother-in-law of the King of Scotland.'

'Go on, François.'

'They searched everywhere—except in one place. They did not think about the drunkards' cells in the gaol. Where, by the grace of God, you spent the night.'

'Well, it proves one thing. As you said the other night, François, there is a special providence watching over children and drunkards. One thing I must do at once. I will have my hair bleached. There is a slight tinge of red in it which I find damned unattractive.'

'No need, Jacques. The king will write a letter to Scotland today, saying that James Stuart was probably murdered in a street brawl. As for Monsieur Jacques, he has been issued a French passport. Here it is. It describes you as a nobleman. I hope you don't mind.'

'In a crisis like this,' Jamie said carelessly, 'one can overlook a trifle.'

'Jacques,' François said, with a sudden surge of vivacity. 'You must be hungry. Between ourselves, I am teaching a certain lady how to make a navarin d'agneau. So, if you don't mind, we'll walk a little faster.'

'I need a shave,' said Jamie, rubbing his chin.

'But where the devil can Alan have got to?'

But Alistair could not answer Jamie's peevish question. And François devoted himself to the serious business of digesting his meal while he contemplated life with a kind of serene gloom and gently stroked his moustache.

They were drinking some exceptionally strong beer which Alistair recommended in the absence of what he called 'drink for men'.

When Jamie went to his lodgings to shave, the tailor had told him that, on the previous evening, a visitor had called to see him, a young man with very red hair, and a foreign accent, apparently mad. Alan! thought Jamie at once. This visitor had left word for Jamie to call on him at the Red Lion.

But the Red Lion had seen nothing of Alan Beaton since the night before. He had gone out before the police raid began.

'Last night,' said Alistair, cheerfully, 'was a night when anything could happen. Anything. He has probably been murdered. Those Danish policemen are a rough lot.'

Suddenly Jamie clattered to his feet. 'Good God!' he cried 'Look who's here!'

A young man with violent red hair and electric blue eyes had entered the tavern.

'Alan!'

Beaton glowered at Jamie.

'Where the hell have you been?' Jamie demanded.

'Where do you think!' Alan exploded. 'In the police head-quarters, that's where. All night. And it's entirely your fault, Stuart.'

Jamie waved to him to keep his voice down.

'For God's sake make less noise, man. These waiters are spies to a man! And my name isn't Stuart. Incidentally, how is it my fault?'

'Because these hired assassins who call themselves policemen insisted that I was a wanted criminal named James Stuart. There was I, sitting peacefully in a respectable eating place, when in came this police lieutenant with some of his thugs. 'What's your name?' he said to me. 'Mind your own damned business,' said I, courteously. 'Arrest this man,' the clown shouted. 'Look at his hair. This is him all right!' Before I could get the napkin from my chin, far less rise from the table, those gorillas had snapped the handcuffs on my wrists. And all because they thought my hair was long and blond and I was Jamie Stuart!

'Long and blond! Look at it! Lucky for me that they had his body in the mortuary all the time and didn't realise it.'

His eyes widened as a new astounding fact struck him.

'But you're dead, Stuart. Dead! And your corpse is in the mortuary. What the devil are you doing here, man?'

'You're muddled, Alan,' said Jamie soothingly. 'Hopelessly

muddled. I'm a Frenchman named Monsieur Jacques. Would you care to learn fencing? I'm the man to teach you. Allow me to introduce my compatriot, the Sieur Carbon de Castel-Jaloux. He may not look it but he's a diplomat. Alistair you know. Now for explanations. Sit down so that I can whisper in your ear what went on last night.'

At the end, Alan said, 'So that was the way of it. By the way, the funeral of the late James Stuart is tomorrow.'

'I will be there,' said Jamie. 'I must attend my own funeral. It is the least I can do. I'll put a card up on the door of the school—Closed owing to bereavement.'

Alistair nodded in agreement.

'What was the religion of the departed?' asked François gravely. 'If he was a Catholic, we can arrange a nice requiem in the embassy chapel.'

The other three looked at one another in turn.

'You must know, damn it all,' said Alan, nodding to Jamie.

'Everybody is a Catholic,' said Alistair piously, 'unless proved otherwise.'

'He had a very Protestant look to me,' said Jamie. 'Better let things take their course.'

The funeral was an unexpected success.

Jamie borrowed a hat with a magnificent black plume from his tailor-landlord. Alistair wore a black cloak which was the property of a guards officer who would be unlikely to miss it, he said. Alan had cleaned his black riding boots for the occasion. Dressed in purple from head to foot, François had the look of a worldly bishop. On their way to meet the cortège, the quartet encountered Dmitri.

'Look out,' said Jamie. 'Trouble ahead.'

But the prince seemed to have forgotten all about the duel in the cellar.

'Why all this black?' he asked. 'One might almost suppose you were going to a funeral.'

'We are,' said Jamie. 'We are. You must excuse us.'

Dmitri threw up his arms with enthusiasm.

'My dear fellow,' he said. 'A funeral! It is only then that one sees people as they really are. In the face of death everyone is sincere. I shall come too. But I insist, Jacques! Your friend was my friend! Now that he has left us, we shall mourn together. In Russia we really know how to bury the dead—the chanting, the weeping, the feasting—you would love it! In this country, I am afraid—ah, well!' he brushed away a tear and began to sing in a voice which shook the window-frames of the houses which they passed. The sables with which his coat was trimmed brushed the snow as he strode along.

The coffin lay, covered with a mortcloth, on a sledge drawn by one dejected horse. They followed it to the chapel in the graveyard, a desolate spot which, for some reason Jamie never understood, was reserved for members of the German community in the town. Before they set off, the priest asked a question which Alan Beaton translated: 'He wants to know who is the chief mourner. I have told him you are, James.'

The chapel was cold, but the service was short. François, as representing the Most Christian King, sat in purple grandeur at the back of the building. His face expressed the notion, suitable to a Catholic and a diplomat, that he was there and not there at the same time.

In front, occupying a chair apart from the rest, was an individual whom Jamie had not seen before.

Jamie thought he recognised one or two phrases in the service . . . 'Dust to dust?' He was not sure. Also, there was someone called Jacob Stuart whom the priest kept talking about.

Dmitri intoned the responses like so many thunderclaps in Slavonic. Frequently he crossed himself, with emphatic plucking movements of his hand.

Jamie noticed that his neighbour, Alistair, was shaking. When he turned with a frown to quell this apparent impropriety, he was astonished to see tears running down the Highlander's cheeks.

'I couldn't help liking the bastard all the same,' said Alistair, sniffing. Jamie glanced at him with complete bewilderment. What the devil was he talking about? And how many weeks had passed since Alistair had vowed he would kill the m whom, under another name, they were burying?

When it was over, the man who had been sitting alone

front hurried out, casting furtive glances at the rest of the congregation. 'Who is he?' Jamie asked.

François said, 'Don't you know? He is a man from your embassy—the Scottish embassy.'

Dmitri pressed a coin into the priest's hand.

'Sorrow is the mother of vodka,' he said solemnly, leading the way through the snow to the nearest tavern.

'Don't you think,' said Alistair, 'that we should mark the grave with a stone? In a sense, you are the next-of-kin, Jamie.'

There was a murmur of approval.

'What name shall we put on it?' asked Alan.

'Initials will be enough. J.S.,' said Jamie.

Dmitri took them to a wine shop which James recognised as the scene of his meeting with the girl, Sophie, on his first morning in the town. That seemed a long time ago now. François, massive in purple, said he must return to the Embassy. A commercial treaty with Denmark was causing a great deal of extra work.

The others sat down.

Sophie served the drinks. When Jamie saluted her with a resounding kiss, she said something which he did not understand.

Alan Beaton translated. 'She says you are much better dressed than you were last time she saw you. She thinks you have gone up in the world.'

'I have,' said Jamie. 'Tell her that I owe it all to the good advice she gave me . . . What did she say?' he asked when Sophie replied to Alan, giggling and shrugging her shoulders.

'It is rather vulgar Danish,' said Alan, with a frown, 'but I think she has a mistaken idea about how you earn your living, James. Perhaps she knows more than I do.'

'Damn you!' said Jamie, winking at the girl.

They downed a glass to the departed, and agreed he was a poisonous little snake and a good riddance.

'I have brought something to show you, James,' said Alistair.

While he watched, the Highlander produced from under his bearskin a bow about three feet long, of an unusual pattern.

It was made, they saw, when they came to handle it, of small pieces of grey wood fitted neatly together with some kind of glue. In a groove along the back ran a strip of sinew to give more propulsive power to the weapon.

'What the devil is it?' Jamie asked.

'You can see what it is. What's more, it's the best one I've ever had.'

Alan spoke. 'Handy,' he said. 'Where did you find it?'

'In the King of Denmark's arsenal—nobody seemed to want it. Guess where it came from. Far away up in Greenland there are savages who hunt seals on the ice with bows like this. They made it. Clever?'

'In my country,' said Dmitri, 'there are Tartars who shoot with little things like that. Very savage indeed. Very horrible.'

'Up there witches live,' said Alistair. 'They weave spells and make the weather.'

'They have marvellous white falcons,' said Jamie. 'And bears as big as elks and as white as snow. And women like queens.'

After a pause, Alan spoke casually. 'There wouldn't be anything else in that arsenal, I suppose.'

'There is a whole heap of swords and targes picked up in the mountains of Norway after the cruel slaughter of some peaceful Scottish travellers. War is a horrible thing! The blood on those swords!'

'I'm sure,' said Jamie. 'Nothing you recognised, I suppose?'

'A pistol is there like the one you had, but it hasn't your initials on it.'

'Has it the initial "G"?'

'How did you guess?'

'Once it was the property of a gentleman.'

'You were not much use with a pistol, James, if I remember rightly.'

'All the same, I should like to have that pistol back.'

'Is that all they have in that arsenal?' asked Alan. 'Some old iron.'

Alistair grinned at him contemptuously.

'Aye, that's all—that and enough pikes and muskets for a few regiments. To say nothing of helmets and armour. Mountains of them.'

'That must be an impressive thing to see.'

'It is. It would put ideas into the most peaceable mind. Anybody who wants to start a war has only to get inside the arsenal and there it is, all ready for him—all he will want.'

'If anybody could be so wicked!' said Alan. 'But of course the king's arsenal is well guarded.'

'As well guarded as anything in this town is guarded! Look —' he began to make marks with his fingernail on the table— 'here is this arsenal, built round three sides of a little harbour, with an entrance from the sea just wide enough to let in one vessel at a time from outside. Pointing this way and that are cannon ready to talk to any ship that might come too near.'

'So it would be difficult,' said Alan. 'Not that I have anything in mind.'

'It would be damn near impossible.'

'Nothing is impossible,' said Jamie. 'But why do you think anyone would want to break into the arsenal?'

Alan looked round thoughtfully. When he saw that Dmitri seemed to have dropped off to sleep: 'No reason at all,' he said, 'unless somebody thought he could use engines of war for some ploy he had in mind.'

Jamie looked up. 'A ploy!' he said. 'You were going to tell me, Alan.'

'Was I now? Maybe I will tell you soon . . . It seems to me we might do worse than take a look at this arsenal. A good brisk walk will harm none of us.'

But Dmitri, when they nudged him awake, wanted to stay drinking. He was willing to stay drinking alone. It was some time, though, before he allowed them to leave.

'At least,' said Jamie as they left the tavern, 'he didn't want to fight this time.'

'Just as well he wouldn't come, the Russki,' said Alistair.

'Why do you say that?' Alan wanted to know.

'Because he would want to go in and take the guns all by himself. He has this idea that he can take the Danish Life Guard on singlehanded. And he can't,' said Alistair firmly. 'Not now he can't.'

'Another idea he has,' Jamie went on, 'is that he is the true Tsar of Russia. When he tells you that, just agree with him—

it'll save you a lot of trouble.'

'People have funny ideas,' said Alan. 'My sister, Mary, clever girl and all that—but she thinks you should be the King of Scotland.'

Alistair broke in.

'When we started on this trip, Jamie—remember?—we were going to set the tsar on his throne in Moscow. Or tumble him off. Or something. Then something went wrong.'

'It went wrong all right.'

'Poor old Sinclair!'

'We should have emptied a glass to him instead of that little rat, Stevenson.'

'You know,' said Jamie, suddenly, 'I have this suspicion about Sinclair at the back of my mind—that he's alive. Somewhere, somehow, the old rascal is alive. Don't you feel it, Alistair?'

The Highlander nodded.

'Maybe, maybe. After all, we are alive, aren't we, and we were in the thick of it, too.'

'And very nasty it was for a while.'

'All those barbarians with axes. A very ungentlemanly weapon in my opinion.'

'Which of these buildings would you say was the arsenal?' asked Alan, who found this old campaigners' talk very tedious.

Talking as they sauntered along, they had come to the waterfront where they looked along the range of buildings between the castle and the sea.

'That long, red brick building,' said Alistair. 'Look, there is a break in the wall facing the sea where those cannon are pointed. That's the way into the inner harbour. Where the galleons load up with their guns and powder. But you'd see it better from a dinghy.'

'Is that a boom I see across the entry?' Alan pointed.

'It might be. It looks as if they opened it by a cable round that what d'ye call.'

'Capstan,' said Alan. 'I should come back some day and have another peep.'

'If a vessel wants to go into the harbour,' said Jamie. 'But does it?'

He pointed to a broad quay which ran alongside the arsenal building and gave on to the outer harbour.

'It depends,' said Alan. 'Is that a small door looking as if it led into the cellar of the building?'

'It might do.'

Alan turned thoughtfully away.

After a few minutes' silence, he said 'Do you happen to know a lady named Countess Rosenkrantz, James?'

'That reminds me, Alan. Whatever became of that girl you brought over from Kirkwall, Margaret Stewart?'

'*I* brought her over—you bloody liar!'

The two young men exchanged wide grins.

'Don't you know that rape is a crime?' said Jamie.

'I found a useful job for her; more than you did.'

'A respectable job?'

'The first she has ever had.'

'Where does she work?' asked Jamie.

Half turning, Alan pointed to the elaborate bulbous spire of the palace.

'There,' he said.

'Good God! There?' James was astonished.

'Yes. In the royal nursery. Looking after the King of Denmark's little bastards. But we were talking about the Countess Rosenkrantz . . .?'

'We were talking about a ploy.'

'We were,' Alan agreed. 'When I went to Hamburg I had the notion that the King of Spain would pay good money for a cargo of arms delivered on the Irish coast. Why not! Five thousand Spanish troops—veterans—are there already at a place called Kinsale. That has wiped the smirk off Queen Elizabeth's face. But what if the Irish themselves had arms— modern arms? Then the trouble at England's back door would be multiplied ten times over.

'So—what if I know where to find the muskets, the pikes, the powder and the shot? What if I have a friend in Hamburg who is ready to charter me a ship of the right kind? Not too big. Fast. Easy to handle. And what if the Spanish silver is already in the bankers' chest? You've followed me so far?'

'And you think it would be a good idea to steal some more

arms from the king's arsenal over there?' Jamie threw out an arm in the direction of the red brick building across the sullen ribbon of water. 'And add them to the collection.'

'I have many good ideas, James,' said Alan stiffly. 'That's only one of them.'

'Go on, man. I'm listening.'

'Then one day on the quayside in Hamburg, somebody I've never set eyes on before slinks up to me and says behind his hand, "Pieces of eight are pretty good pay. But what would you say to the yellow boys?"'

'Yes. What did you say?'

'I said, "I'm never too busy to say good morning to a stranger." After a bit he talks about a scheme to run arms to the English coast where the Thames runs into the sea. From what he says, it seems that a cargo of the right commodities would find a market there. And it seems there would be friends waiting to welcome the goods ashore. What do you think? Better money and a shorter crossing. And it's all in the same good cause, isn't it?'

'You spoke of a lady—the Countess Rosenkrantz,' said James.

Alan's sidelong glance hovered about his face for a second or two before he answered.

'Yes, Jamie. How well do you know her?'

The Traitor Has Been Found

A cloud of grey smoke with a scarlet tongue swelled suddenly outside the fortress and was blown away by the wind. A boat was rowed out from the shore with a square-jowled official sitting in its waist.

'That will be our pilot,' said the stout, plain woman on the fo'c'sle to the excited girl beside her.

A few hours later, and many miles farther south, they caught sight of the city.

It was much bigger and much stronger than Mary Beaton had expected. So many ships. So many ramparts bristling with guns. So many twisted spires swirling up into the sky.

This was where her brother, Alan, went about his business. And where Jamie Stuart was in danger. Not that she cared. On the contrary, she felt that it served him right in a way.

Certainly, he was nothing to her. Nothing at all. Ridiculous, feckless, and thoroughly untrustworthy. Those cunning letters which any girl in her senses could see through. And the roses! How often had he tried that trick on a girl? And probably succeeded . . . Some girls are stupid enough to be taken in by that sort of nonsense! Of course, in a way, she was under some sort of obligation to him, although nothing to make her lose any sleep.

He had once, in an Edinburgh close, saved her from a disagreeable experience. Naturally, a girl ought not to forget a thing like that.

And if, as they said, he was really in danger . . . No doubt it served him right. As Lady Anstruther had said, he was probably a traitor, a criminal.

At any rate, a bad lot, as she herself had always thought. The funny thing was, however, that she could not feel as angry with him as she ought to.

Just when a frown of moral condemnation was clouding her brow, a faint betraying smile was curling the corners of her mouth.

Cautiously the ship was edging towards a curving quay on which the snow lay, half a foot deep. A drawbridge was raised ahead of them. Mary had the impression that they were about to land in the main street of the city.

It was time to go and see that her mistress had finished the small, last-minute packing which (she had insisted) only she could do.

At the last minute, when Lady Anstruther was about to set foot on the gangway, two men had thrust rudely in front of her and scurried ashore.

Mary had seen them once or twice before during the crossing, and noticed that they seemed to keep apart from the others. 'Who are they?' she asked the mate.

He shrugged his shoulders. 'The ship is not sinking, but the rats are leaving it. Rogues, lassie, rogues, and going abroad to finish some bad work which they've begun at home.'

When she looked a question, he drew a finger across his throat.

'What do you mean?'

'I mean they are killers,' he growled. 'Men who have left some mischief behind them and will make more mischief where they go. Have you ever heard of a man named Jamie Stuart? They are looking for him.'

Mary felt chilly forebodings clutch her heart as her eyes followed the pair as they vanished into the crowd loitering on the quay.

That evening, Lady Anstruther came to her with wide, excited eyes.

'You will hardly believe it, Mary. But there is to be a ball at the palace. And I am invited. Look, here is the invitation, not that you will understand it! But there is an invitation for you, too. Lady of the suite . . .'

Before darkness closed down on the city, Mary scribbled a

few lines and sealed them. She beckoned to one of the servants of the ambassador's lodging, a boy she thought she could trust.

'Do you know an inn called the Red Lion?' she asked and, at last, after many attempts at explanation, she succeeded in making him understand. The note was addressed to her brother, Alan.

That night she was surprised to see two men leaving the lodging. Their eyes did not meet hers but she had seen them both before. The rats that had left the ship had found shelter beneath the Scots ambassador's roof.

What surprised Mary even more was that they seemed to have come from the ambassador's quarters.

She watched them as they went out into the cold, gripping their cloaks at the throat as they went. Two burly ruffians, on some unavowable mission.

That night her mistress said, sitting at the mirror while Mary brushed her hair: 'I told you about the ball at the palace. Pay attention, Mary!'

'Yes, ma'am.'

'It seems that we are expected to wear masks. Masks! The court here has a reputation quite unlike our own in Edinburgh. I don't mean that it is licentious—not like Paris, thank God—but—freer in its manners than we are used to. Really, I don't think I should let you go, lassie. After all, you are hardly more than a child.'

'But I shall be waiting on you all the time, ma'am.'

'Well, I hope so. I am not sure your mother would approve.'

'My mother would expect me to do my duty, Lady Anstruther.'

'Yes. No doubt. But you are so young. The wild life of a foreign court! It's so easy to be taken in by that kind of thing. And all these handsome young Danes.'

'I don't care for blond men, ma'am.'

'Just as well, girl. That reminds me. That traitor, James Stuart. He has been found—'

'Found?'

'Yes, found here in Copenhagen. But dead. Stabbed to death in the street. Girl, you are tugging my hair!' cried Lady Anstruther.

A Man Interested in Pearls

Like a visitant from some gulf excluded by distance or custom from the lawful business of the sea, the black ship came into view beyond the northern battery and stole across the stretch of shallow water before the city. She had shortened sail. Now she was barely moving.

Jamie watched her approach from the quayside of the outer harbour. There is always interest in seeing a ship make her landfall. After a voyage there is sometimes a thrill of pleasurable anticipation. Not always.

He was not the only person who noticed the new arrival. A man ran across the quay to the water's edge, evidently enraged. He put a speaking trumpet to his lips and shouted something in Danish. When he had finished, he made emphatic gestures with both hands: Keep off! Keep your distance! We don't want your kind here.

It is easy enough to interpret what he was saying.

Jamie grinned. He thought he understood why he said it.

Black, foul, disreputable, with sails patched in various shades of soiled grey, an affront to the quiet waters she floated in, a ship he had seen all those weeks ago in a narrow Norwegian seaway, was coming to the roadstead of Copenhagen with all the shameless insistence of a piece of bad news.

The *Gloire*!

He remembered what Ingrid had said: not a pirate, yet hardly within the law; not a trader, yet able to pick up a living, somehow. Port of registry, doubtful; name, derisive. Wherever she went, an occasion of disquiet.

The man with the trumpet scrambled into a dinghy and sculled vigorously out towards the new arrival. Every now and then he would pause, turn around and bellow a fresh string of imperatives across the water.

'They won't let her come too near!'

James recognised the light, ironic voice. It was the Englishman, Edward Carey.

'I wonder they allow her to come at all,' he said. 'Although one must learn not to judge by appearances.'

'In a town like this, there is usually some business for a ship that is not likely to ask too many questions.'

'Can you see the skipper? He has a red beard.'

'By God, I believe you're right. You have pretty good eyesight, Stuart.'

'Stuart is dead, Carey. I attended the funeral.'

'De mortuis,' said Carey, touching his hat.

'His assassins did a quick, thorough job. Obviously they were old hands at the game.'

Carey's eyebrows rose.

'You saw the affair? But of course you did! So *that* was how the scrap of parchment was found on the body with your name on it! I wondered at the time.' His eyes shone with admiration. 'You think fast, Monsieur Jacques.'

'That way I stay alive.'

'That person—the one who died—might have stayed alive, too. But he played in a game that was too big for him. A warning to all of us, Monsieur Jacques, don't you think.'

The faint rumble of a chain running through a hawser hole came from out at sea.

'They are allowing that ship to drop anchor far out,' said Carey. 'But I have the idea we shall see your Captain Redbeard ashore before very long. Some people will want to do business with him. Are you, by chance, going to call on Caroline Gyldenstierne? Let us stroll along together. And you can tell me about Redbeard.'

'For one thing,' said Jamie, 'he's French.'

'So many people are French nowadays.'

'Yes. Also I gather he is a real artist with the dagger. Next time you are in need of a murderer, Carey, you might bear him in mind!'

'I shall make a note of it,' said Carey, politely.

At Caroline Gyldenstierne's the usual four were playing the usual game of cards, while they talked the political gossip which, a month or two earlier, had been the latest news in Whitehall or the Louvre . . .

How long would it be before Spain launched the new armada against England? How long before the King of France took a new mistress? Marriage, notoriously, gave a man a new impulse to adventures. And the King of Scotland? At least from him there was no danger of that kind of thing. His tastes . . .

And so on.

'I see you are looking around,' said Caroline to Jamie. 'She is not here . . . Are you heartbroken?'

'I was going to ask her a question. Who is this Giovanni, said to be her servant?'

Caroline looked at him seriously.

'That answer she will never give.'

'If he is her servant, she is his slave.'

'You have not wasted your time, Jacques. Already you know as much as anyone.'

'I don't think so,' he said. 'Where does Giovanni's power come from, Caroline?'

She hesitated a moment before answering in a hurried whisper.

'She has an old servant called Lucrezia. Lucrezia could tell you.'

'But will she?'

After a week, during which the fencing school was busy, Jamie felt rich enough to buy himself a short velvet cloak which he wore hanging from one shoulder and also a pair of shoes. Boots at a court ball? They would not do at all.

Stepping carefully in his new shoes round the heaps of slush in the streets, Jamie called at the Golden Crayfish where François was already at table with a napkin tied round his neck. After a quick glance of sombre appraisal, he covered

155

his eyes in horror.

'No! ' he cried.

'No—what?'

'You can't wear those shoes with heels! It's effeminate.'

'Anything that makes me effeminate is miraculous. Don't you know the new style when you see it?'

'The new style! How do you know? And *red* heels! '

'I am a nobleman. Look at my passport if you doubt,' James pointed out.

François smoothed down his moustache thoughtfully.

'That cloak—hanging from the shoulder . . . affected! '

'You will find that it is the latest thing from Paris,' said James. 'Before weeks have passed, everybody will be wearing it.'

'Not everybody will be able to. It needs a touch of—'

'Vulgarity? I agree. Now tell me what is there to eat? That soup smells good. I have the most damnable appetite.'

'I brought in some garlic in the embassy bag. It is the only thing the English spies will not think of stealing.'

'While I eat, you will tell me the news, François.'

'News? A ship has arrived from Scotland with an ambassador's wife aboard—if you call that news—'

'Oh. What is the lady like?'

'Not your taste at all, James. But I am told that she has brought a beautiful girl with her.'

'I'm not interested,' said Jamie, frowning.

At the guardhouse, Jamie found Alistair sullenly polishing a cuirass.

'Is this work for a gentleman, James? I tell you, but for the thought that I would soon be free of this damned trade, I would bring this piece of plate down on the sergeant's head.' He screwed up his eyes as he contemplated James. 'Where did you get those fancy shoes from, man?' he asked. 'You were not dressed like this when we were roaming the mountains together like two hunted beasts.'

'Things are different now, Alistair. I have to look my best for tonight. The ball at the palace.'

'The ball! That's why I'm rubbing up this old soup tureen.

Ceremonial duty in the palace. Full dress uniform! Wait and see. None of my family has looked so grand since my father of blessed memory went to court in Edinburgh. Those were the days, boy! My people were still on calling terms with the House of Stewart—that nest of vipers—but you're one of them yourself, aren't you, of a kind? So just forget what I've said. Was there something you wanted to see me about, James? Just go on talking while I work.'

'Have you seen Alan Beaton by any chance?'

'Beaton? No, that I have not. He's been out of the town on that ploy of his. But I can tell you this. He is due in any minute now. At least, that's what he expected. By a boat called the *North Star*. So if you haunt the quay, you'll be sure to see him. Oh, and Jamie—I can see you have something in your purse. Won, God knows how. We'll have a dram together, you and I, and I'll tell you about the wonders in that arsenal. God save us, if my people and those guns could only be brought together, we'd sweep that little tod off his throne in a month. You know who I mean.'

'I know,' said Jamie. 'My namesake in Edinburgh.'

'Weak-kneed James, the so-called King of Scots.'

Alistair spat ceremoniously on the cuirass and rubbed more vigorously than ever.

'A dram,' he said.

'Later.'

On the crowded quayside, while he waited for the *North Star* to appear, James became aware of something like a drop in temperature. When he worked the problem out, a second or two later, the sensation seemed to be associated with two men who had passed him in the throng.

He turned to have a second look but, by that time, the men were indistinguishable from the general press of people on the quay. He had the impression he had seen the men before somewhere—and that they, for their part, had recognised him. A trick of memory? A hallucination? Why the devil did he have these fancies?

The question troubled him for a little while he walked to and fro on the quayside waiting for Alan's boat to come in.

157

'That's her,' said one of the loafers who were always hanging about. 'That's the *North Star*. Regular as a clock, she comes in.'

The three young men were not giving their minds to the game of dominoes set out on the table before them.

'So we do it tonight' Alan explained. 'At the stroke of midnight. The ship, a flyboat from Rostock, is there, lying offshore, out of sight, loaded with the pikes and the powder—the best quality I could get in Germany. After dark, she will come as close inshore as the skipper dares. Then, when the palace clock strikes the half-hour, the ship's longboat will begin to row to the arsenal harbour—'

'Where a lantern will have been left burning,' said Alistair, 'before the door which, by accident, has been left unlocked. The sentry will have been given a drink by one of the masked ladies who have been at the ball.'

'You have found one you can trust to do what's needed?'

Alan grinned. 'We've found one,' he said. 'The drink she gives him will make that sentry fall asleep on his feet. After that, there will be no problem. What do you think of it, James?'

'As a plan, it's like other plans—all right if all the parts fall into place at the right time.'

'And why shouldn't they?' asked Alistair.

'Because they usually don't. Haven't you noticed that? But have I any part to play in this comedy.'

Alan laughed. 'What do you think? That we'd leave out our best actor?'

'Tell me.'

Alan rubbed thumb and finger together. 'The yellow boys, Jamie. The yellow boys. That's where you come in.'

Alan leant forward and spoke in a soft, urgent flow of words. Jamie listened intently. Then he tapped the table where the dominoes were set out. 'It's my turn to play first,' he said.

After looking at the pieces that faced him, he put the double six on the table.

'At midnight, we unmask,' he said.

'A lot will have happened before then!' said Alistair, gleefully.

The notion of going back to his old trade excites him, Jamie thought. Perhaps it is just as well I am not the King of Scots. One of the first things I'd have to do would be to string up this robber.

Alistair went on: 'So we take a boatload of muskets from the King of Denmark and hand them over to the Queen of England's rebels! What could be better? As elegant a theft as ever I heard of.'

'Theft?' said Alan severely. 'This is not a crime, boy. This is politics.'

'My father warned me to have nothing to do with politics,' said Alistair. 'But I don't think this would count. Where are you off to, Jamie?'

Stuart had pushed back his stool and risen to his feet.

'The game is finished and I have won. What's more, I know a man who is interested in pearls.'

Alan looked up. 'Has your friend money?'

'All the money in the world,' said Jamie.

Alan followed him out and, after a few quick words to Alistair, went to the Red Lion where he found a note addressed to him. It was in a hand he knew.

Mary Beaton! Of all the wonderful and mysterious things! How the devil did his sister come to be in Copenhagen?

Half Silver, Half Black

After that first moment, when she was brushing her mistress's hair, Mary showed no sign of emotion during the days that followed. And what was it she felt, and did not show? Regret. Above all, regret that she had not understood until it was too late what she felt about that preposterous young man. And now what had happened was something that, all the time, she had known was likely to happen.

The news that Alan had arrived reached her through the kitchen of the ambassador's lodging. She found him sitting on the edge of the cook's table with the wild gleam in his light blue eyes that she remembered.

'Alan!'

She threw herself into his arms, which surprised him a great deal. As a family, the Beatons were not given to shows of affection. Then she astonished him even more by bursting into tears.

'What's the matter with you, Mary?'

It was no way for her to behave. Homesickness? A bullying mistress? But these were troubles that a girl of character, a girl like his sister, should not allow to get the better of her.

But here she was sobbing on his shoulder.

'What the devil's wrong with you, lassie?' he asked irritably.

She wiped her eyes on her sleeve and was calm at once.

'It's Jamie. Jamie Stuart. You'll have heard?'

'Heard what, for heaven's sake?'

'He's dead. And Alan, I love him.'

Her mouth was firm but the tears had begun to run down her cheeks once more.

Alan's face wore the expression of one who has heard two impossible statements in one breath.

'Dead!' he said indignantly. 'Jamie's dead! Don't be a damned fool, Mary. Unless he died this morning.'

'You mean that he has not been stabbed in the street?'

'Certainly he hasn't! Listen. This is what happened.'

Lowering his voice and speaking quickly, Alan told his sister how—and why—the murder of a spy named Jock Stevenson had become in popular belief the assassination of a gentleman named James Stuart.

At the end, the wonder in Mary's face changed into a look of pure horror. Clutching her brother's arm, she cried, 'Forget that other thing I told you. It isn't true.'

'You mean? *That*! Of course it isn't true. You wouldn't fall in love with a ruffian like him.'

Mary's eyes flashed.

Ruffian? He's not such a ruffian as you are. But you're not to breathe a word.'

'All right. All right. If you want to see him—'

'Of course I don't want to see him!'

With an impatient shake of his head, Alan dismissed the subject. Women were impossible. And his sister was more of a woman that most.

'I came here,' he said, speaking with quiet emphasis, 'because you left a word for me at the Red Lion. What was it about?'

'What do you think? It was about this—about Jamie. What else! He is in mortal danger.'

'But that's all finished now,' he pointed out. 'All finished and done with.'

'If you believe that, Alan Beaton, you're even dafter than you look. The men who are hunting Jamie will not give up so easily. They have sworn a solemn oath at a secret meeting in Edinburgh to have him killed. They think that he may stand in the way of King James becoming King of England.'

'Who are they, lassie?'

'Nobles, most of them. Gentry, and all friends of the king.

His toadies and fancy boys!'

'Do you think that Jamie is the kind to let himself be taken so easily?'

'Then let him leave this town—quickly. They have traced him to here.'

'How can he leave? Business keeps him here. Big business!'

'Some girl!' She tossed her head.

'No. Not a girl.'

'Then he has changed a lot.'

Alan smiled at his sister.

'Not so much as all that,' he said.

Mary sat sewing in the tiny room that opened off the ambassador's study and was used for storing the official boxes. 'Go in there, girl,' Lady Anstruther had said. 'Make no noise and Sir Robert will be none the wiser.'

Her ladyship had a woman who was coming in to dress her best wig—the red one—for the evening. Mary's room had been earmarked for this ceremony.

And Mary was intent on altering one of her mistress's dresses, which had already appeared in the court at Edinburgh, so that she herself could wear it at the ball that night.

She had sat there, as quiet as a mouse, hearing only the occasional rustle of paper from Sir Robert's desk, now and then a dry cough (the ambassador swore that the Danish winter climate would be the death of him) or a tap on the door leading to the ante-room. Maybe an hour had passed before she heard something that made her sit rigid, listening.

The door to the study had opened quietly. A few seconds of silence followed as if the ambassador was unaware that someone had come into the room. Sir Robert was somewhat deaf.

Then she heard his voice saying peevishly, 'How long have you been standing there? And who are you, anyway?'

The man's voice that answered spoke in a stumbling English, with so many misplaced accents and twisted vowels that Mary could understand little of what was said. But she heard the words, spoken softly . . . 'the Signor Stuart, my lord.'

'Yes. You wish to see me about him, do you?'

The other voice was as soft as before, but it had an ill-omened quality—of sleekness, perhaps. It said, 'My lord, it was you who wished to see me about this person.'

'Go on, man. What is your name?'

'Call me Giovanni.'

'What have you to say, Giovanni?'

'It might be that you and I have something in common . . .'

Mary could hear the papers on the ambassador's desk rustle as if he was annoyed by this remark.

'It might be that some people—people in high places—wished to . . .'

At this point the voice fell to a quick murmur so that Mary could not hear.

'What then?' Sir Robert asked. 'Assuming for a moment that it be so—which, of course, it isn't—what do you propose?'

The foreign voice went on, speaking quickly, coolly, like a lame pony trotting on a bad road. Mary heard it speak, with emphasis, of the court ball—the signore would be there, wearing a mask of black and silver.

'How do you know that?'

Mary thought a new ingredient came into the answering voice. It was as if the man whom she could not see had spread his hands in a gesture of cynical apology.

There was talk of a signora, a contessa, although it was not clear what this lady had to do with the matter they were discussing.

'That will be the moment—it can be arranged, my lord.'

The ambassador's chair creaked on the floor as it was pushed back.

'Enough,' said Sir Robert, impatiently. 'I must hear no more. I will take you to some men you can talk to.' The bell on the ambassador's desk tinkled. 'They are ruffians,' he said, 'but not the same kind of ruffian as you.'

'I understand, my lord. I have done business of state before.'

'I believe you,' said the ambassador.

Someone knocked at the study door. Sir Robert muttered an order. Silence for a moment. Then, 'One thing, Giuseppe—'

'Giovanni, my lord.'

163

'Giovanni. I am curious to know why you want so much to harm Stuart?'

The answering voice was calm and deadly. 'Because the threatened man strikes before he feels the knife. It is a custom among us Italians.'

In the silence, Mary was aware of the ambassador's distaste, although she did not understand why a reason so straightforward and reasonable as the Italian's should seem so shocking. One had to be older than she was to realise that murder needs a robe of state to cover its nakedness.

The ambassador's voice was as light and dry as an autumn leaf. 'I will lead you to the men I spoke of. One thing more. Stuart should come to no harm here, on Danish soil. That could be embarrassing for us all. But at sea—that would be different.'

'My lord, there will be no need for anything against the law. There are other means available in this case.'

'I don't understand you.'

'I am sure you don't.'

After a brief pause, the ambassador spoke again:

'There is said to be a ship, a captain with a red beard.'

'I know the man, my lord.'

'Then follow me.'

Mary heard the ambassador's private door open and shut.

For ten minutes Mary did no needlework. She sat in the little room, motionless, expressionless, looking apparently at nothing. Then, as if some inward command had been uttered, she resumed her task furiously.

By the time the stitching was finished and a quick tug had broken the last thread, Lady Anstruther's old court dress was a simpler and smaller garment.

Mary whisked it away to her mistress's dressing-room where there was a tall mirror. She stood there for a minute, holding the dress up to her bosom. But, by a curious optical illusion, she thought she could see over her shoulder a face in a mask, half silver, half black.

The Ball at the Palace

There are occasions, Jamie told himself, when prudence should not altogether command one's life. A masked ball is one of them.

He had dressed that evening with more than his usual care and had treated his hair to a perfumed preparation which not only brought out its golden light also emphasised its natural curls. When a whistle sounded behind him in the street he decided that it was probably an expression of honest admiration, surely permissible in the circumstances. This was an evening for indulgence towards others as well as to himself.

He could, just for once, relax the cautious behaviour which he had made his regimen.

A ball in a court he had not visited but of which he had heard the most agreeable reports . . . A king who, in addition to being a formidable toper, was a man of taste. A nation unusually well-endowed with pretty women, the possibility that he might fall in with some minx who would seek to lure him from the path of virtue—the certainty that he would see Leonora . . .

At these thoughts, Jamie's steps along the cobbles of Copenhagen grew lighter and more rapid. He found himself humming that air of which he alone in the world knew the words. And thus he passed the fish market, the ships in the harbour, the gaol in which he had recently lodged, to his great advantage, the point at which he could see the lights of Caroline Gyldenstierne's house . . . He had promised to dance with the baroness . . . To dance . . .

165

It was a long time since he had danced. Two years at least. But he thought he remembered the steps well enough.

The pavane where you strutted slowly with a stiff carriage of the body and an absurdly solemn expression on your face. A stately dance, suitable for a church, or the opening of a court ball with the king and his queen leading. And the volta where, at one moment, your partner as good as sat on your knee—a natural position for a girl—that would present no difficulty at all.

But the volta, he thought, was not danced so much nowadays. It had given way to the galliard, in three-time, energetic and exciting. Queen Elizabeth of England was said to dance it first thing in the morning as an exercise. Amazing woman.

The sarabande you danced with gliding steps while the girls marked the time with their castanets—very slow and Spanish and, somehow, very provocative.

And all those romping dances that belonged to barns and inn-yards rather than to courts. At the thought of them Jamie breathed more deeply and with a heightened sense of anticipation.

It was a long time since he had danced but he thought that, somehow, he was going to enjoy King Christian's ball.

If only his bad ankle did not let him down.

He was now passing the spot which marked Jock Stevenson's demise, poor wretch. But that, after all, was something which might have turned out worse.

In fact, to Stevenson's death at the hands of those assassins—whom, incidentally, the Danish police had never caught—to that tragedy he, Jamie Stuart, could be said to owe his life or, at least, his freedom. A sobering thought which he, Monsieur Jacques, promised to ponder gravely when he had dealt with more pressing matters.

By now he was approaching the sentry at the palace drawbridge who came smartly to the salute and waved him on to the gateway where a chamberlain examined the king's billet of command. While that formality was being gone through, James put on the black and silver mask that covered all but the tip of his nose.

Then he sauntered across the courtyard towards the main entrance to the palace. If he had been anyone but a finished product of M. de Pluvinel's Academy, it might have been said that he swaggered.

Hand lightly on sword-hilt, hat neither too straight for a festive occasion, nor too tilted for propriety; cloaked, and wearing that extraordinary mask, Jamie looked like some strange bird. Slightly sinister and, probably, with no good intentions.

His first glimpse of the courtyard raised his expectations one notch higher.

A path had been cleared through the snow with spruce-branches strewn to carpet it. A score of flambeaux burned smokily from tall masts painted in stripes.

At the foot of the great staircase he could already hear the music. The light was gently glimmering from hundreds of candles. A faint odour of burning pine-wood perfumed the air. A deliciously blonde young woman ran across his path, casting him a sidelong glance. Jamie thought it a good omen.

As he handed over his fur cloak to a servant, he felt that the night was going to be all that he expected of it. And maybe more than that. He adjusted his mask and walked rapidly upstairs.

To reach the ball he passed through a room lined with long tables charged with golden dishes on which an immense variety of cold meats was displayed. In the background, from roof to floor, Flemish tapestries hung—a series of hunting scenes which had apparently been woven specially for the room.

Contemplating the army of dishes with absorbed interest was a plump figure in crimson velvet whom he recognised at once. No mask could hide François's widow's peak. In passing, Jamie gave him a nudge.

'When you are tired of dancing there will be something else for you to do,' he said, nodding in the direction of the tables.

'It is very promising,' said François. 'I don't intend to wait too long before trying it. Those Danes are devilish greedy.'

After inspecting the liveried footmen, Jamie decided that the king had reinforced the palace staff from among the peasants on his farms. As the evening wore on, these recruits became noticeably more unsteady on their feet. In fact, they were not alone.

'The peerage of Denmark is drunk to a man,' said a voice in English at Jamie's elbow. 'No doubt out of loyalty to the sovereign.'

Jamie now entered the great ceremonial hall of the palace. Banners hung from the rafters. The candlelight was reflected from round silver plates on the walls. And here the dancing went on.

At that moment the dancers were filing past in a pavane, ceremonial and complex. It was early in the evening and movements were restrained. But the allure of the bodies showed, as the stateliest dance should do, that when the time came to put stiffness away, they would be able to respond.

Jamie contemplated the scene with the eye of one who was expert in picking out the essential features.

Never before in his life, he decided, had he seen so many beautiful young women. This was a thought that had occurred to him not more than a dozen times before in life, and always with the same sense of delighted surprise. Those golden shoulders, those gleaming heads, those glowing cheeks . . .

Beware, he reminded himself, all girls are lovely when they are wearing masks. It is one of the first things a man learns. And forgets.

Looking at the beauties of King Christian's court, Jamie cast aside the last faint vestiges of depression which the recollection of Jock Stevenson had caused him. Life, he was sure, was about to begin one of its most brilliant chapters.

He scanned the throng, the many dancers and the few who watched, for figures he could recognise. For Dmitri. For the Englishman. They would be somewhere here. For Caroline and—

There was the king. No mistaking His Majesty. He was simply the biggest man in the hall. Enormous, blond, ruddy, and gleaming with perspiration. Masked like everyone else and quite easy to recognise.

Standing there in a corner in the hall, he was like a Northern deity of revel and concupiscence. When he threw an arm round a buxom young woman and pulled her towards him, he guffawed with laughter as he kissed her.

It was etiquette to take no particular notice of him until the moment of unmasking arrived.

Standing at a respectful distance from the monarch was a soldier of the bodyguard, in gold, silver, scarlet, blue, gleaming, magnificent. If he were meant to symbolise the power and wealth of the Danish monarchy, he was succeeding very well.

While Jamie admired this effigy, another exactly similar arrived and, with an exchange of salutes, took his place. It was only when the first guard was pacing solemnly backwards from the hall that Jamie recognised him. If he gave the curlew's cry, the guard would answer. It was Alistair.

But, just then, Jamie's search was for something else—for one woman's shoulders. He would have no difficulty in recognising them. They would be an extraordinary, lustrous white. And they would be adorned by a necklace of magnificent black pearls. In all Europe there would be no necklace and no shoulders so—

'Dance,' said a voice he had not heard before. 'Dance, stranger.'

It belonged to a small dark-haired young woman wearing a purple mask who was standing at his elbow. A second earlier, she had not been there.

Her features were aquiline and she had the kind of bones that make men want to test their strength. Her voice was soft, with slurred undertones. Her French—she spoke French— seemed to have too many s's in it. It was a trifling defect which should not affect her dancing.

He bowed over the hand she lifted towards him.

'Why have you kept me waiting so long?' he asked.

The new chapter in his life was opening well.

Mary Beaton arrived late for the ball. Late, excited, and, as is suitable to a young girl at her first ball, apprehensive.

Lady Anstruther had hurried so much over dressing that, in the end—it was inevitable—there was a mishap. At the last minute she discovered that the wig-maker had made a botch of his work so that Mary, death in her heart, had to frizz up the second-best wig.

By the time she had put it on the old lady's head, Sir Robert was angry and impatient. Stamping about, throwing his eyes to the ceiling and making sarcastic remarks. When a king asked you to his palace, you arrived with two minutes to spare! And so forth. Then the hired sleigh kept them waiting. The drowsy driver had to crowd in another order . . . And, when all was ready, Sir Robert had mislaid his new gloves.

So Mary Beaton arrived late for the ball.

Worse, she was forced to stay beside Lady Anstruther and explain to her that it would be a breach of etiquette to make her curtsey to the king at this stage.

Eventually, she found her mistress a chair in the room where the food was laid out, a gross, pagan, inordinate spectacle. There was enough on display to feed a town of starving people. Mary should have been shocked, and was shocked with herself that, on the contrary, she was enchanted by the sight.

It took Mary some time to find someone with whom Lady Anstruther would gossip and not until then did she go to see the dancers in the great hall.

She stood for a moment in amazement. She had never seen such dresses, or such beautiful people, such a swirl of movement, ordered and controlled by the music, at the same time monotonous and moving.

Pulses were throbbing in her. It was all strange and unexpected. She looked round eagerly.

'Can I help you?' said a man's voice.

'I am looking for somebody in a black and silver mask,' she said. This man was wearing a crimson domino and his voice was agreeable.

'That should be easy to find. Black and silver. No, I haven't seen him. He *is* a man, of course?'

Mary turned sharply to the person who had made such a stupid remark.

But already he had disappeared before Mary had time to ask why he had spoken to her with an English accent.

In his place was another man, rather fat and bowing effusively. He was apparently asking her to dance. Mary used up her Danish vocabulary thanking him and saying no. These stiff and courtly dances were not for a girl like her, brought up in a small hill town on the margin of the civilised world. Later, her chance might come.

But it was possible that she would have no time for dancing tonight. She turned to find her way back to Lady Anstruther. Then she saw a man she had surely seen before. A man with a scar.

Gold, silver, scarlet and blue, with a silver breastplate and a silver helmet, a knight in armour who hàd been to the wars. Where else could he have got that terrible mark under his cheekbone. Disfiguring. It was then that she recognised him. 'Alistair!' It was the Highland veteran who had been James Stuart's companion in Scotland.

He put his finger to his lips.

'I am attending on Lady Anstruther,' she whispered.

'Alan told me.' His lips hardly moved.

'Have you seen James Stuart?'

Alistair shook his head.

'He is in danger,' she said. 'Awful danger! I must see him.'

Alistair's eyes lit up.

'On no account tell him that,' he said softly. 'He will be sure to do something daft.'

She looked at him hard. He was probably right.

'What is likely to happen to him?' he asked. 'And when?'

'Tonight, here, in this palace, they will kidnap him and—'

Alistair listened impassively.

'It's my duty,' he said gravely, 'to see that no disorder takes place in the king's palace. How will I know him?'

'He is wearing a black and silver mask.'

'Black and silver.'

He nodded and disappeared quietly into the crowd. The beat of the music changed to a three-time rhythm.

From where they were lying, two miles offshore, the palace was no more than a mass of more solid black uncertainly outlined against a dull orange glow in the thick air. The glow came, Alan knew, from the flambeaux they were burning in the courtyard. To the west, the grey of the sea merged into

171

a black cloud which he knew was land. Eastwards, the town stretched, picked out here and there by the lights of houses, and ending in a long finger of blackness which was the site of a battery.

The ship, the *North Star,* rode lightly, held by a single anchor. She was losing a little way but not enough to matter. The wind was light and from the north. The anchor would hold her for as long as it was likely to be needed.

He put his head in at the wheelhouse where a lantern was burning. There he pulled out his watch. Two more hours before they needed to move.

He walked round the ship. The longboat was moored alongside, with the water slap-slapping against its side. Its oars were neatly shipped and the rowlocks were well padded with canvas.

He had gone to some pains to pick as its crew the half-dozen best oarsmen in the ship, taciturn North German sailors experienced in this kind of business.

There was no need for him to feel nervous. But the disgraceful truth was that he did.

He had embarked on a big adventure, and this was only the beginning of it. As for the later stages . . . All I will have against me, he told himself with sarcasm, is the English fleet. Nothing more! It happens to be the best fleet in the world and maybe the biggest. Its captains think, in their arrogant way, that every other ship on the seas is probably a pirate. Shoot first and have the survivors aboard for questioning afterwards.

They tell me their gunnery has improved lately. I never heard that it was all that bad anyway . . .

Cheer up, Beaton, the English fleet can't be everywhere at once. While they are watching the Irish coast or hovering about off Corunna, you will run inshore near Lowestoft, as the lady said. Or will you? . . .

He shivered slightly. Nine-tenths of being brave is keeping warm.

Looking upwards, Alan could see the outline of the ship's spars and rigging more plainly than before. The sky was clearing. Here and there an angry star glimmered, entangled in the web of clouds like a fly caught in a blanket.

But he ought to be finished with the business ashore before the moon rose. There was nothing to do but wait.

Alan pulled his sea cloak more tightly about him. It was going to be a long, cold time of idleness.

Just then his eye picked up a black object sharply outlined against the darkness of the water. Slowly it moved, ever so slowly, between him and the shore.

A ship. A big fishing boat? She was showing no lights. That made her interesting.

'What is she? Do you know?'

The German mate had been silent a second before answering.

'She's French. At least, she has a French name!'

'What name?'

'The *Gloire*—Glory!' The mate was sneering.

'Ever heard of her before?'

'Many times. She is one of those craft that loiter about the coast waiting for something to offer.'

'In other words, a smuggler.'

'If there is nothing better to do,' said the German.

But there usually is, thought Alan. Piracy, for example. Pirates earned more money than smugglers and the risk they ran was no graver.

The night grew older, darker, colder. From time to time lights winked on the snow-covered quays below the palace. Signals of some kind, made with a lantern that had a shutter. Once a voice called something across the water and was answered by a lamp showing for a moment on the *Gloire*.

Perhaps a warning.

After this, there was some movement on the *Gloire*—movement and voices. A longboat which the vessel had been towing was pulled alongside; someone dropped into it; oars were pulled up from under the rowing benches; there were other noises which he had no difficulty in interpreting—a rudder was being mounted on the boat's stern.

Silence fell, and lasted a long time.

Alan heard a bell strike somewhere on shore, twice.

A few minutes later, noises came across the water from

the *Gloire,* as if something—such as a man's body—were falling heavily into the longboat from the deck above.

Cautious splashes came in a slow beat. The faint grey on the surface of the water shook into facets of light and blackness. A boat was being rowed, so quietly that only a sharp pair of ears would pick up the sound.

A shape detached itself from the blackness of the *Gloire.* After a minute, it was lost in the confused shadows which the shore cast over the water.

A lantern was burning over there. Unless his sense of direction was misleading him, it would come from the break in the quay wall at the entrance to the arsenal harbour.

The music came to an end. Jamie could see the players reaching for the mugs of beer which were waiting for them.

'You must have Spanish blood,' said his partner.

Her hand was trembling perhaps from the exertion of the dance and perhaps from another source of excitement.

'I am a gypsy from Transylvania,' he said. 'It is much the same thing. Later, let us try again.'

'We shall.' Her eyes stayed in his until, with a nod, he turned away. He had meant to ask her who she was—but, it appeared, there would be time for that before the night was ended.

In search of Leonora, he was jostled by a large, aggressive man wearing a black bearskin hat more than a foot high. Jamie was about to give this savage a hard push in the middle of the stomach, between the diamond-dangling gold chain round his shoulders and the belt of gilded Venetian leather round his waist, when he realised that it was the Pretender to the throne of the tsars.

Dmitri, the spectacular dancer, the soul-awakening singer from the steppes. Dmitri, without whom no funeral was complete. Putting his hand to his stomach, Jamie whispered something in the Russian's ear. Dmitri swung round and clasped him in the embrace of a bear. A bear drenched in sandalwood.

'My friend, the Frenchman!' he bellowed. 'The man who knows about the pearls. Listen. She has shown them to me.

You are right, Jacques. A thousand times right. For this discovery I am ready to forgive everything. It is a necklace for a queen! No, for a tsarina! For my tsarina. Incidentally, the tsarina is here tonight, incognito.'

At Dmitri's elbow was standing a small, young woman with glistening black hair and a skirt covered with spangles and shorter by six inches than that of any other woman in the palace. Jamie recognised his tawny beauty of a few nights before. The gitane.

They looked at one another with the smouldering impudence which the wearing of a mask encourages. He pressed her hand.

'I ought to thank your imperial majesty for my fur cloak which you saved from thieves the other night.'

'There was no difficulty. Remember, I was armed. Although the dagger was not in my stocking.'

'Are you certain Leonora will sell the pearls?' asked Dmitri.

'About that lady, it is impossible to be certain of anything,' said Jamie.

He had resolved that at some early moment he would exchange gypsy secrets with the gitane. But just then his attention was diverted. He had caught sight of a neck glowing white, and encircled by a necklace of bizarre splendour.

Even if she had not been wearing it, it would have been easy to recognise her. When a face is a mask, another mask is no disguise.

Murder Is a Game for Two

'The Russian will buy,' he told Leonora.

'And now I am not sure that I shall sell,' she said.

'You have until midnight to decide. So there is no reason for haste. And we have not danced.'

She shook her head. Taking his hand in hers, she led him out of the crowded ballroom, and out of the sound of the music which had sprung up again.

'Where are you taking me, Leonora?'

'There is a private way to my room from the queen's apartments. If we take it we shall not be seen.'

The room was reached at the end of winding corridors and steep, twisting flights of stairs. Two tall candles lighted it. Through a chink in the shutters he could see the dark water below and the lamps that marked the line of the quayside.

Leonora undid her mask. Then she locked the door of the little chamber. 'Now we will not be disturbed. Only Lucrezia is here. She is the only being in the world I trust.'

'Not Giovanni?' Jamie asked. She did not answer.

He kissed her and was surprised to find her trembling. He drew her over to a small canopied couch in one corner. But she remained ill-at-ease.

He did not ask why. Very soon, she would tell him.

'Jacques,' she said at last. 'The other night I wanted you to go to England. There is something to be done there which needs a man of your kind.'

'A man without principles?'

'No. A man for desperate action. I do not know whether

you would have gone. Probably, yes. Because of the devil that is in you.'

'You have never told me plainly what the action is,' he said, reproachfully.

She looked deeply into his eyes.

'Plainly—to overturn a throne,' she said, a sudden harshness in her voice.

'These things are never so easy as one thinks, Leonora,' he said lightly. 'But go on.'

'Not easy and, in this case, very likely not possible. Although—who can say? If there were two armies marching on London and a rebellion in the city, with the Scots king invading and the Welsh squires gathering—'

Jamie gave a short laugh. 'Did you say the Scots king invading?'

'Yes. Why?'

'Only that it would be comic if King James and I had found ourselves on the same side.'

'You are enemies?'

'That would be going too far. But he would like to cut my throat.'

She gave him a penetrating look. 'I don't think he is alone in that.'

'No. Apparently not. But go on, Leonora.'

'I do not ask you to go to England. I thought that you might shame a certain man to act—or give him the resolution that he lacks. But it would have been madness. A peacock cannot be transformed into an eagle. Your head would have adorned a pole at London Bridge—and all for nothing. So—'

'I am not to go?'

'No. But you are not to stay here either.' Suddenly she took his hand in hers and pressed it to her bosom. Strange—and strangely exciting—that so strong a tide should run beneath so still, so sullen, a surface!

'Can't you feel that you are in danger here?'

'From old enemies or new ones?'

'From old *and* new ones, I think—no, I do not think. I know. Although half I know is guess and the other half is instinct.'

He held her breast more firmly while his other hand stole round her waist. Looking into her eyes he found them brimming, not with tears, but with a presage of doom. An unexpected tenderness invaded him, as if for some strong and beautiful bird fluttering in the fowler's nest.

'Leonora,' he said, and kissed her lips which seemed to shudder into a wild response. Then she pushed him away—with long tapering fingers hard on his chest—so that her haunted eyes could look more deeply into his eyes.

'Jacques,' she said in a low voice, 'if I were to tell you that I love you, what would you say?'

'I should say, liar.'

'But what if it were true?' she said. 'After all, it has been true before.'

'It was true of the beautiful one!' His voice taunted her. 'The man who sent the pearls!'

She laughed.

'Do you think he was the only one, Jacques?'

'Certainly I don't, but he is the one who sent the pearls.'

'Let me warn you, Jacques. The men I love have been of many kinds—old, young, rich, poor. Once I fell in love with a gondolier. He insisted on being paid. After all, why should I be treated any differently from other girls? The men I love have one thing in common. Disaster overtakes them. All of them. All! One day it will come to the peacock, too. His feathers will be trodden into the mud by an old woman's feet. So beware, Jacques! Beware, my blond gypsy from Transylvania. The men I fall in love with say goodbye to fortune. Even the gondolier was drowned.'

'But I have yet to bid fortune good morning, Leonora,' he said.

She did not seem to hear him.

'It is years now,' she went on, her voice as animated as her face was not. 'Years since I fell in love. But I seem to remember a feeling very like this.'

Jacques shook his curls.

'Put your mind at rest. Blond gypsies from Transylvania do not have the same kind of misfortune as other men.'

She took his shoulders and shook him impatiently.

178

'Fly, Jacques, fly!' she whispered. 'In the meantime, learn how to undo a woman's dress without disarranging her necklace.'

'There will be time for everything,' he said. 'For pearls and plotting and love—'

'And disaster,' she said.

A door had been thrown open somewhere. Or the wind had changed. A shutter was banging. A frail gust of music coming from far away burst into the little room . . . Jamie recognised an air he had heard before. It was a sprightly, emphatic tune to which one trod the steps of the coranto, a dance of flirtation, of courtship, of desire.

His hand ran down her spine from link to link. When he touched certain places, her lips trembled. Pain or pleasure? She would have new bruises there.

There was no moon but the water was as sharply broken into black and pale grey as the fragments of a smashed bottle. Alan kept his eye on the shore. He had seen the longboat from the *Gloire* make its way, with extraordinary caution, towards the quays which stretched between the palace and the water and which were interrupted by the narrow entrance to the arsenal.

With not a sound of an oar, the longboat of the *Gloire* approached that point and vanished, swallowed up by the blackness of the land.

He counted ten slowly. She had not appeared again.

'Did you see that, Mr Beaton?'

Alan swung round irritably to the Rostock skipper.

'Of course, I saw it. So—?'

'Others are at this game. There has been talk!'

'There has been no talk. Nobody knows but you and I—'

'And somebody else, Mr Beaton. How could we hope to enter that harbour if somebody else had not opened the gate? So someone else had to know.'

'They have passed into the harbour, skipper. Our task is to bring the boat alongside the outer quay. There, where the lantern is burning.'

'The water there will be very choppy, Mr Beaton. And with

the wind like this—'

'In the north.'

'North by east. We'll have the devil's work to keep our little boat out of trouble.'

'Rubbish, man!'

'I hope so. And there is this. Whatever the *Gloire* is up to, her longboat will raise the alarm in the palace. The sentries will be alerted.'

'Tonight there will be no alarm. The king is giving a ball. Music. Feasting.'

'We had better wait, Mr Beaton. The king has a battery of cannon over there. They make a music I don't want to hear.'

'The gunners are drunk. That has been arranged.'

'You hope so. I hope so. But drunk or sober, I don't want to hear them. Not tonight. Better wait awhile, Mr Beaton.'

'We have half an hour. After that, we must get under way,' said Alan.

The cold had eaten into his bones and the thought that the skipper might be talking sense made him even more irritated than he should have been.

He held her elbows for an instant before he spoke.

'Tell me, Leonora, why does Giovanni have this power over you?'

She tore herself free from him and spoke passionately.

'What power? I do what I like. You imagine things, Jacques.'

He shook his head. 'Let me imagine an answer, Leonora. You and Giovanni have travelled far together, upwards—'

'Most of the way.'

'He knows the secrets of the firm.'

She laughed shortly. 'You are not such a fool as you pretend, Jacques.'

'And some of the secrets could be dangerous . . . Giovanni hates me. I find that interesting.'

'Hates you!' she cried. 'He means to kill you.'

'Murder is a game for two.'

'Not as Giovanni plays it. He is an Italian. Do you think you will be the first man Giovanni has killed? And don't ask me why. If you need to ask why, you are a fool after all.'

She unlocked the door softly. Outside, the corridor was dimly lit and silent.

Suddenly, she pulled him towards her.

'One power a man will lose only with his life,' she whispered. 'Go now and be on your guard. Beware of dark corners and dark women.'

'I am always on my guard,' he said. 'Later, we shall meet, Leonora.'

'Perhaps,' she said. Her lips reached swiftly for his. She shut the door.

Jamie found his way back to the ballroom. Standing with a group of other women was the dark aquiline girl he had danced with before.

'A coincidence,' he said.

'Of course,' she said.

'Tell me.' said Jamie. 'What is the power that a man will lose only with his life?'

'That depends on which nation he belongs to. Where does he come from, your man?'

'Oh, the South. A Spaniard or, perhaps, an Italian.'

She laughed.

'A Spaniard thinks most of the power to look himself in the eyes. Surely you know that. An Italian thinks of his power over a woman.'

'Her beauty, her mind, or her conscience?'

'Let us dance, my lord, and I will try to explain.'

In her dressing-room, Leonora sat at the looking-glass between the tall candles long enough for the image there to fade into mists in which memory and fantasy swirled together and then slowly re-assembled. She shook her head as if only some physical effort would shake the brooding intensity from her eyes.

'What time is it?' she asked.

From the shadows of the room Lucrezia's voice, dry as a lizard, gave the answer.

Leonora rose from the stool on which she had been sitting and began to unfasten the bodice of her dress. Lucrezia watched. Her bright old eyes were two motionless points of light in the gloom.

'What dress, Contessa?' she asked, when Leonora stood before the glass, naked except for the parure of pearls. Leonora shook her head.

'No dress, Lucrezia. My fencing suit. This is a masquerade—I may go in travesty, may I not?'

The old woman opened a deep armoire and brought out blue hose and a green doublet. With swift, determined movements, Leonora put them on. When she looked at herself in the glass a faint smile touched her lips for the first time. Worn over the green velvet of the doublet, the rows of black pearls had a macabre quality.

'Do you wish to take off the necklace, Contessa?' said Lucrezia.

'Take it off! By no means. Like this, I shall be the most brilliantly dressed man at the king's ball. Look! . . . Give me my dagger, Lucrezia, the one with the ruby hilt.'

She tied on her mask and went towards the door, lengthening her steps to mimic the walk of a man. Too slight, too softly tinted to be a man, she was, it seemed, a boy, the sketch of a boy. Graceful, slender and dangerous.

At the door she turned, knowing that Lucrezia was about to speak.

Out of the darkness of the room, 'Contessa. Why do I not kill Giovanni?' asked the harsh old voice, as if it were a question she had asked many times before. Leonora was silent.

'There are ways to do it,' said Lucrezia. 'No bleeding. No struggle. No noise . . . Only a needle driven in at the right place by one who knows. He does not deserve so kind a fate. When I think of what he has done—what he does . . .'

'You know why, Lucrezia. Because one day he will tell me.'

'Tell you. Where he has hidden the—'

'Be quiet, you old bitch!' She took a step forward.

Lucrezia's eye did not quail.

'He will never tell you, Contessa. Never! He is a monster, that man.'

Leonora looked at the servant for a moment, her face motionless in the mask. Then she shut the door quickly behind her.

Lucrezia shook her head sadly and mumbled some words in a peasant dialect spoken in the mountains behind Bergamo.

Mary looked round the ballroom—too crowded, too warm. She was still looking for a mask half black, half silver. Looking from one to the next as they glided past her. Then the music changed, became livelier and a man took her by the hand. He did not even say, Dance!

But this was a measure that she had danced all her life, a whirling peasant fling which had reached the palace without losing the romping zest of the barn where it was born.

The man who was her partner said something to her with a flash of teeth. He was friendly; perhaps he was more than that. Mary answered with a brief smile and threw a new abandon into her steps. She came from a country where dancing was still a fine art and a barbarous one. She knew that she could dance better tonight than she had ever done in her life before.

If only she could see *him*. But probably some girl . . . If she knew anything of Jamie Stuart . . . Why should she worry about the man?

She could see that this unknown she was dancing with was finding the pace too hot. Drops of perspiration were running down his cheeks.

With a charming smile, Mary increased the energy of her movements, remembering steps from a dance in Scotland, a Highland brawl.

A few minutes later, she caught a glimpse among the press of dancers of a man whose back was towards her and thought she recognised him. The height, the breadth of shoulder, the mass of blond curls. Surely, it was! She steered towards this man.

He swung round in the dance and her heart sank. The man had vanished. She must at all costs find him, pass close to him and murmur in his ear a message he would understand. If he were, indeed, the man she was looking for.

At one moment, Mary thought that she saw him with a small dark-skinned girl. They had paused near one of the doors of the ballroom, as if they were about to go out.

Just then, Mary's partner, with an unexpected burst of energy, swept her into a whirling movement and, when she looked again, there was no sign of the man with the long blond ringlets. He had gone. But had he been Jamie?

Mary hesitated for a moment—excusing herself to her partner. A hand to her forehead and a circular movement of her fingers—in any language, it meant giddiness. She saw Alistair and went over to him.

'Guess who I've seen,' he said. 'Two hired killers from Scotland. Here, in this palace!'

'You are sure?'

'Certainly I'm sure. Last time I set eyes on those two they were trying to murder James Stuart in Edinburgh.'

Mary wrung her hands. 'They are going to take him out to sea and—'

'Which sea?'

'That one out there—or the North Sea.'

'Or maybe the Atlantic Ocean!'

'Why the Atlantic?'

'It's deeper,' said Alistair.

Minutes passed after Leonora left the room, closing the door behind her. Minutes of absolute silence. Then from a further room Giovanni, the servant, entered. His livery was concealed by a long, dark cloak. He carried in his hand a black mask as big as a hangman's.

He and Lucrezia looked at one another for a long minute without saying a word. Then the old woman said in her voice as dry as sticks crackling in the fire of some encampment, 'You will not touch her again, Giovanni.'

The servant looked at her. If he had any expression at all it was that of astonishment. Astonishment that a creature so near to the original mud as she was had acquired the gift of speech? Or astonishment that she had dared to address some words to him? It was impossible to say.

He went towards her, fixing her with a gaze intended to reduce her to subjection. He said nothing. Lucrezia's glance did not flinch.

'Do not touch her,' she said, her fierce old eyes on his.

He sneered wordlessly.

'You have done enough,' she went on. His eyebrows rose. 'And she has done enough, too, one way and another. Things she did alone, things you made her do and things you did to her. But now, enough!'

'Let her be finished with it, then,' he said, his eyes like drops of poison. 'Why does she not? You know, you old hag. You know. Because she dare not! And something else—because she loves it.'

'Devil, devil, devil!' she spat out, clawing at the air before her face.

Giovanni stepped forward quickly and struck her across the face with his glove. Lucrezia cowered, waiting. He left the room quickly.

As soon as the door closed her moans ceased. She rose and, with the energy of a young woman, ran across the room and opened a box of inlaid wood. From it, searching about feverishly with her fingers, she took out a long needle and held it up for a moment in the candlelight. Then, scrabbling again, she came on something she wanted and pulled it out.

A thimble. Lucrezia fitted it on to her thumb. Her fingers had stopped trembling. She went out.

It had been like having his pocket picked. But different. In the riot and rustle of the dance, when the music was, every minute, more intoxicating, Jamie was aware that he was being jostled. Someone had touched the hand which rested elegantly on his hip.

When he glanced round, it was impossible to say which of his neighbours had done it. All of them, men and women, were absorbed, absorbed in the business of the dance. Their lips had a faint curl of pleasure or, perhaps, of secrecy. Their eyes were downcast. It might or might not be in evasion.

A second later, Jamie realised that a folded scrap of paper had been put in his hand. When the music fell silent, he un-folded the paper. It was not the first time he had received an invitation from a lady at a ball. But usually one was given some warning that it was going to happen.

The message on the paper consisted of three words: 'Arsenal. Help. Alan.' What it meant was clear enough. But who had written it—that was not clear at all. And there was only one way to find out.

Jamie turned to his partner.

'It is hot in this room, don't you find. Perhaps we could take a stroll for a little and see if we can find some fresh air.'

'Fresh air!' she said, mockingly. She was certainly a Spaniard. 'My Lord is from the north. You are more used to snow and ice than we are.'

'I do not mean the open air, madame. But perhaps we could walk as far the the arsenal together.'

'The way will be dark and winding.'

'You need not be frightened. I will be there to guard you.'

'When we reach it, all the doors will be shut.'

'For you, I will open every door,' said Jamie. 'But you must lead the way.'

'No,' she said, shrinking back.

'At least come with me on the first part of the journey.' His voice was coaxing. He pulled her hand towards him gently, but insistently.

'You madman,' she whispered, yielding.

His hand in hers, Jamie Stuart walked with his unknown partner into ever darker and narrower corridors in which the roof was, second by second, nearer his head and the lights— mere tallow dips—were fewer.

The seed of caution in his nature which he was constantly encouraging to sprout was, at times like these, stifled by a sudden and monstrous growth of curiosity. The girl, thin, small, aquiline, was not at all his type. But she had one source of appeal which he had never been able to resist.

She was the Unknown.

The unknown, with a slight whiff of danger to make her more alluring.

The way led, downwards on the whole, into what was evidently an older part of the castle, where the walls were rougher and the footing more uneven. We are going to the dungeons, thought Jamie.

At the Stroke of Twelve

Somebody had left a lantern lighted on the ground. Thoughtful of him whoever he was. For just at that point the way forked and one branch led down a steep flight of stairs into blackness.

'Which way to the arsenal?' he asked.

'Why do you want to go to the arsenal?' she said.

It seemed a strange place to be going with a girl at that time of night.

'Because there's a pistol there that I'd like to see again.' Although, in the circumstances, he did not think he would ask the King of Denmark to give him his pistol back.

He thought he heard a noise somewhere behind. He thought she heard it too.

Just for a moment her hand stiffened in his.

His grasp tightened.

'You take the lantern, beautiful,' he said. 'There's something I want to do.'

With the hand that had been holding the lantern, he slid his sword a couple of inches out of the scabbard.

'Always feel easier in my mind with this thing nearer to hand,' he said. 'Nerves!'

After half a dozen steps downwards, he listened again. Yes. Somebody was moving softly nearer in the gallery they had just left.

Underfoot, the way was paved no more. They were walking on a surface of naked rock, wet and uneven. The vault above was low, less than an inch from Jamie's head. It had been built long, long ago by men who wanted to be sure their work would last. Huge blocks of stone were held together with thick iron bands.

His nerves pricked him as he strained to catch the faintest variation in the air; the almost imperceptible weakening of an echo which betrays that a body has been interposed between the listening ear and the resounding stone; the noiseless puff of air made by a cloak that has been cautiously put aside; breathing that was almost soundless but not quite.

The blind see more easily in the dark. The man on his guard sees as easily as the blind.

Something dripped from the vault. The lantern showed a brilliant and slimy green on the walls. They were underground. Perhaps under water. He did not know. But it was certain that the palace was built at the water's edge.

Now the way ahead of them was rising once more. Stone steps, leading upwards this time.

Sounds of noisy breathing. Jamie's hand, quick as a snake, slid to his side. His sword made a livid yellow arc in the darkness.

The woman pulled back, whimpered. Jamie would not let her go.

At the top of the steps a corridor ran each way and a stone arch opened in front. On the ground, a sentry lay, snoring. A lantern stood on the ground beside him.

'He has been drinking with friends,' said Jamie.

At that moment, she pulled and twisted. The lantern she was carrying swung into his face and, when he drew back from the flame, fell with a crash to the ground. At the same time, he felt a sharp pain at his wrist. Her teeth had torn into his flesh. His grip yielded. The echoes of scurrying footsteps faded away. He was alone with the snoring sentry. The lantern was still alight.

Jamie picked it up and made his way cautiously under the stone archway ahead. A few yards farther on, an iron grating blocked the way. It was heavy and ancient, with enormous bolts that slid into square holes cut into the stonework of the wall. Somebody had pulled the bolts back. He put his shoulder to the grating. It swung back with a creak. It was open.

A moment later, Jamie stood on the threshold of the King of Denmark's arsenal.

He hung the lantern on a hook on the wall. Then he looked round. Alistair had not exaggerated. This was a treasure house of the god of war. Swords, pikes, axes, helmets, breastplates, cuisses—all the sombre accoutrements of slaughter were here, dully gleaming in stand after stand. Battle axes that must have been swung by Viking raiders, lances that had been levelled in charges during the Crusades, and the crossbows, arquebuses, muskets of modern times. In the distance, Jamie could see dim steel cylinders recumbent in rows. The Cannon Hall.

He looked round. No sign of Alan. Not that he had expected to see him. No sign of anyone. He was alone, surrounded by enough weapons to start a fair-sized war. Alone?

Not so alone. Two tiny noises, apparently unconnected, drew his glance first in one direction, then in another.

From behind a full suit of armour in the style of a century before and set up on a wooden dummy, old-fashioned Death lurched into sight a few yards away. He came on with a forward roll of his cloaked left shoulder and a twitch of his fingers towards the dirk at his right side.

Jamie sprang back and to the side. Fast, but not fast enough. Death had brought a friend.

Out of the darkness behind Jamie something hard and heavy struck. The blow had been aimed at his head and, when he turned quickly, struck his left shoulder, deadening his arm. The man in front stepped forward and swung at Jamie's jaw with the fist that had been holding the cloak to his face.

He lurched back against an armour-clad effigy, and, on a sudden inspiration, used his crippled shoulder to pull the armour down between him and the attackers. It fell with a crash on the stone paving of the arsenal.

Jamie had a moment in which he could shake his head clear. No more than a minute. The two men came at him again, one with a cudgel, the other with dirk and knuckleduster. He thought wildly that he had seen them before somewhere.

Give me a minute to recover and this pair will be meat for

the crows! Why the devil don't they come at me with the steel? . . .

He had them both in front of him now while he retreated among the weapons of old wars. An ancient mace was stacked where his hand could reach it. Jamie snatched it and threw. One of the two—the man with the dirk—ducked as it flew past his ear.

At this rate, thought Jamie, I can hold them off for ever. He laughed. It was a stupid thing to do, for one of the ruffians growled in English, 'We've played with the bastard long enough.'

The other said, 'You ken our orders.'

'To hell with orders. Give him the point, Mac.'

Their blades flashed together and they came on circumspectly, one on either flank with a heap of arms laid out tidily between them—the accoutrements, horse and man, of a squadron of horse.

Jamie grinned. The idiots!

He waited until they were close up before springing forward at the man on the left, levelling at him a lance which he had torn from a rack of arms and held firmly against his side. At the same instant he uttered a blood-curdling yell that echoed from the walls.

The wretch had no time to flee or defend himself. The lance caught him full in the shoulder. He staggered back, making a barking noise. It was either anger or pain.

Jamie wasted no more time on him. He leapt over the hedge of arms and faced the second assailant.

This man could fight. He held his weapon the right way. He made the right passes. In the dim light of the armoury he could be dangerous; above all, if Jamie took risks. He had to take risks. He moved swiftly in—one, two, three! and thrust! He heard a grunt. The fellow's sword rose. Jamie thrust again.

He turned. He had heard something.

A third antagonist, cloaked, masked and dangerous, had entered the arsenal. Jamie thought he had seen him before too. Not long before.

But the light was too uncertain and the need was to keep his eye on the man's blade, like a fan of cold light, glittering in his hand. It would probably be all right if only he had frightened the other two off. But although he had hit both, and one of them twice, he did not think they were out of the fight. If he could find a place where his flank could not be turned . . .

In the archway that opened into the darkness of the Cannon Hall? The light, such as it was, would be in his face. But he would have all his enemies in front of him.

The third antagonist, the newcomer, seemed to be waiting to see if the other two were fit to carry on the battle.

'Come on, coward,' said Jamie.

Two of them came towards him. One hung back, holding a hand to his shoulder. Good! he thought. I have crippled one. The others will not be so eager to engage. For a moment he stood there in the archway, at his ease, balancing first on one foot, then on the other, his blade making a supple, enticing dance of light in his hand.

It would be wise to stay where he was and await the attack. Jamie was not wise. He leapt forward, gracefully, with no pretence at a feint, his point aimed at the man he had already hurt.

The third man, the newcomer in the cloak, entered the fight at that moment. Aware, by intuition, and the sense of what he could almost see out of the corner of his eye, Jamie struck down hard at a blade licking out at him. There was a sharp pain below one knee; something tearing; something that soaked through his stocking. Jamie countered viciously with a mad flurry of strokes that made the cloaked man step sharply back.

The cloak fell open. Jamie saw a livery he recognised. He was fighting a man who meant to kill him!

For a servant, Giovanni knew how to use a sword. He had learned to fence in the same school as Leonora. Or from a master of the same authority . . .

Stylish, wary, dangerous—it would be interesting to give him a match one day, on even terms. Interesting, but it was going to be one of those things that did not happen.

Giovanni was going to end the business, there and then. He had brought his two friends—just to see fair play. If the two friends did not seem as eager for the fray as they might be, they had some excuse. They had already been hurt. But

Jamie had only to make one mistake and they would be on him like the jackals they were.

Giovanni came on again, this time with all caution put aside, and everything thrown into a dazzling attack which had Jamie warding off the strokes for his life as thrust followed slash, and head, flank, heart were, one after the other, the target. The sweat ran down his breast and stung in his eyes. Not since he fought against a big Swiss behind the Louvre stables had he been in such desperate danger.

By God, he thought, if I survive this bout I am a better swordsman than I thought I was.

One thing now was in his favour. The Italian, a hard, experienced fighter, malignant as a devil—master of all the tricks by which men take lives—had lost something of the sparkle of youth. Jamie sensed it in Giovanni's stance, the flat feet on the ground, the ungainly angle of the knees.

Assurance swept over him. His sword play became bolder—a darting, daring, bounding exhibition, pressing forward in airy confidence that the two others would not intrude on this conflict of champions, and bounding back to his base in the archway.

Then without warning all was changed. A blast of icy wind came from the dusky Cannon Hall at Jamie's back. A clatter of feet on the stones. The rumble of voices growing louder.

Jamie hesitated for an instant. The newcomers, whoever they were, were close behind him. Men were talking French. His blade rose, hesitantly. Behind Giovanni he saw a vision which astounded him. A slim, masked figure in green coming forward out of the darkness, sword in hand. A bitter pain stabbed his shoulder. Giovanni's face wore a grin of triumph.

'Leonora!' Jamie cried.

At the name, the Italian turned on the girl, his face distorted with rage. He lunged at her. She parried, elegantly. Christ! The girl is good. My money is on her.

Jamie had no time to see any more. Men were jostling him from behind. Out of the darkness something hard and heavy fell on his head. He wanted to yell with the agony of it. Perhaps he did. Hands pinned his arms to his side. From somewhere a fist struck his jaw—a fist that was harder than any fist of bone and muscle could be. His mouth was full of salt, warm liquid. His teeth had become pebbles. Iron fingers gripped his throat, squeezed.

Somebody said, 'No need to kill him.'

Somebody said, 'That can wait.'

Somebody laughed.

In the distance there was a scream as if somebody was being killed. Puzzling.

Then there was nothing at all. Not even pain.

The coldest hour of the night was approaching.

The longboat from the *Gloire* could no longer be seen. It had vanished into the inner harbour.

Alan was peering into the night, screwing his eyes up against the cold air.

'They've gone ashore,' said the mate.

Alan scrutinised the shore for a moment.

'You're right,' he said.

Stealthily, black figures could be seen crossing the snow-covered quay between the harbour and the arsenal. A minute later, a dim light appeared, outlining a rectangular shape in the blackness of the building as if a door had been opened there.

'It seems that somebody else has had the same notion as we had.' said Alan.

'We can take the dinghy and wait for the longboat as it comes out,' said the German, urgently.

Alan made an impatient sound.

'And finish in the dungeons before daylight!'

'No,' said the German, earnestly. 'It need not be like that.'

'How do we know what they are doing over there?'

'We know they are doing no good.'

Alan could see shadowy figures in the lighted doorway. Then darkness. The door had been closed.

Alistair thought there would be no trouble about finding his relative, Roderick. For a strictly brought-up member of a family of gentlemen cut-throats, Roderick had an inordinate partiality for women. In the glens mothers had kept a watch on their daughters when Roderick was in the neighbourhood.

And there he was, sure enough, in the royal nursery with that girl, Margaret Stewart, sitting in his lap—the girl Stuart had brought over from Kirkwall.

Alistair shot at him a stream of Gaelic. Roderick rose, frowned, pushed the girl from his knee and reached for his halberd.

'Manners!' said Margaret Stewart, haughtily, smoothing down her skirts.

'Manners can wait, woman.'

The two guardsmen hurried back towards the ballroom where the revels of the night were turning into a carouse.

Roderick began a systematic search in the corridors of the palace, enlisting every guard he met in the search for two men, foreigners, unmasked, rough-looking. They were to be arrested at once.

Alistair went to look for Mary Beaton.

'Roderick is alerting all the guards,' he told her. 'The trouble is that most of them are drunk. Roderick is none too sober himself. I thought that I'd take a stroll now to the vaults.'

'I'll come with you, Alistair,' she said eagerly.

'But what about her ladyship?'

'Her ladyship finds Rhine wine very tiring, poor lady.'

'Come on, girl,' said Alistair.

Alan had pulled himself up on the rigging so that he could see better. In a few minutes his fingers were numbed with cold, and the danger of frostbite was near when he saw something ashore that made him slip down to the deck in a rush.

Staggering as they walked, three men were carrying a long, unwieldy bundle from the door that led out of the mass of buildings of the palace. The burden was heavy and they carried it with difficulty across to the quayside where the *Gloire's* longboat was lying. The bundle was clumsily wrapped up. Apart from that, he could not describe it.

He summoned the mate.

'The dinghy,' he said. 'Every rower to have a weapon.'

The mate's teeth flashed in a grin. He showed the cudgel he was carrying. The picked crewmen were squatting on deck in the shelter of the wheelhouse. One after another, they slipped over the side. In less than a minute, the boat was making at speed towards the shore.

'There she comes,' Alan muttered.

The sharp black shape of a boat appeared, a solid mass of darkness on the broken gray of the water. It was gliding fast out of the harbour entrance. The rowers stopped pulling.

'Ship oars—but quietly! —and wait until she comes nearer.'

But noises ashore drew his eyes from the boat. Figures appeared running to the water's edge from the palace buildings. A man; another man; and—by God! —a woman! And, by an extraordinary trick of eyesight or imagination, Alan thought he recognised her.

A man's shout came across the water from the quay.

'Help there—help! To the rescue!'

'That's the voice of a man I know!' Alan caught the mate by the arm. 'Row in there fast and we'll find out what is happening.'

He knew that Alistair MacIan would not call out unless there was good reason.

Rowing fast into the harbour, which now that the boat had entered it he saw was hardly bigger than a tennis court, Alan heard the clock on the great tower of the palace strike. One, two . . . *twelve!*

Midnight. The hour when he had planned to fetch the parcel of arquebuses from the King of Denmark's store. But now it seemed that there was something more urgent to do.

The music died and the dancing stopped.

Footmen in gala livery had draped an ermine cloak over the ivory throne that stood on the dais at one end of the ballroom.

Twelve men in livery carrying silver trumpets entered, followed by two kettle drummers. They blew a fanfare while the drummers beat a long roll.

Beautiful, challenging, declamatory, the music echoed from the walls.

Then the king entered at the head of a file of halberdiers. His face was shining and rubicund, his small blue eyes had a roving, humorous glint. His gait was not of the steadiest. He stood, in front of the throne, facing the company. At that moment, a bell could be heard outside. The king counted the the strokes with his finger. At the twelfth, he tore the mask from his face and burst into a roar of laughter.

The guests unmasked. The women sank in a curtsey. And His Majesty of Denmark collapsed on to the ermine-draped throne. He clapped his hands once for the musicians to play again.

Scarcely had the dancing begun when an officer of the guard hurried in with drawn sword, and saluted the monarch. He spoke in a low voice, hurriedly. The king rose, frowning.

'Disorder, you say, Klaus? In my palace? Incredible!'

'One of your majesty's guests, a foreigner, it seems, has been attacked and carried off.'

The king uttered a long curse. Before the end of it, he had drawn his sword. It looked very small in his hand.

'Alan!' Beaton heard the name carried across the narrowing space of water in the arsenal harbour, the sound wavering as the night wind plucked at it. He saw her tear the mask from her face.

'Mary!' he cried.

The dinghy nudged the stones of a flight of steps which led down from the quay to the basin of the harbour. A boat-hook was held out and seized by Alistair, who with another guardsman stood beside Mary.

'What is it?'

She began to tell him. Before she had ended, he was throwing out orders.

'They have taken him to that old tub there. If we are quick enough we'll overtake them.'

A third guardsman appeared, a Dane carrying a lantern. With the others, he tumbled into the dinghy.

'Push off,' said Alan.

But by the time the dinghy had cleared the harbour entrance, the *Gloire* was beating against the wind on her way to deeper water. She was showing no lights and, it seemed, her skipper was steering by landmarks his eyes could pick up.

'You are not clad for a night at sea, sister,' said Alan.
'I will be all right,' she said.
He could hear her teeth chattering.
By the time the Rostock flyboat got under way there was no sign of the *Gloire* among the shoal waters.

The World Is at Sea

He was still smiling faintly when he woke up.

What time was it? He did not know except that he thought it was after daybreak. Not much after daybreak. And where?

He had been dreaming, that at least was certain. But at what point the dream world passed into reality—if it really was reality—and just how real *was* reality? At a question so profound and so ridiculous Jamie began to laugh feebly.

After a while, another thought crossed his mind. In one respect, the world had changed since he knew it last. If this, in fact, was the world! It was rocking slightly from one end to the other—so! —with a complicating crossways motion, like a—No doubt about it. The world seemed to be at sea . . . Yes, by God, it had turned into a ship.

He thought it was a change for the better.

He opened his eyes cautiously and shut them quickly. He was evidently having a bad dream. A dream about a man he had seen before somewhere, but he could not remember where. A man with a red beard, who seemed to be sharpening a knife on his thumb. For some reason this man was looking down at him. Somehow or other, Jamie decided, he was in a ship with a preposterous name which in a minute he would remember . . . Oh, yes. The *Gloire*. He smiled at the thought.

Now a man was talking; but somehow he knew that it was not Redbeard, although this man, too, was talking French—the French of the south, spoken in a thick, rusty voice.

'What are you going to do with him, Captain?'

'You know damned well what I'm going to do with him.

Take him out to sea a bit and drop him overboard with a cannon-ball tied to his ankle.'

'You shouldn't do that, Captain.'

'Orders are orders, boy.'

'Sometimes orders are better ignored.'

'That's what you say. *They* say differently. And they have paid the money.'

'Money!' There was the sound of a man spitting.

'Yes, money. Have you heard of it?' asked Redbeard. 'They don't want to have him found anywhere near the town. Alive or dead. See? There are reasons. Reasons of state. So we are going to take him out to sea before we do the job.'

'You shouldn't do it, Captain.' The voice had a grating stubbornness in it.

'Who says?'

'I do.'

'And what makes you think you give the orders on this ship?'

While Jamie blinked and twisted with pain, somebody leant over him. Rough fingers pulled his shirt open at the neck.

'Look at this! See that mark on his shoulder. Burnt in. That's a brand, if you know what that is. And what does it say? Read. G—A—L. Do you know what that means? It means he has been a galley slave. Just like me, Captain. Look at my shoulder. See. Same brand. G. A. L.'

'Meaning you are cattle from the same herd.'

'That's it. Cattle that have escaped.'

'So! What's that got to do with our business?'

'It has everything in the world to do with it. He's a member of the Brotherhood, Captain. Ever heard of it? The Brotherhood of Galley Slaves. You shouldn't touch him.'

'No?'

'No. It could be a mistake.'

'Oh-ho. Mutiny, eh?'

'Don't lay a hand on him, noble captain!'

'On this ship, only one man gives the orders. That's me. Understand that, espèce de maquereau?'

'Maquereau! Maquereau! You who lived on the earnings of your mother because your sister had the pox.'

The voices had gone quiet now. Jamie thought that they would not be quiet for long. He thought that the speakers were moving about as they spoke.

Peering through his eyelashes, he took in the scene. He was lying on the wooden floor of a ship's cabin. The beams above it were so low that even a middle-sized man could not stand upright. The light from the outside was cut off by men who crowded the doorway, watching the pair with hungry eyes.

Redbeard had finished stropping his knife blade on his thumb. The other ruffian was a hunchback, low-visaged and powerfully built. He had begun to tremble quite noticeably.

Jamie thought he knew what that meant. It was a weakness he had himself. It meant that Redbeard should look out.

Edging round one another and then moving apart and prowling like animals, the two threw at one another a stream of words in a gaudy vocabulary he had not heard since his student days in Paris.

'*Hareng, Turbineur, Gironde*'—and, at last, the epithet which cannot be overlooked even among the most degraded of men. '*Empaffé!*' The insult that is the signal for battle.

Silence. The hunchback was trembling more violently than ever.

Then, all of a sudden, it began. Jamie was aware of something singing in the wood a foot above his head. Redbeard had thrown his knife and missed. Now he had whipped out a scimitar from his sash. Just in time! For the hunchback had leapt at him. The broad triangle of a dagger took the light as it rose and fell.

And, after the silence, a tumult of noise.

A rabble poured into the cabin from the door which led to the deck outside, men brandishing weapons and snarling curses, in all the seamen's tongues north of Cadiz. At the tail came two women, screaming, waving their arms and tugging at men where they could reach them.

If these angels join the discussion, thought Jamie, we'll be here all day.

Cautiously, unnoticed in the fracas, he sat up, clenching his teeth at the pain every movement cost him. The cut on his shoulder was no more than a scratch but it burned damnably.

Feeling about with his good hand, he found his doublet crumpled beneath his body, worked it free and put it on. More important, there was Redbeard's knife which had hardly stopped quivering in the timbers.

This was hardly a moment for a man to be unarmed.

Above him, the straining, stinking bodies went on with their muddled conflict.

The battle seemed to be going the captain's way. The hunchback, badly slashed on the face by Redbeard's scimitar, reeled back—his hands to his face. It seemed for a moment that the next sweep of the scimitar would behead him.

A tall negro, wearing only a ragged pair of breeches, leapt forward and flashed a dagger at Redbeard's ribs. The captain, bellowing, fell to the deck. The big African leapt on Redbeard, the knife raised for another blow, when two men threw themselves on him.

Jamie thought he had seen enough. It was not his quarrel, although he could not pretend he was indifferent to the outcome. He worked himself upright and was shocked by a hammer of pain that came down on his skull.

Unsteadily, he made for the door which, at that moment, was blocked by the two furies. Apparently, they had decided that they were on opposite sides in this war.

Between rage and exhibitionism, each was tearing the clothes off the other's shoulders. The shoulders were powerful, the breasts enormous. Each was weeping, mewing with rage, and driving red furrows down the other's cheeks. One woman's shoulder bore ten bloody teeth marks.

Jamie staggered past the hunchback, who was holding somebody's shirt to his bleeding face. 'Merci, frère,' said Jamie, taking care to touch the man's hump. Then, when he came to the door, 'Excusez, mesdames,' he said, politely.

He was careful not to separate the viragos but instead, as he pushed past one, to thrust her into the other's arms.

Outside on the deck, he stood for a moment, swaying in the sudden cold, the overwhelming freshness of the dawn wind. Quickly, he steadied himself by the ship's rail for a minute. Dragging himself up to the poop, he looked back over the stern-post. The helm seemed to be unattended.

Through the grey morning mist he could see a small cloud on the horizon. Or was it a sail?

The land on either shore of the seaway was low-lying, with sandy beaches on one side shining in the pale light and rocky slopes on the other. A look-out shouted something down from the masthead.

'He's seen her,' said the helmsman to Alan who stood beside him, his face pale blue and rigid with the long, cold vigil.

'He's sure of that?'

The helmsman spat over the side.

'To mistake that ship a man would have to be blind.'

Alan called down to Alistair, who lay sick on deck.

A minute later, he pointed, excitedly. He had seen a small, dark speck rising in the restless expanse ahead.

'We should overtake her in—how long?' he asked the mate. While the seaman's eyes were calculating, the helmsman said something in German which Alan did not hear.

'He says there is something strange about that ship,' said the mate. 'As if nobody was steering her. She has lost the wind and nobody is tending the sail. At this rate, we'll be alongside her in half an hour.'

He shouted an order. A few minutes later, with her sails more tightly hauled, the ship leaned over in the wind and moved more swiftly through the water.

'Not long now, Alistair,' cried Alan down to the green-faced Highlander.

Alistair had made a quick recovery from his seasickness. White-faced but sharp-eyed, he was crouching on the deck of the Rostock flyboat with an arm on the rail. He was ready to jump and he had discarded his halberd.

'For me, the family weapon,' he had said, apologetically waving a broadsword. But, unobtrusively, he had put a small bow on the deck beside him. It was the Eskimo bow Alistair had found in the arsenal. So far, he had never put it to serious use.

'But,' he had said to Alan Beaton, 'a man has to try everything once. The time may come. If these savages up there in

Greenland can use it, why not a Scottish gentleman like myself?'

'Go below, Mary,' Alan had commanded. 'This will be a serious business. No time for girls.'

She had not seemed to hear him. From somewhere, perhaps, from one of the Germans, she had armed herself with a pistol. Alan shrugged his shoulders. He was sure she had no idea how to use it. She would try to fire at the wrong time, causing him embarrassment at a moment of crisis. But he had frowned and said nothing. His sister was a foolish, stubborn girl.

The ship had worked its way to a cable's length from the *Gloire* before the action began. Suddenly, the deck of that down-at-heel vessel was crowded with an assortment of criminal faces, a repertory of all the misdeeds of the seas, men with bloody faces and bandaged heads, men with drawn swords and brandished knives, women tattered and half-naked.

A red-bearded man who had thrust his way to the front shouted orders. A porthole slammed open and the mouth of a cannon appeared. It was fired once and once again as the distance between the two ships closed. The Rostock ship shook with the impact as the shot struck her timbers.

The *Gloire* was drawing away, when she suddenly hesitated for a moment. Alistair had sprung forward to the gunwhale and bent his little grey bow . . .

'My God, you Highland wizard, that was a shot!' cried Alan.

The helmsman on the *Gloire*, bawling with pain, was plucking at an arrow in his arm.

'These savages up there in the ice,' said Alistair. 'They make quite good weapons all the same. But look, Alan, look! See who that is!'

His curls nonchalantly taking the morning light, Jamie Stuart was waving to them from the poop of the *Gloire*.

The two ships came together in a shuddering crunch. Agile as cats, Alistair, Roderick and a handful of German seamen clambered aboard the *Gloire* which rode a foot or so above the flyboat.

The two Highlanders swung their swords in glittering arcs of menace.

Horrified by the noise of the cannon, Mary Beaton was quite

sure that nobody could have survived so terrible an explosion.
While she was glancing wildly about, amazed to find that
she, at least, was alive, Alan leapt to the gunwhale, brandishing a cutlass.

'No, no!' she cried, or thought she cried, for in fact no
sound passed her lips. 'Alan! You know I can't stand the sight
of blood!'

She shut her eyes tightly, expecting every minute to fall in
a swoon on the deck, to the disgrace of her family. All about
her, she was aware of hard-breathing men making threatening
noises and leaping from one ship to the other.

From the gloomy innards of the *Gloire*, men poured out.
Fighting at their head was a sinister, half-naked ruffian with
a red beard who shouted in French, 'Give the fishes their
dinner, boys!'

In a half-circle on the slimy deck, Alan, Alistair and
Roderick, with a Dane in guards uniform and a couple of grim
German seamen, harassed the *Gloire*'s defenders with fierce
aggressive play. A woman, almost black from the sun, the salt
air and dirt, rushed to the front and threw a blazing firework
into Alan's face.

Mary heard his shout of pain and opened her eyes. She saw
her brother duck and hold both hands to his face.

In her hand she held the pistol somebody had given her. She
lifted it, shut her eyes and pressed the trigger. To her amazement, something exploded. She shut her eyes to keep out the
smoke. In a minute she would faint . . . when this excitement
was over. She opened her eyes and saw James.

On the poop of the other ship he crouched over the deck
of the flyboat, all his teeth showing in a pale grin and a naked
sword in his hand. A boasting, showing-off, deplorable young
man, about to make a fool of himself as usual.

Crash! Now he had jumped down to the deck and, strangely
enough, a hush had fallen on the battle. Jamie Stuart was
shouting:

'Get back all of you! This is between the skipper and me.
Would you like to change swords, Redbeard?'

From Redbeard's mouth came a torrent of quayside French.

'Good,' said Jamie. 'Keep back, the rest of you. Alistair,

Alan, if one of them moves, put a knife between his ribs. On guard, Redbeard.'

I shall faint, Mary told herself; any minute now, I shall faint. I should have fainted long ago. Where is that woman I aimed at? God, I hope I did her no harm.

But she could see nothing, nothing but that big show-off in his shirt, making passes with his sword, so confidently, so elegantly it made her sick with irritation to see him.

And then, suddenly, it was all different.

One of those shameless whores had leant forward. Something in her hand had glinted. And Jamie was staggering on the deck.

What happened after that was something she could never understand or never accurately remember without a laugh, half-horrified, half-believing. She found herself without the boat cloak that had protected her from the cold, wearing only the balldress she had stitched a few hours before.

She had gripped her pistol by the muzzle and, somehow or other, she was using it to beat the brains out of the woman who had attacked Jamie, and who was now screaming with the pain of this new attack.

Then Mary felt herself being pulled backwards. She heard somebody cry 'Mary!' in horror. It was her brother, Alan. When she looked again Jamie, white as his own shirt, had struck Redbeard's sword from his grasp. Redbeard had raised his arms. The duel was over.

'Throw down your arms, all of you,' shouted Alan.

'No. Let the hunchback keep his. He and I are brothers,' said Jamie.

And now, for the first time, he saw Mary Beaton. His jaw fell. His eyes widened.

'Mary!' he cried. 'You here! What in God's name?'

'I suppose I have a right to visit foreign parts like other people,' she said.

He stood for a moment before her, grinning, very pale, and swaying from side to side. 'But you are a girl who can't stand the sight of blood,' he said, and began to laugh. Once he started, he could not stop.

A moment later, Jamie Stuart collapsed in a heap at her feet.

With a sudden cry, Mary dropped to her knees beside him.

After a glance, Alan said, 'He'll be all right.'

Mary shot an upward glance at her brother from eyes dilated with indignation.

'Yes,' he said. 'All right. Give him half an hour . . . He has a good thick head, has your friend Jamie.'

Just at that moment from somewhere quite close at hand came the shock and roar of a heavy cannon.

Alan turned to look out to sea over the ship's quarter. 'A pinnace flying the Danish colours.'

'A ship of the king's,' said Alistair. 'Telling us to heave to.'

The Rose of Kirkwall

A pale, melancholy dog of great size hoisted itself from the floor and surveyed, dispassionately, the young man who had been ushered so abruptly into the room. The dog had the black muzzle and pointed ears of the breed and the man who had come in thought it stood nearly three feet from the ground. After giving him a long stare from its calm, honey-coloured eyes, it folded itself and collapsed once more in its place.

At a nod from the man seated at a desk, the door closed behind the newcomer: Jamie Stuart looked cautiously around.

The room was quite small and hung from floor to ceiling with faded tapestries. It was furnished with a desk and an armchair set on a dais. There were books and writing material. On one wall hung a handsomely engraved map of northern Europe.

It might have been the study of a university professor or a merchant interested in the Baltic trade. It was the private cabinet of the most powerful monarch of the North.

At that moment King Christian sat leaning forward in his chair with his huge belly comfortably between his knees, tugging at his beard and glowering at Stuart with a mixture of kingly authority and human curiosity.

Jamie, from his position below the dais, returned the curiosity in full measure. At a rough estimate, he had decided that King Christian could give Captain George Sinclair a couple of inches across the shoulders and an inch in height.

'I can see you looking at me, Jacques, with a calculating eye,' growled the king. 'Be good enough to tell me what's in your mind.'

Noting that the monarch's French was tolerable, although marred by a strong German accent, Jamie replied politely:

'Your majesty misses nothing. I was measuring you in my mind against a certain friend of mine whom I have always regarded as the most impressive figure of a man I have ever seen?'

'Am I bigger than he is?'

'By the breadth of a finger, sire. Each way.'

'Can your friend wrestle? Send him to me and we'll try a fall. What is the man's name?'

'You won't know it, sire. It is Sinclair.'

The king looked at him suspiciously.

'I've heard that name somewhere. In a minute I'll remember where. Now as for you, Jacques, you are no doubt wondering why I don't have you hanged, or deported, or at least put in gaol.'

Jamie opened astonished eyes.

'Yes,' said the king, 'and don't pretend you don't know what I'm talking about. Hanged as a known criminal. Deported because some people in Scotland would like to see you. Or gaoled because you are living in Denmark under false pretences.'

Jamie bowed and said nothing. It seemed to him that he could make no useful comment.

'Let me satisfy your insatiable curiosity, monsieur. There are two reasons for my royal clemency. First, certain persons had the damned impudence to assault you in the precincts of the palace. On sanctified ground! That is something I cannot overlook. Secondly—but come along with me and I'll show you something in the royal collection.'

The king rose and walked briskly towards a small side door. Jamie followed. The dog followed Jamie. A minute later, they came out into a long panelled gallery hung with pictures. The king stopped abruptly in front of one of them.

'Stand over there, beside it.' Jamie did as he was bidden. King Christian's gaze went from picture to man and back again. Then:

'By God!' he cried. 'Wasn't I right? When I saw you for

the first time that night in the courtyard, I thought you reminded me of someone. Look! This is it! You might be brothers!'

Jamie stepped back. His eyes fell on the portrait of a tall, bony, youngish man in the costume that was worn half a century before. There was something familiar about the face. It reminded him of—

'Do you know who that is?' asked the king. 'His name is James Stewart. Have you ever heard it?'

'I was going to say, sir, that he minds me of my father—but he is not so handsome.'

'Is that so, indeed! Well, my boy, he was the king of Scotland in his time. King James the Fifth. Much good it did him, poor devil. Now perhaps you'll explain one thing to me. Why are you so like the man in the picture?'

'Coincidence, perhaps,' said Jamie.

The king shook his head vigorously and tugged at his beard.

'No. Not coincidence,' he said, with emphasis. 'Now let me tell you something. Your name is not Jacques. You aren't French. Who are you?'

Jamie hesitated only an instant before answering. It is always as well to tell the truth to somebody who has guessed it.

'They call me James Stuart.'

The king beamed. 'By God, I thought so! You belong to that family—on the wrong side of the blanket, no doubt.'

'Not everybody thinks so.'

'Oh-ho! No wonder my brother-in-law hopes that somebody will cut your throat. Do you know, if I were in his shoes I would think the same.'

'And if you were in my shoes, sir, what would you do?'

The king looked at him for a moment with knitted brows, then,

'Come on,' he said, and led the way back to his study. There he took two glasses from a cupboard and filled them up from a tall jug of wine on his work table. He handed one to Jamie.

A smile broadened on his face.

'I'd give the little bugger a run for his money.' He lifted his glass. 'Skaal!' he said. 'Also, M. Jacques, if you take my advice you'll leave Denmark as soon as you can arrange it. Let me fill your glass,' said the king, filling his own. 'And you'll stay to dinner. I want to ask you some questions about that fight in my arsenal. For instance, who killed that Italian servant of Countess Rosenkrantz? Did you?'

Jamie shook his head.

'But he tried hard enough to kill me,' he said.

'Somebody killed him,' said the king, emptying his glass. Later, many hours, many glasses later, the king leant across the table. His head was swaying a little from side to side.

'I understand now,' he said, 'why Brother James is so anxious to be rid of you. Remember, he is playing a big game. And he may not look much, but he has brains. Don't underrate him. If you were wise—which you aren't—you'd keep out of his way. If you don't, you may find yourself up against more than Brother James.'

'I'm not sure I follow,' said Jamie.

'No? Well, listen. Among us kings there's a kind of—what do you call?—a camaraderie.'

'A brotherhood,' Jamie suggested.

'Call it that if you like.'

'I belong to one myself, the brotherhood of galley slaves. It did me some good once.'

'Kings are different from galley slaves,' said the king, frowning.

'For one thing, they don't pull oars.'

'Don't interrupt so much, Stuart. What I was saying was that kings are apt to close their ranks against outsiders. So, if you work against Brother James, we will probably work against you. It's our instinct. So—'

'But it's he who is working against me,' Jamie pointed out.

The king waved his hand majestically.

'All I'm saying is, be careful,' he said. 'Incidentally, there's another matter I want to discuss with you.' He pulled a pistol from an inner pocket of his doublet and laid it with a smack on the table. 'Is that your pistol, Jamie?'

Jamie looked at the initial 'G' on the ivory handle of the little gun.

'It looks very like one I bought in Scotland.'

'It was found in a river valley in Norway.' said the king.

'That's very strange, sir.'

'Strange! I should have thought it was the most natural thing in the world,' said the king. 'Why did you invade my kingdom of Norway? You would have been caught, even if we hadn't been warned you were coming. Why were you such a damned fool?'

'Have you ever heard of a place called the Kremlin?'

'Yes. It has sixteen gates and twenty-four churches.'

'Yes. And emeralds as big as pigeon's eggs. We were going there.'

'You would have found it a sight colder than Copenhagen, boy.'

'Cold! Poof!' said Jamie.

'Maybe. So you were going to Moscow?'

'And then somebody interrupted us.'

The king's fist crashed on the table. He shook with laughter.

'You should have asked my advice first, boy. I could have told you about those peasants. A rough lot, eh?'

'On equal terms, we'd have cut them to pieces, sir.'

'Maybe,' said the king, solemnly. 'I agree that you have one quality besides conceit. You're a trained soldier. The sort of man I am looking for. Listen carefully. There is going to be a war, Jamie, a big war. I see it burning Europe from one end to the other before it's put out. You could help me to train an army. But Brother James wouldn't like it and Brother James must be treated with respect. He is going to be a big figure one of these days if I'm not mistaken. So I can't ask you to stay here, can I? In fact, boy, the sooner you vanish, the better.'

'And where does Your Majesty suggest I should go?'

The king looked at him for a moment, narrowing his eyes as if he needed to bring them into focus.

'If it were any other man but you I'd say London. But any day now, Brother James may be there.'

'Somebody else said London. A woman I know.'

'You know too many women, Stuart, like your grandfather, the man in the picture. He was a hell of a womanizer. Terrible! And that reminds me of something.'

King Christian rang a handbell. A liveried page appeared.

The king spoke a few quick words in Danish. The page bowed and left the room.

'I owe you a debt of gratitude, Stuart.'

'Happy to think so, sir.'

'Yes. Had it not been for you, I should not have met the light of my life. One minute. Ah, there she is!'

The door flew open. Margaret Stewart, the rose of Kirkwall, curtseyed to the king.

'Margaret!'

Her eyes opened wide.

'Jamie Stuart!' she cried.

'Isn't she a beauty,' said the king, with enthusiasm. 'Come here, darling. You know this young man, don't you? If I were the jealous kind, I'd wring your neck, Stuart. As it is, I am going to reward you for bringing this beauty into Denmark.'

He drew Margaret down on his knees.

'Name what you want, Stuart. Come on. Out with it, sir!'

Something came into Jamie's mind.

'There is a young woman in Norway—'

'God! Another woman! But go on!'

'She was kind to me. Your Majesty could do something to prevent them taking her farm from her.'

'People don't have their farms taken from them,' said the king angrily. 'Not in this country.'

'I was sure of that,' said Jamie.

'Her name? Her name?'

'Ingrid Sigurdsdottir.'

'How do you spell it?' On the table in front of the king was a small tablet and a pencil.

'I-n-g-r-i-d,' Jamie began . . . The king wrote.

Jamie watched, his eyes glazed, a faint smile on his lips.

If the King of Denmark was able to read his own handwriting in the morning, it would be a miracle.

Mistress and Servant, Slave and Master

Four elderly people sat at their usual table in the corner of Caroline Gyldenstierne's room, playing cards.

'Leonora is late this evening,' remarked the French woman. The woman sitting on her left made an impatient movement of her shoulders.

'Are you surprised? To have lost her major-domo so suddenly. And in that dreadful way!'

A man spoke next. 'Major-domo . . . So that's what he was! I used to wonder.'

'A heart attack, they tell me.'

'No.'

'A single scream. Blood-curdling. Apparently it was heard by dozens.'

The Frenchwoman's voice descended to a lower register, suitable to so sensational a theme.

One of the players was about to put a card down. He thought better of it.

'He seems to have had a great influence over Leonora.'

'To put it no higher!' said one man dryly.

'An extraordinary thing to happen in the palace!'

'As if it were the only unusual event that night!'

'You have heard about the king?' asked the Frenchwoman.

'The king?'

'He has found a new girl, it seems, from Scotland and already installed in the royal nursery. Very convenient.'

'How many does that make?' asked a man player.

'Hush! . . . Somebody has come into the room. The gypsy.'

213

Silence, broken only by the light sound of cards falling on the table, then—

'I take with the king,' said the Frenchwoman.

'The king wins!' cried her partner, pouncing on the cards.

Jamie Stuart, strolling across the room towards the card players, saw the Russian.

Dmitri greeted him with a scowl. 'She has not sent me the pearls. And I have promised them to the tsarina. I am a man dishonoured.'

'But you have your roubles still.'

'Roubles! What do you take me for? A pawnbroker? Must I fight you, Monsieur Jacques?'

'Prince Dmitri, I have a better idea. Fight *her*! Fight the Countess Leonora.'

'Idiot!'

'Your Highness has not seen the lady fence, I have.'

Jamie, with a gesture of disengagement, turned and looked into the quizzical eyes of the Englishman, Edward Carey.

'How are the bruises, Stuart? Admit I warned you.'

'You said, "Come over to the other side of the street." Tell me, which side of the street was I on when those rogues attacked me?'

Carey laughed pleasantly.

'The wrong side. You had the bad luck to be attacked for two reasons. One man thinks you have designs on the Scottish crown.'

'To hell with the Scottish crown!'

'Quite so. Although any day now it may have become the British crown. A different proposition, don't you agree?'

'You said there were two reasons.'

'Yes. The other one was also a man. Giovanni. He was frightened of you. You were a danger to him. Yes, it must have been something like that.'

'It could have been pure dislike. Antipathy.'

Carey shook his head.

'No. Not strong enough. It was fear.'

'You are guessing.'

'Of course I'm guessing.'

'Carey,' said Jamie after a pause.

'Yes.'

'What *was* Giovanni?'

The Englishman shrugged. 'An Italian. Not a peasant, not a nobleman, one with a talent for dreams, and a hankering for secret power. One who was taking the King of Spain's money and had schemes of his own.'

Jamie thought about that for a moment.

'And nothing else?'

Carey shrugged his elegant shoulders. 'You are thinking of the woman?'

'Of course.'

'When we explore the secrets of the heart,' he said, 'we have to be content with guesses. Giovanni had some power over Leonora—witchcraft, blackmail, or plain brutal terror—he was using her to advance some vast project of his own. And you—he probably sensed this from the beginning—you were a danger to his schemes. It seems,' he smiled, 'that you have your own kind of magic, Stuart. You used it to bewitch her.'

'Not true.'

'He was taking no risks. In his eyes, you were an enemy. And it was logical to sweep you from the board.'

'As a pawn?'

Carey leaned forward and lowered his voice.

'It would still be a good idea,' he said, 'to cross the street. But there is not much time.'

Stuart looked at him hard for a moment and then shook his head. But by that time, Carey's eyes were fixed on some point over Jamie's shoulder, on someone who, in the middle of a sudden quiet, had entered the room.

Leonora.

She wore black. No pearls. Her face was a still, white-hot sheath. Snowflakes still sparkled in her hair. She greeted Jamie with an imperceptible nod.

'Beaton is ready to sail,' he said. 'He has recruited seamen and will take them to Hamburg. There the ship is waiting.'

She made a slight gesture of dismissal.

'Too late,' she said. 'All too late.'

'Too late?'

'Everything. Lord Essex plucked up courage ten days ago.

He tried to raise London against the queen, and London shut its doors on him. Now he is in the Tower. The end can be easily guessed. If you are in doubt what it will be, ask that Englishman you have been talking to, Mr Carey.'

'At least the peacock had the courage to ape an eagle.'

Her shoulders moved faintly.

'Courage? Or his nerve broke under the tension of waiting? Like a child shut in a cupboard, not knowing whether the nurse will come with a whip or the order of release? Anyhow, he is a dead man now. I told you that the men I loved were unlucky. Now, Mr Beaton must find another market for his cargo of arms.'

She walked slowly out of the room and Jamie walked half a pace behind her. When they came to a small panelled room which might have been a study or a bedchamber, but was probably neither, she turned to him.

'Giovanni,' she said.

He nodded.

'He was going to kill you. You know that?'

'You warned me. Remember? I only half believed you.'

'When he had made up his mind to kill, a look came into his eyes. I have seen it before. I saw it again, that night of the ball.'

She paused and looked at him out of her implacable eyes. But he knew that he need not ask the question that was on his lips. She was going to tell him.

'Giovanni,' she said at last with a laugh. 'You wonder what he was. It is quite simple. He was the Devil. If there can be a devil on earth, it was he. When I saw him first, I was no more than a child. That was years before we were brought together. You must understand that my family were musicians, and Giovanni was a peasant woman's son, a bastard. His father was—who knows? A priest, they said. At that first glance I knew that he was wicked and that he was my fate, as girls know that some men they see in a crowd for a moment will be the love of their life. You do not believe it? Say so, then. No?'

He said nothing.

'At that glance something passed between us, cold and

decisive. A recognition. We were, somehow, the same kind. But in the world we both lived in, the world of wickedness, he was more accomplished than I.

'Some years after that, I found that I needed him. I was going to have a child by a patrician of Venice who had gone to the embassy in Madrid. Imagine how much my lover cared! If he knew! I had to do something and I knew that Giovanni would tell me how to do it. I haunted the streets where I would be sure to meet him; near the palazzo where he was a servant. And, of course, we met.'

'You told him?'

'I did not need to tell him. I could see from the way his eyes wandered over me, adding me up, estimating how much I might be worth to him—and how—that he knew. Oh, he knew. Well, he arranged the business—the excuses, the lies, the accomplices—he did it all as if he had been doing nothing else all his life. Perhaps he hadn't! And from that day we were together—mistress and servant, slave and master, tool and guiding hand.'

'And the child?' asked Jamie.

'Ah, the child. He took it away and hid it. He would never tell me where. That was the secret he would not divulge, knowing that it was his final power over me.'

'Perhaps . . .' he said, and stopped, making an abrupt sweeping movement with his hand.

Leonora shook her head.

'He would not do that. One day, somehow, the child might be useful. He would not give it up.'

Jamie waited for her to come back from the clouds of sullen thought.

'Was he your lover, Leonora?' he asked.

She turned on him with a quick, angry laugh. 'How like a man to ask that!'

'How like a woman not to answer it!'

'Clever,' she said. 'But does it matter now? He belongs to a world that is dead. And, it seems, strangely enough, that you belong to it, too.'

He nodded. He was not surprised.

'You will find a new lover, Leonora,' he said.

'Of course. But what I need is a new accomplice. He will be harder to come by.'

'One thing,' he said, 'not important. What of the pearls?'

She shrugged.

'Dmitri will be inconsolable,' he went on. 'But you may not want to sell them now.'

'No,' she said. 'I have a different idea. My husband is going to Whitehall on a mission for the king, one day soon. Queen Elizabeth thinks that the Danes are too possessive about their fisheries off the coast of Norway. My husband will be discussing the question with her ministers. Needless to say, he understands nothing at all about it. I shall go with him, as a good wife should. And when Her Majesty asks us to dine, I shall be wearing the pearls that were once Her Majesty's.'

'Do you think she will recognise them?'

She laughed.

'That queen forgets nothing,' she said.

'I should like to be present.' In Jamie's eyes interest had kindled.

'Why not?' said Leonora.

'I shall tell Dmitri you mean first to show them to the English queen. After that . . .'

'Tell him I will give them to the poor.'

'He will certainly want to fight me. Oh damn! The last thing in the world I want to do is kill that Russian!'

'Goodbye, Jacques.'

'Later—' He had put a hand on her arm.

'No. Another day perhaps. If a dead world can come to life again!'

'In London—'

'Who knows? Au revoir, Jacques.'

She left him alone in the room. Slowly, thoughtfully, he went back to the lights and the chatter.

'Ah, Jacques, there you are!' It was François. 'I have been looking for you everywhere. Listen. Yesterday, I was not feeling well—a pain here—' he patted his stomach. 'So I consulted my astrologer. A very good man. I can recommend him especially when the liver is upset. While I was there, I talked about your case. What he said was most extraordinary! Either you are going on a long sea voyage, or you are about to receive a proposal of marriage. Apparently it is not certain which.'

'I have taken a vow of celibacy.'

'Very wise,' said François. 'I recommend you to make that voyage as soon as possible. At once, Jacques!'

'There is one visit I must make before I go.'

It had been his hope that he would slip unnoticed out of Caroline's house. But while the footman was helping him on with his cloak, he was aware that Carey stood there, dressed for the road.

'My sledge is coming to the door. Where will it take us? Yes, I am coming with you, Stuart. Don't argue. Incidentally, have you a pistol?'

'In my lodgings. Unloaded. I have never had much luck with firearms anyway.'

The Englishman smiled and showed a horse pistol under his cloak.

'This may be useful. Where do we drive to?'

'To the Scottish ambassador's lodging,' said Stuart.

'Good God! Into the lion's mouth! Listen to reason, man. I can take you to a stable where a good horse is waiting. You can leave town in half an hour. And don't look so stubborn. Two paid bully-boys, armed with pistols, are out with orders to kill you.'

Jamie shook his head.

'I'll be gone before daybreak, Carey. But one thing I must do first.'

Carey shrugged his shoulders.

'Come on,' he said.

'Listen, Carey—'

'Come on, man.'

Five minutes later, Jamie knocked at the kitchen door of the Scots ambassador's lodging.

'The name is Jacques in French and Stuart in English,' he said to the servant who opened. 'No hurry. I'll wait here.'

The man gave him a startled look and retired.

Suddenly, she was there. His heart did what it always did when he saw her. She was holding something out.

'There it is,' she said.

'There what is?'

'What you came for. Your grandmother's marriage lines.'

'Damn my grandmother's marriage lines! I came to tell you I love you.'

Her laughter was so musical that it delighted him while it enraged him.

'You are hopeless, Jamie!'

'I am not in the least hopeless! On the contrary, I am the—'

'James, James!' She wagged a finger at him.

'Damn it, Mary. I have to leave in a hurry. Will you send my regards to your mother? Tell her, I wear the shirt she mended. By the way, someone has sewn a crown on it.'

'Why not, Your Majesty?'

'Now I must go. I am told that some friends outside are anxious to see me.'

'Be careful, Jamie!' Her face was suddenly drawn and white.

'You know me.'

'Only too well.'

'Is that all you have to say?'

'No. As a matter of fact, it isn't'

'What else, Mary?'

'I love you, Jamie.' She took a step towards him and kissed him on the lips.

The shooting started when he stepped out of the sledge at the entrance to the Red Lion. Out of the corner of one eye, he caught sight of the yellow flame. The sound was flattened by the snow. The puff of air passed his ear. From beyond the sledge came another shot. By this time Carey was on his feet, firing. Jamie, bent double, zig-zagged fast towards the first man. The second bullet struck the sealskin of his cloak. He thought it had gone through without harming him. The pistol man saw Jamie's sword. After a brief appalled glance, he turned on his heels and disappeared.

'A bit of luck,' said Carey, putting the muzzle of his pistol to his nose.

'You hit your man?'

'I think so. He thought so, too.'

'Come in and have a drink, Carey.'

The Englishman shook his head. 'Maybe I'll see you in London óne day,' he said.

'What makes you think that?'

Carey smiled and shook the reins. The sledge jingled away into the darkness.

Jamie pushed open the tavern door.

'What the hell was all that noise?' asked Alan.

The waiter said that there were letters for Mr Beaton. Alistair arrived. He had just come off guard.

'So you think we should take the cargo of arms to Ireland,' said Jamie.

Alan nodded his head vigorously.

'Our market is there, made for us by the Spaniards. Don Juan de Aquila has landed at Kinsale, in the south. I'll show it you on the chart—with five thousand professionals. The Irish rebels are coming down to join him, marching from the north-west, over wild country—almost as bad as our Highlands.'

'Who says the Highlands are bad?' asked Alistair, fiercely.

'Nobody,' said Jamie, firmly. 'Go on, Alan.'

'Marching down to the south,' Alan continued, 'are the Irish lords, Tyrone and Tyrconnel. They have more fighting men than arms. And between them and the Spaniards is the English Lord Deputy, Mountjoy. They mean to crush him— so!' He brought his fist down on the table. 'In the meantime, they are the best market in the world for honest men who have guns to sell.'

'And then?' asked Alistair.

'What do you mean, and then? We are not there yet. First of all, we have to get through the English screen of ships— not so easy, let me tell you. The Channel Watch is never less than a dozen galleons strong. And there are as many more on the Irish station.'

'You'll get through,' said Alistair. 'But after that—what?'

'What does it matter to you, anyway?'

'Because I'm coming with you,' said Alistair.

They looked at him.

'And the Guards?' asked Jamie.

'To hell with the Guards.'

'What about your regiment?'

'Fancy uniform and no fighting. After all, I am a gentleman. I'll come with you.'

Alan stared for a minute, then,

'It's for you to decide, boy,' he said, equably. 'You asked, What are we to do after selling the guns to Don Juan? That's a reasonable question. There we are, loaded with money and all the time in the world to spare. What do we do?'

'Why don't we go to enjoy some sunshine?' suggested Jamie.

Alistair frowned and jerked his thumb towards the cold night beyond the door, the darkness diagonally streaked with snow falling in large flakes.

'What sunshine?'

'There are places where the sun shines,' said Jamie. 'Lemon groves that you can smell from twenty miles out at sea. Beaches bone-white and stretching as far as the eye can carry. Olive trees as old as the Roman Empire—'

'Any mosquitoes?' Alistair sneered. 'Any fever?'

Jamie waved impatiently.

'You talk too much,' he said.

'Me,' said Alan. 'I should like to see the South Sea.'

'Why the South Sea, man?' asked Alistair.

'Because it's the biggest thing of its kind in the world. That's why. I'd like to sail into it—far, far into nothing, and see what nothing is like. Besides, there's gold there.'

'I think I'd like to stay in Ireland,' said Alistair, thoughtfully. 'It seems to be a country where a gentleman would find employment.'

The waiter brought letters to the table. They were mostly for Alan. He broke the seals one by one. After a few minutes, he looked up.

'What a pity Lord Essex lost his head! There's news of a Genoese captain at Dunkirk. A man named Spinola.'

'Spinola,' said Jamie. 'The family is rich. They are bankers.'

'This one is a captain. He has a squadron of galleys which

he uses to plunder the English. These galleys would have been just what we wanted to convoy the arms over to Essex. What damnable luck!'

'Perhaps we could make use of him yet,' said Jamie. 'He might lure the English fleet away while we slip through the Straits to Ireland.'

Alan brightened up.

'The cargo is ready at Hamburg,' he said, 'greased, crated, everything!—Oh, here is a letter for you, Jamie. Someone who knew where to find you.'

Jamie took the packet. It was addressed in a hand he did not recognise. He opened it. 'Good God,' he said. 'Listen to this. And guess who it's from.'

He read aloud in a voice that shook with excitement:

' "Stuart. I hear a rumour that you are alive. It must be true. Madmen like you are not easily killed . . . Now, to speak of more serious matters—" '

His eyes danced with pleasure. He brought his fist down on the table with a crash.

'It's from Sinclair!' he cried. 'From Captain George Sinclair of the Swedish Service. The old devil is alive. I didn't think they would be able to kill him. Now his wounds are healed. He is in Stockholm. Waiter, fill up these glasses!'

'Go on,' said Alistair. 'What else does he say?'

'What do you think! He is going back to Scotland to raise more men. He wants us all to go to Moscow with him.'

'Not in this weather,' said Alistair, with a shudder.

Alan got up from the table.

'Time to go,' he said. 'We cast off soon after midnight.'

Jamie had feelings of regret, as if somehow his stay in this city should have ended differently, as if he should have done more, as if . . .

Under his arm he held the board on which an artist had painted a sign, 'Monsieur Jacques. Escrime'. It might come in handy one day. He was a provident young man.

The gangplank had been pulled on land. The longshoreman threw the last mooring cable on deck where a sailor began to coil it neatly. There was already a slight tremor in the ship, as wind nudged its hull and spars and the helmsman moved his rudder. Inch by inch, the space between ship and quay widened.

'Either you stop humming that tune,' said Alan, 'or you sing it properly.'

Jamie looked at him guiltily.